Zombies Versus Aliens Versus Vampires Versus Dinosaurs

Jeff Abugov

Zombies versus Aliens versus Vampires versus Dinosaurs
Jeff Abugov

Copyright © 2015 by Jeff Abugov

J-Stroke Productions, November 2015
2015 Print Edition

ISBN-13: 978-0692581032
ISBN-10: 0692581030

Cover design by Will Kleist
Formatted by Polgarus Studio

Author Website
jeffabugov.com

Printed in the United States of America

J-Stroke Productions
Los Angeles, California

Contents

PART ONE

THE GOOD, THE BAD
AND THE GORGEOUS

CHAPTER ONE

Alma's Bar and Grill was the most popular bar and grill in all of Heartsoot Creek because it was the only bar or grill in town. It was where smatterings of local farmers and ranch-hands would come for breakfast, or lunch, or to drown their sorrows Monday through Thursday nights. (It was closed on Sundays because of Jesus.)

But this was Friday night. Everyone in town had just been paid or received their welfare checks, and the joint was a'hoppin'. Johnny Cash, Toby Keith, Taylor Swift and Tammy Wynette blasted from the souped-up jukebox as Alma's patrons danced, drank and even brawled the night away. It was a Friday night like any other Friday night, at least that's how it seemed.

Julius sat alone at the bar. That is to say that he had no company as of yet. Crowding him on his left was Bobby Joe Mackelroy who was putting the moves on Candy Mae Swinson, and not getting very far. Crowding him on his right were Mikey Johnson and Lenny "Ponyboy" Webster who were arguing the merits of President Addison's new economic plan even though neither of them really understood it, and it was only a matter of time till their debate devolved into fisticuffs. It was a Friday night like any other Friday night, and Julius was bored.

He could get any woman he wanted—he barely remembered a time when he didn't have that skill. He could also get any guy he wanted for that matter but he far preferred women these days. He was a good-looking man, movie-star good-looking. Early thirties and fit with jet-black hair, sleek, alabaster skin and dark, hypnotic eyes, he was the coolest dude in the joint right down to his Stetson hat, cowboy boots and tatts. He also owned the sprawling Long Tooth Ranch, making him one of the richest men in southeast Georgia.

He scoured the dance floor for a prospective mate for the evening, but nothing appealed to him. They all danced the same slutty moves that they had learned from television, wore the same kind of trashy outfits, each girl virtually indistinguishable from the other. He had wanted something special. The only question now was whether he would settle for ordinary or go home unfulfilled.

Then he saw her. At a small ice cream table in the far corner of the packed space sat a petite little waif of a girl. She had blonde, curly hair, a cute little button nose, and she was all alone. She couldn't have been more than eighteen, Julius thought, probably less, but there was something so ridiculously sweet about her that he didn't care. She wore a fancy evening gown and sipped on a colorful umbrella drink. She was so out of place, so didn't belong, Julius simply had to have her.

She was looking around everywhere in wonderment, taking it all in, when she caught Julius's gaze upon her, caught his killer smile, so warm, so hot. She smiled back instinctively then quickly turned away as a good girl would, must. But she couldn't stop herself from turning back to him to find his sultry, dark eyes still upon her, his killer smile now bigger, warmer, hotter. She blushed as she turned away once more, then back again to find him gone.

She sighed in disappointment only to realize that he was standing right next to her, his hand held out for her to take, his fantastic smile showering her with a sense of love that she couldn't remember ever having felt.

"What?" she asked, referring to his hand, as if she didn't know.

"Come," was all he said in return.

She blushed, smiled coyly, then took his hand and let him lead her out of the joint. She never had a chance.

*****

4

HER NAME WAS MARY, and she was living up to everything Julius had wanted for the evening. They walked along the empty street swinging their hands like little kids as she dodged one of his questions after another, too shy to talk about herself, fascinated to learn more about him. She spoke with a strange accent that Julius couldn't quite place—and he had been to most everywhere in the world at one point or another. The mystery surrounding her was a massive turn-on.

He agreed to take her to one of his favorite places so he led her off the road and headed into the Heartsoot Creek Cemetery. It was so quiet at night, he explained, so romantically dark with the only illumination sourcing from the moonlight. The Georgia grass was always perfectly groomed and sweet smelling, and one could truly lose themselves in the peacefulness. But Mary found it amusing.

"You take I to graveyard?" she said through a small laugh. "Not usual place for to seduce young girl, no?"

Julius laughed back. He was busted, and he was so rarely busted. This girl was more than special. As much as he was enjoying the seduction, he didn't know how much longer he could wait before he took her.

"Your accent is killin' me, m'darlin'," he said in his light Southern drawl.

"No, my accent is bad," she said, now deadly serious. "But I work hard for it. *On* it. I work hard *on* it. One day it will be gone, all gone."

"Don't worry too much about your future, Mary," he said good-naturedly. "You don't have one."

And with that, he opened his mouth to reveal his long, sharp fangs. He hissed as he grabbed her by the shoulders and bit hard into her neck, devouring her luscious red blood.

She screamed wretched yelps of shock and agony that only made the vampire's meal all the more satisfying when, all of a sudden, her girly cries morphed into a hideous, otherworld growl. Her delicious, red blood turned to a slimy, green pus on which the vampire began to gag. She shed her taut, teen body like a trick suit to reveal a terrifying, bug-eyed, insect-like creature within, then grabbed the vampire's head and snapped it hard across its neck. CRACK! Julius dropped to the ground like a bag of nails.

She tried to regain her composure but she was in too much pain, and she knew that her wound would have to be treated. Aware that her assignment was now blown, she tapped on alien-symbols on a keypad strapped to her insect-forearm. The ground shook. A tall, black oval roughly the size of a phone booth suddenly materialized beside her. Clutching her gushing wound with one hand and dragging her human-skin costume with the other, she limped into the wormhole, and it snapped shut behind her.

Barely a moment later, Julius opened one eye to make sure she was gone. He sat up and sighed, thoroughly dumbstruck. Close to three thousand years old, he had never seen anything like this before.

CHAPTER TWO

"Ding! Ding! Ding!" sounded the alert on a never-ending loop.

Jean-François dropped his Maxim magazine and leapt up from his chair, knocking over his Angelina Jolie coffee mug and drenching his pants as he raced to his underling's terminal, barely aware of the intense burn to his thigh.

"Jeff! It's another one!" shouted Lance.

"I know, I know," he answered, running. "This makes what since he last said no? Fifteen? Sixteen?"

They were the only two working the Astronomy Wing of NASA's Johnson Space Center at this late hour, not counting security and janitorial staff. Jean-François, midforties, bald, chubby, the brilliant French-Jewish astrophysicist laughed out of the EU for his overly bold theories and now relegated to the Houston graveyard shift as punishment for being smarter than most of his superiors, and also for being French, or Jewish, but probably French; and Lance, the twenty-six-year-old geek whiz kid along for the ride because after selling his app to Google for an ungodly sum of money five years prior, he wanted to do something historically special with his life, and Jean-François's controversial papers had blown him away.

(Lance was the creator of the No-More-Crash app, the one that detects and warns users of impending computer crashes early enough for the user to take the steps necessary to avoid crashing entirely. You probably have one.)

"This makes twenty," Lance told his adopted mentor as he stared at his

7

monitor and calculated their exorbitant wormhole data. "It's a perfect match. Again. Dead-on perfect! Less than a minute ago for the one here on Earth, and it's absolutely identical to the one that's five-point-three light-years away."

"All right then," Jean-François said as he sighed the kind of sigh one sighs as they embark upon political suicide. "Let's get the big guy in."

"He can't say no again," Lance said with certainty. "Not with the data we've got."

"He can," answered the Frenchman. "Let's just hope he doesn't."

INTERLUDE

Montana. One hundred million years ago, give or take.

It was an egg. A large egg but not the kind we're used to seeing because its shell boasted every color of the spectrum. A rainbow egg, one might say, surrounded by three other rainbow eggs of equal size in a very large nest. But this egg was the first of the four to shake, and with the shaking came a small pecking from within.

The mother of the eggs lay in the nest snoozing, but she lurched her massive head right up the moment she heard the pecking. She was a proud Deinonychus mother (pronounced "die-NON-ih-kiss"), a colorful, feathered, highly intelligent biped, roughly five feet tall, ten feet long, with three six-inch claws on each of her front paws and hind legs. (The Deinonychus was the real inspiration of *Jurassic Park's* Velociraptor which was actually a rather small dinosaur albeit with a much cooler name.) To her new offspring she would be "ma" even though the Deinonychus lacked speech or even the concept of words, but like all animals they recognized each other's individuality from their actions, their appearance, their smells, their very essence. So for the sake of narrative simplicity, let us call this one Dinah.

Dinah beamed as her firstborn struggled out of his egg. She instinctively knew not to help him for that would only weaken him to the later struggles of life. She watched as he shook his little feathered body to rid himself of the shell remnants that clung to him, then she looked up to the sky and shrieked as if announcing to the world the blessed event. The hatchling, already tuckered out, laid down and cuddled against his mother who tenderly licked the top of his plume when a second egg began to shake.

A male Deinonychus, just slightly larger than Dinah, came running out from the woods and leapt into the nest beside her, as if answering his mate's call. Let's call this one Claw even though, of course, again, he didn't really have a name either. Claw dropped to all fours to get a better look at his newly hatched son, then shrieked out a cry of his own. Dinah nestled her sixteen-inch head upon her male's shoulder and cooed. Claw cooed back as their second hatchling pecked her way out of her shell and entered the world.

An early American family.

CHAPTER THREE

Julius stood alone atop the Heartsoot Creek Observatory. The three-minutes-for-fifty-cents-telescopes were useless for his quest, which is why he had brought his own—a super high-powered thing he had bought for fun years ago only because he had more money than he knew what to do with. Still, it was rendering no more results than the touristy crap.

"What nature of beast are you, my friend?" he asked unto the heavens in his real voice that still had a tiny trace of Brit-German accent. "From where do you come, Mary? What is your purpose? And why can I not see you?"

He then noticed a lovely young couple in love walking the pathway below, and it reminded him of how hungry he was. Mary's thrashing had taken so much out of him that it was no longer about the delight of a great meal. Now it was just about sustenance, nutrition.

"Hey, y'all! Wanna see somethin' cool?" he shouted out in his best redneck.

"You talking to us?" asked the young man.

"Check it out, man!" Julius answered. "It'll blow your mind!"

The young couple looked at each other and shrugged—yet another future memory of their wonderful early days together. Why not?

They climbed the tiny mound as Julius savored his next boring yet nutritious meal. "What is it?" the young man asked.

"I dunno," Julius answered. "Just look at it. Maybe y'all can tell me."

The young man smiled then looked into the vampire's telescope. "I don't see anything. What am I supposed to be looking for?"

Then in one crazy-fast, fluid motion, Julius jutted out his right arm to grab the young woman by the throat to hold her in place while simultaneously ripping his fangs into the young man's neck to suck him dry of all his blood. And even though the young woman opened her mouth to scream for help, not a sound came out of her.

With the young man's body depleted of all its vampire nourishment, Julius let him drop to the ground like a deflated blow-up doll, then sucked the life out of the young woman, letting her fall to her demise in the same manner.

Julius burped. A boring meal, but still, maybe he overdid it. Then he returned to his telescope, the true mission at hand, as if nothing of importance had just happened. Still, he saw nothing in the skies.

"What nature of beast are you, my friend?" he repeated towards the heavens.

CHAPTER FOUR

It was one of the most lavish fund-raisers the Watergate Hotel had ever showcased, and President Michael Addison was eating it up. A former governor of Montana, forty-five years old with a Kennedy-like sex appeal, a Reagan-like geniality, and the political instincts of FDR, he had the billionaires right where he wanted them. No way was he going to be a one-term president.

The superrich barraged him with their questions, trying to pin him down to precise answers, but everyone knew it was an idle exercise. They were going to give Michael everything he asked for, no matter what. They had to. The thought of his opponent taking the White House was unacceptable, and the consequences of being the only billionaire who *didn't* contribute were even more daunting. All Michael had to do was not offend any of them.

"But which side are you on, Mr. President?" pleaded a corporate demigod.

Michael knew the answer they wanted but he also knew what the voters wanted, and he had learned long ago never to say something to one group you didn't want another to hear—not in this day and age of social media and tiny cameras. Far too easy to get Romney'd.

"It's a fallacious debate, Charlie," he told the demigod. "It's not a question of big or small government. It's a question of how to grow big and small businesses while still tending to the lowliest of our citizens so that they too can become proud, productive members of the greatest country on Earth."

"And to get the answer to *that* question," piped in the stunningly charming forty-year-old woman on his arm, "Just ask him. But I wouldn't 'cause he'll tell you."

The crowd laughed, just as the First Lady intended. Laurel Addison, dressed to the nines in a fabulous evening gown, subtle diamond earrings, and a sparkling silver crucifix necklace that drew the eye to just a hint of cleavage, was the perfect asset to her husband's career. Laurel could lighten any mood when Michael seemed too calculating or wonky, good-naturedly teasing the great man, bringing him back down to Earth, and reminding the nation that the Addisons were the couple you wanted at your home barbecue. The most beloved First Lady since Eleanor Roosevelt, she had the ability to make you feel like she truly cared about you— because she did! In fact, the worst her detractors could ever say about her was that she was a bit of a social butterfly, shallow when it came to affairs of state, a college dropout who could never quite finish any project she started. Frivolous. A lightweight. This was all true, of course, but she was so warm and decent that no one really seemed to mind, not even her detractors.

But if Laurel was the President's greatest asset, not too far away stood his greatest liability.

Vice President Peyton Willis, formerly General Peyton Willis, formerly Chairman of the Joint Chiefs of Staff Peyton Willis. It had seemed such a no-brainer for Michael to put him on the ticket. A beloved military leader with no political leanings, he could publicly endorse any policy Michael put forth with no accusation of "flip-flopping." He fully complemented then-Governor Addison's lack of experience in foreign matters, and Michael genuinely admired the man. Well, till he got to know him.

For the General had one fatal flaw when it came to national politics— when asked a direct question, he spoke his mind with the honesty and integrity of a soldier. Lacking the cunning nuance that great political leaders like Michael must employ on a daily basis, Peyton actually found the practice distasteful. And although he had been a fine running mate—

delivering every electoral state he had been counted on despite his many political blunders—it was clear by the end of the election that his partnership with Michael was to be no partnership at all.

It was hard on him. Having begun his career as a young lieutenant fighting in the jungles of Vietnam, there had barely been a war since in which he hadn't been involved be it combat or planning. He was a man of action, catapulted to the second-highest office in the land, without anything to do. His wife of forty years had passed away just a few years prior so, after spending his days doing nothing at all, he would return to a home that was empty.

And so, the widowed warrior took to drinking, and the drinking made his honesty worse—or better, depending on your point of view—and it really ticked off the President. For there he was, on this all-important fund-raising night, surrounded by his own conclave of one-percenters, shooting off his mouth like the drunken clown that Michael had come to know him to be.

"You know, it's tricky what I, as Vice President, can say at a fund-raiser like this," Peyton began, just slightly tipsy and feeling fine. "Because we don't want it to look like we're asking for bribes . . . because let's face it, we kinda are. And thanks."

The captains of industry did not take to the comment well. Of course they wanted access, of course they wanted influence, of course they wanted what they wanted, and they were willing to pay for it. But calling it a "bribe?" That makes it a crime. That makes the President's administration corrupt, and they part of the corruption. That's not how the game is played! Their donations are their exercise of free speech as American citizens, and that's all that should ever be said about it.

What if something happened to Michael and this bozo had to take the Oval? they began to wonder. And the wondering made them nervous.

None of this was lost on Michael—very little was ever lost on Michael. How drunk *is* the old drunk? Next he'll be telling them we'll be raising their taxes. Peyton had to be muzzled and fast, but Michael couldn't walk away from the billionaires in front of him so he looked to Laurel for help.

15

"I'm on it," she mouthed to him then turned to the crowd. "Excuse me, I must go mingle. You can't have us both to yourselves all night. But I'll leave you with the one of us that matters."

And off she went, whipping across the room as she worked it flawlessly. "Love your gown, Emily . . . Congrats on the big promotion, Tom . . . Still on for lunch next Wednesday, Nora."

But she couldn't get there fast enough because Peyton was on a roll.

"And I'm the worst bribe there is," he continued. "I have no power nor purpose in this administration. Give no advice, and I don't know squat. Plans to get our budget through Congress? Don't know. Trade negotiations with China? Beats me. Middle East peace talks? Who the fu—"

"Mr. Vice President!" Laurel called out. "It's been far too long!" And with that she took his arm and kissed him on the cheek.

"Ah, the only member of the royal family worth a damn," Peyton said warmly. "Well, your kids are okay. And the dog."

"We must catch up," she said then turned to the offended rich. "Excuse us." None of them seemed to mind as she whisked Peyton off to a quiet, empty spot across the room.

"How we holding up, General?"

"Gotta be honest, ma'am," he began. "This is the most boring bachelor party I've ever been to."

She couldn't help but laugh. Despite all the friction between Peyton and her husband, she had always respected the ole coot.

"Think maybe you've had enough?"

"Don't worry. I'll stop as soon as the strippers get here."

"You do know this is really a fund-raiser, right?"

"Then I guess I'd better keep drinking," he said with a wink.

Again, Laurel laughed—it was so hard not to like the man. But her laugh was cut short when she suddenly sensed a strange vibration, an odd feeling that something was off. Wrong. She tilted her head back and sniffed at the air. Sour.

"Are you all right, Laurel?" Peyton asked, all kidding aside.

"Yes, fine, fine," she lied. "Thank you. Excuse me."

POTUS would have to put someone else on veep patrol for something far more pressing was at hand. She headed back to her husband to tell him she'd be leaving the party early—another migraine coming on, she'd say—then she shot a fast glance at a large, African American man in a dark suit standing against the wall.

Secret Service Agent Denison had been protecting Laurel for a very long time and was the only member of the Montana security team that the Addisons had brought with them to Washington. He knew what all her looks meant without the necessity of words, especially this one.

"Bring up the First Lady's car," he said into the microphone on his wrist.

*****

HE WAS QUITE A handsome man actually, thought the crack-addicted streetwalker, if you're into that whole well-dressed, pale-skinned, shiny-shoes kinda thing. He must be some kind of big-shot political freak coming down to the southeast side for some exciting excitement, but that could be good for her. He probably wouldn't know the going rate so she could take him for an extra fifty—and that's fifty her pimp wouldn't know about, so a real fifty. Maybe she could use it to get into rehab, get herself clean, see her daughter again. It'd been how many years now? Damn, she missed her baby.

"Hundred bucks, sugar," she told the mark, hoping he wouldn't know she'd doubled the price. "Plus hotel."

"No hotel," he grunted as he dashed her into the alley. "Right now, right here."

"Simmer down, sugar," she said with a smile. "Wherever you want it, but it's the same hundr—"

But he didn't care what she had to say. He grabbed her shoulders, pinned her hard against the wall, and then opened his mouth wide to reveal his long, sharp fangs, ready to devour her!

What the Christ! she thought as she gasped in terror. It's a goddamn vampire!

It wasn't the pending loss of her own pitiful life that made the prostitute scream and struggle in mortal fear but rather the realization that her poor daughter would never know how much her mother actually cared about her.

So she screamed and struggled, but it was no use. The vampire was just too strong. He leaned in for the kill, his sharp fangs less than an inch from her pimply, tawdry neck when a hand reached out from nowhere and threw him across the alley, sending him crashing into the garbage cans on the other side.

The whore didn't understand what had happened, but she didn't care. She bolted off, certain this was a sign from God, vowing to the Lord Almighty that she'd go into rehab as soon as she could, right after her next hit.

The vampire laid on the ground, covered with garbage, looking up at his assailant. And what he saw scared him to the depths of his dark soul. For there before him stood one of the most notorious vampire slayers in all of vampire lore.

First Lady Laurel Addison was fresh from the fund-raiser in her fabulous gown and jewelry. The only difference was a burlap satchel slung over her shoulder, a wooden stake in each of her hands, and a look of sheer determination on her face.

"Didn't you get the tweets?" she said to the creature. "D.C. is *my* town. Clean town. Vampires persona non grata."

The vampire knew it was kill or be killed, knew his chances against Laurel were slim—but if he could take her down with him, he would at least perish a hero.

"Slayer!" he shouted as he charged her.

Laurel dodged his assault with ease, slashing at his chest with her wooden stakes as he passed, but missing. But her own chest was now wide open to him, and the vampire charged again. Laurel leapt straight up to grab hold of the balcony above her then kicked out her legs for the vampire to rush past her below. She then let go and crashed down upon the creature, knocking him to the ground, pinning his shoulders with her knees to hold him in place. She raised her wooden stake to plunge it into his heart when she heard voices approaching.

"Slayer!" the voices shouted as two new vampires emerged to save their brother. The first knocked Laurel off the fallen vampire while the second moved in for the final kill. She back-flipped out of his way with lightning speed, grabbing hold of the other who she shoved against the wall. She raised her wooden stake once more, then proceeded to ram it into his heart.

The vampire hissed and transformed into mist, virtually invisible and utterly incorporeal. Laurel's wooden stake sailed harmlessly through him, bashing against the brick wall behind him with full force, shattering to dust. The other two then morphed to mist as well, converging upon the First Lady to her imminent doom.

With all seeming hopeless, she quickly reached into her satchel, grabbed a handful of an ancient beige powder and threw it at the lot of them, rendering their physical forms to return—and just in time to spot one of them flying at her at full speed, fangs poised for the kill, barely a foot away. She buckled her knees and dropped herself prostrate to the ground as she thrust her remaining wooden stake upward, nailing the creature perfectly in his heart as he soared past above her, taking her weapon with him as he crashed against the brick wall, already dead.

One down, two to go, she thought as she raced toward the corpse to retrieve her weapon, but she was grabbed from behind before she got there. Pinned in a full nelson, helpless! She struggled ferociously but despite her many skills, her impeccable physical training, and her vast knowledge of the creatures' foibles, she knew she could never overpower one with sheer strength. And although she had a free hand, she held no wooden stake, no weapon with which to fight. The vampire who restrained her sprouted his fangs and salivated as he moved to tear into her infamous neck flesh while the other charged at her fast.

In one fluid motion, she used her free hand to grab hold of her silver crucifix necklace and whisked it back and upward, jamming it hard into the forehead of the vampire who held her. The creature screamed in mortal agony as his skin sizzled, smoked, burned aflame, a crucifix tattoo permanently embedded above his eyes. And before he even fell to the ground, she kicked out her right leg as the other monster charged chest first into the wooden heel of her Louboutin stiletto.

It took all her strength to yank her designer shoe out of his heart before he hit the concrete, his evil existence done with forever. Panting, exhausted, two enemies dead and one writhing on the ground, Laurel looked down on the pathetic creature with pity. Then she raised her leg high and stomped down hard upon his chest, driving her expensive wooden-stake heel deep into his heart, ending him too.

Secret Service Agent Denison stood patiently by the parked limousine outside the alley awaiting his Mistress. The moment he saw Laurel approaching, he opened the back door for her to enter.

"How'd it go, ma'am?" he asked with polite deference.

"The usual," she said with a shrug as she got into the car.

CHAPTER FIVE

"Okay, from the beginning," said the NASA administrator with the annoyed tone of someone who'd rather be in bed so early on a Monday morning. "Tell me how you'd tell it to the President."

Jean-François stood at the front of the conference room, and he knew it was make-or-break time. His budget was already small for NASA, and he needed significantly more funding to take his project to the crucial next level. He also knew that it was on the top of the cut list because Raymond Saticoy, NASA's fifty-five- year-old head honcho, simply didn't like him—probably the French thing again.

"It's okay," said Gloria Ames softly with an encouraging smile. Gloria was the deputy administrator, Raymond's number two, who had initially found Jean-François's theories preposterous like everyone else. But she went from his biggest critic to his greatest supporter once she saw his data. A true scientist, Jean-François thought admiringly, unlike their boss who was a true bureaucrat.

"Go ahead, Jeff. It's okay," she repeated.

Jean-François took a deep breath. He was a scientist, not an actor, and he hated these dog and pony shows. Why couldn't Raymond just read his report? But he knew that life at NASA didn't work that way, so he took another deep breath and began.

He nodded to Lance, the only other person in the room. Lance sat alone at the far end of the conference table hovering over his laptop. He pecked at a few keys, prompting a map of the Orion Arm of the galaxy to appear on the LCD television on the wall.

"We spotted the first wormhole by accident several years ago," Jean-François began as a red dot popped onto the galactic map.

"A wormhole is like a shortcut through space and time," Lance said helpfully.

"I know what a wormhole is," Raymond replied annoyed.

"You said we should say it like we would to the President."

"Fine. Go on."

Jean-François started again, "It was roughly six light-years away —"

"Which means that at the moment we saw it open and close, it had actually happened six years earlier," Lance explained.

"You do get that I run NASA, don't you?" Raymond snapped.

"Let them talk, Ray," Gloria said insistently.

"We searched for others, but it was like a needle in a haystack," the astrophysicist continued. "Two years till we found the next one," he said as another red dot popped onto the screen. "Then another year till we found two more." Pop. Pop.

"Then we noticed something startling. The wormholes were forming a single line." A curved green line appeared on the galactic map, connecting the dots, visually displaying Jean-François' thesis. "So we extended the line outward, and we discovered that there were wormhole remnants everywhere along the way." Pop. Pop. Pop. Pop. Pop.

"But how far back, how long ago did these wormholes begin? we wondered. So we extended the line in the opposite direction, backward in space, back in time so to speak. Now that we knew where to look, now that we had a precise track to follow, we were able to scour with precision every photographic plate, print, or sketch of the area from past research of other projects. And lo and behold, in the faint corners and ignored parts of so very many of these images lay the wormhole remnants we had been seeking." Pop. Pop. Pop. Pop.

"It's called 'precovery,'" Lance piped in. "Short for 'pre-discovery.' It's the process of using —"

"Will you stop already?!" Raymond barked at the boy.

Jean-François raised his hand to his protégé—he'll take it from here.

"The furthest remnant we found was on a photographic plate from research done in 1986, which we calculated at close to fifty light-years away. This is not to say that the wormholes don't go further back than that, only that we have yet to find any plates to support it.

"And it all begged the question: if the wormholes in space are akin to one side of a door, where is the other? So, on a hunch, we studied the Earth for the same phenomena."

"Wanna hear about the cool equipment I invented to do it?" Lance piped in boastfully.

"No," Raymond yawned without even looking at the boy.

"And our theory proved valid," Jean-François went on. "Not only were we finding wormholes appearing and disappearing with alarming regularity, but each wormhole on Earth perfectly matched one specific, unique counterpart in space. The size and shape, the spectral composition, the temperature, the duration of its very existence. So this green line—clearly the source of the wormholes—seems to be the pathway of some interplanetary vessel. Which would in turn imply that extraterrestrials have been visiting us for roughly fifty years, if not more."

On screen, the green line continued to jut out across the stars, faster, faster, with red dots popping up all along the way, the camera swish-panning across the galaxy to keep up.

"And if we continue to extend the line forward, we can see that the vessel itself is heading straight . . . toward . . . Earth!"

And there it was on screen—the green line stopping at our very doorstep.

The room went silent as they awaited Raymond's response. It was only a matter of seconds, but to Jean-François it felt like hours.

"That's a giant assumption, fellas," the boss said at last.

Jean-François and Lance were crushed. Gloria was exasperated, frustrated beyond belief, angry.

"You gotta be kidding me," she said forcefully. "You don't think there's enough here to warrant amping up this project? Ray, there's something going on out there and we should know what it is."

"Then why haven't the guys at SETI found it?"

"For all we know they have!"

"SETI tracks radio waves," Jean-François calmly interjected, fully prepared. "We can't determine what kind of waves the alien vessel emits, if any."

"There is no alien vessel!" Raymond shouted with finality. "Guys, this is exactly what you've been bringing me for years. I can't take 'aliens' to the President."

"Then we should at least bring him the wormhole findings," Gloria offered as a pale compromise. "I still don't know why we didn't years ago."

"Because anyone who hears this will make the same unsubstantiated leap you did, and then we're right back to where we started. Aliens."

"Ray, it's our job to report these kind of findings."

"No, it's your job to do what I tell you. It's *my* job to keep this place running. And right now it's the President's priority to get his budget through Congress."

"What's that got to do with anything?

"Addison's going to compromise to get what he wants, he always does. Right now we fly under the radar, but if we go public with this alien nonsense, we'll be the butt of every late-night comic's joke. It's just begging Congress to slash our funds. No more manned mission to Mars, no exploration of Jupiter's moons. It will be the end of the advancement of mankind for a generation."

"The American public will eat this stuff up," Jean-Francois pleaded.

"Some will, others will kill us with it," Raymond said as he stood up and headed to the door. "You guys want to go public with an alien, get me an alien. Till then, the only aliens the President wants to hear about are Mexicans."

And he was gone.

CHAPTER SIX

The jeep was less than a mile from the Fort Brooks Army Base as the two MPs drove their prisoner along the South Dakota dirt road. At the wheel was Staff Sergeant Harve Sedar, a true patriot who just happened to have turned eighteen on September 11, 2001. The Kentucky boy had taken the attack as a personal insult and went to enlist that very day, but everything was closed. He enlisted the day after.

Eleven years and four stints in Iraq and Afghanistan after that, the buff six-foot-two man was redeployed home and resolved to make the Army his life. He saw no better way to find purpose and meaning, no better way to serve his country and his God. When he learned of a shortage within Army law enforcement, he requested Military Police as his new specialty because his other best career option—drill sergeant—seemed no option at all.

Harve knew that most of the young boys and girls he would train would be deployed somewhere, someday, and most of them wouldn't come back—not in one piece anyway. He himself had had no problem killing enemy combatants, and he respected the heck out of the fine men and women by his side who had died for their country—but the notion of looking fresh-faced young recruits in the eye every morning as he prepared them for their end was simply too much for him to stomach.

It was the right choice. Harve took to his new assignment like a fish to water. The Army couldn't function without rules, he knew, and those who broke them had to be removed or the whole system would break down. He was protecting the military from collapse, and the local townspeople from the military's bad seeds. Barely a day went by that he didn't feel content with the life he had chosen.

Today was not one of those days.

"Come on," cajoled the boyishly handsome, handcuffed prisoner in the backseat as if Harve's best bud. "One grunt to another, lemme go. No one'll be the wiser."

"It's not our call, Private," Harve began with no emotion attached. "You broke the law. You'll stand trial."

"I didn't though."

"You were AWOL."

"I just lost track of time," the prisoner said a little too glibly for Harve's taste. Perhaps the soldier was too dumb to realize the severity of his situation, or perhaps he really just didn't care. Either way, his smart-ass attitude combined with his disheveled uniform and longer-than-regulation hair was causing Harve to develop a serious dislike for the man.

The truth was that the prisoner didn't care—but he had good reason.

Johnny Kester once cared about things—cared about the same things as Harve and just as strongly, minus the Jesus part. The Southern Californian boy had served his tours in the Middle East with the same degree of pride and patriotism as his current jailer. Then the incident happened, and everything changed.

What Johnny had done was unforgiveable, he knew that—but how the Army handled it afterward was even worse. So if he couldn't forgive himself, he certainly would never forgive *them*. On the other hand, they could never touch him.

On the other other hand, he could never get out.

All that was left for him to do was enjoy himself.

Which he did in droves.

And given that he was handcuffed in the backseat of a jeep on the way to a court martial that would never happen, getting under the skin of a fanatically religious, gung ho G.I. Joe seemed as fun a way as any to pass the hours.

"Lost track of time? My hot patootie!" Harve said in response to his prisoner's lame excuse. "You were in a bar fight!"

"The guy came at me," Johnny answered innocently.

"Because you'd been messing around with his wife!"

"She was hot and she liked me. What was I gonna do, *not* mess around with her?"

The MP in the passenger seat laughed. "This guy's hysterical."

Corporal Frank Hatteras had met Harve on their first tour in Iraq, and they had remained brothers-in-arms ever since. He was a gangly, goofy-looking guy with bad teeth and not too much upstairs, but Harve had learned long ago that there's more to a man than smarts. Frank was brave, loyal, a crack shot and a fine soldier, and that was all that mattered.

Still, he couldn't let the prisoner's wrongful attitude be encouraged.

"He is not hysterical," Harve replied coldly. "He is a disgrace to his uniform."

"I can be both," Johnny said with a friendly smile.

Frank laughed again. "I'm telling you, Sarge, the guy's a crack-up."

Harve barely grunted, and Johnny could tell which one of them was calling the shots. But he also knew something they didn't.

"Fine, bring me in," he told them. "They won't do anything to me."

"I dunno, buddy," began Frank. "AWOL's pretty serious."

"Ten bucks says I don't spend one night in that base's holding cell."

"You're gambling on your own liberty?" Harve countered with a fury. "What the heck is wrong with you?!"

"Easy, Sarge," cautioned Frank. "If the man wants to give us his money, who are we to stop him?" Then he turned back to the prisoner and said, "You got a bet."

"Ten bucks," Johnny spelled it out. "Not one single night in that base's holding cell."

BOOM!

The military base a half mile ahead suddenly exploded in giant bursts of fire, the force of which thrust the jeep back and into the air, flipping over and crashing onto its roof on the road's edge.

The Army barracks and the other wooden buildings on the base ignited in flames with the wrath of hellfire. The buildings of brick shattered to rubble. Tanks and metal structures melted to liquid goo. Every building, man, woman and child, all of it, the equivalent of a small town ablaze in giant balls of death until nothing existed at all but a sprawling expanse of desolate land.

And at that very same moment, at every military installation in every corner of the world and beyond, identical destruction was taking hold.

Giant bases and airfields, fighter jets and rockets, battle cruisers and aircraft carriers, space stations and satellites, weapons bunkers and munitions factories both military and civilian, all suddenly exploded in simultaneous violent flame. Submarines underwater burned impossibly. Underground nuclear silos and the atomic missiles they contained disintegrated into a sandy nothingness. Scores of hundreds of millions of men, women and children died in an instant. Iran, England, Pakistan, Israel, Russia, China, Korea North and South, enemies and allies alike. Everyone! Everything!

The entire military capability of our planet was gone.

CHAPTER SEVEN

The news of the planetary destruction had not yet reached the White House. Although late morning, Laurel was still asleep in her bed in the East Wing, Saturday night's vampire battle having taken much out of her—they always did. The President, concerned for what he believed to be his wife's increasingly occurring migraines, had returned from the Oval in between meetings to do his budgetary readings at the small bedroom desk by her side.

Michael gazed at his wife with admiration as the sunlight beamed through the sheer window drapes, casting an angelic hue upon her. Look at her, he thought, as he sipped his black coffee. She was still so sexy to him even after all these years together. Critics often said he had been lucky to win the primaries—the truth he knew was that winning the primaries had been skill, winning Laurel had been lucky.

She began to stir awake.

"Morning," he said with a smile.

"Hey you," she yawned back groggily with affection. "You got home late."

"More hooey with China," he said casually, then added with a smile. "I got all these nukes. Such a pity I can't use them."

"You're bad," she laughed.

She started to get up when he noticed a scratch on her neck—a remnant of her battle's close calls. "What happened there?" he asked.

Drat, she thought. She forgot to conceal it before going to bed. Careless.

"Oh that," she said. "It was just—pfft, nothing, it was stupid. So are you going to get a deal? With the Chinese, I mean."

Before Michael could answer, the phone rang. Laurel was closer to it so she picked it up, playfully answering in a hushed Marilyn Monroe whisper.

"Mr. President's bedroom."

But her playful smile quickly vanished, and she passed Michael the phone. "It's the Chief of Staff. He seems freaked out."

Michael grabbed the phone from her hand. "What?"

And as he listened to the voice on the other end, he grew pale.

"What happened?" Laurel asked him.

He held up his hand to hush her—something he had never done before, which only made her realize how dire a situation this must be. China? Russia? Middle East?

"What I thought I heard you say is not possible, Tom," Michael emphatically said into the phone. "I must have misheard you, Tom. So, slowly, carefully, Tom. What . . . the heck . . . did . . . you . . . say happened?"

Then the room went dark, very dark. But it wasn't just the room, Laurel realized. The outside, the current source of their bedroom's light, had gone dark too. While her husband dealt with his frightening phone call, Laurel went to the window, pulled back the drapes and looked up to the sky.

Something was blocking the sun!

*****

JOHNNY WAS THE FIRST of the three to gain consciousness. With his hands cuffed behind him, he dropped to his knees to face the back of the jeep, then wriggled his palms between the two front seats and into Harve's breast pocket. He lifted the Sergeant's keys, clumsily unlocked his shackles, then shimmied and twisted his tall, thin frame out of the wreckage, only to be utterly astonished by what he saw next.

The base was gone! Actually, physically, completely gone. A billow of smoke here or there but other than that, it was just . . . just . . . gone.

It was impossible.

The crash must have done something to his memory, he thought. The base must not have been as close as he had imagined. This smoldering expanse of nothingness was something else, and the base must be miles down the road.

That made no sense, he then thought.

Were we attacked? Are we at war?

Focus, Johnny, he told himself. Figure it out later. You're free! Run!

Yes, he thought, he should run. If ever there was a time to run now was it. The Army will be consumed with whatever it was that caused the base to vanish—his own existence would be a mere afterthought to them. He'd have the time to get away, find some nice remote place to live out his life, fake a new identity, and never have to think about the incident again.

Run is exactly what he should do.

And he would have ran, if not for the two unconscious men lying in the overturned jeep with gasoline leaking on one end and sparks sparking on the other; two men who would surely die if he didn't intervene.

I'll run later, he sighed as he moved to the jeep to save the lives of his captors.

"Idiot, idiot, idiot," he said aloud as he proceeded to pull them out.

*****

THE WEST WING OF the White House was in pandemonium. Aids and staffers were zipping from one office to another, and all the phones were ringing off the hook. Michael sped toward the Situation Room surrounded by his senior staff, trying to garner as much information as he could before speaking to his generals. But there was little information to be had.

"No one knows who's behind this, sir," answered the Chief of Staff. "The Russians thought we did it until the Chinese accused *them*. Egypt thought it was the Israelis, and Israel thought it was Iran. India and Pakistan assumed each other."

"Nor is anyone claiming ownership for the giant spacecraft overhead," added the Communications Director.

Of course not, thought Michael. What nation on Earth could possibly have the resources to pull off something like this? What human being could be so evil as to kill so many so quickly? So who was it? There seemed to be only one possible explanation but it was too preposterous to accept—and Michael sure as hell didn't want to be the first to vocalize it.

"Set up a conference call with the leaders of the G8," the Commander in Chief barked to his inner circle. "Then put me in a room with the Speaker of the House and the Majority Leader of the Senate. And get the Secretary General of the UN on the phone."

"He was visiting the Erdek Naval Base in Turkey," the Chief of Staff responded sadly. "He died in the explosion."

"Then get me the Deputy Secretary!" the President shouted. "And if he's goddamn dead, get me whoever the hell is in charge over there! Jesus."

Michael and his entourage turned down the hallway where the Vice President awaited. Peyton knew that Michael would be headed to the Situation Room so it wasn't hard to plant himself along the way.

"Mr. President. My God, "he said softly as he approached his running mate. "I was just briefed. What can I do to help?"

Before Michael could answer, two Secret Service agents approached with urgency.

"Sir, we have to get you out of Washington."

"No," Michael told them firmly. "The American people need to know that their President is at his desk and on the job."

"Mr. President, the enemy craft is overhead and –"

"And if they had wanted to take out the White House, they would have done so by now. Your task is to get the First Lady and the Vice President to safety."

"Mr. President," Peyton piped in, "I believe I can be of value here."

"Your only value to me right now is to stay alive."

Peyton looked around, wishing there was a way to speak to his one-time friend and protégé privately, but that was not possible amidst the chaos. He would just have to humble himself in front of the whole entourage, not one of them an ally.

"Michael, please," he began softly. "I understood keeping me out of the political side of things, but this is a military situation. I'm your military guy. It's why you put me on the ticket."

"No, Peyton," Michael responded. "I put you on the ticket to get me the South, and you did. Now, go."

Then he turned and headed off, his senior staff in hot pursuit, leaving the Vice President all alone.

Son-of-a-bitch, thought the former General.

*****

JOHNNY COULD NOT REMEMBER ever having sweat so much, barring only a few close calls during combat. But as he lugged the second MP through the blistering August sun, far away from the burning jeep, he knew that he had done his good deed for the day, the week, the year. He had saved the lives of two jerks who had only wanted to put him behind bars. If that wasn't good karma, nothing was.

He dropped the very large corporal next to the even larger sergeant whom he had lugged to safety minutes earlier, wished them well, and turned to go when he heard a gun being cocked.

"You're still under arrest, soldier," Harve said, lying on the ground where Johnny had left him but now conscious with his pistol pointed at his prisoner's chest.

"You gotta be kidding," Johnny said in amazement. "I just saved your life!"

"And I thank you for that, Private," Harve replied, his cocked gun unwavering. "It showed tremendous character on your part. Nonetheless, you broke the law so, like I said, you're under arrest, Private."

"For the love of . . ." Johnny began, then paused, looked at the sprawling empty land where the base had once been, looked at the still unconscious Frank, then blurted, "Well, he still owes me ten bucks!"

*****

JEAN-FRANÇOIS DIDN'T THINK HE should be allowed in the White House

Situation Room. He was just a physicist, not even a US citizen yet, but Gloria Ames, NASA's deputy administrator, had insisted. These recent horrific events were clear validation of Jean-François's theories, she had told Raymond Saticoy, NASA's big cheese. She could relay those theories competently but not with the expertise that Jeff could. And this was to be before the President! If Jeff couldn't come, she blackmailed, neither would she.

And much to Jean-François's chagrin, she had won.

His plan was to stay in the back and not say a word . . . unless directly asked a direct question . . . and then in as few words as possible . . . and he hoped he would be asked nothing at all. The highest-ranking officers of every branch of the US military were in attendance, as well as the President himself. Despite his many academic accomplishments, Jean-François felt like a little boy on the football field all over again. Please don't kick me the ball, he thought. Please don't kick me the ball.

"From what we know so far," began General Mitchell, the highest-ranking officer in the United States Air Force, "the alien vessel hovering above us is roughly the size of Rhode Island, but it's the only one they seem to have."

"So it's confirmed that they're *aliens?*" Michael asked, almost relieved that there was at least a clear course to pursue, relieved that someone other than he had first said the word, and relieved that the NASA bigwigs were on hand to explain it all. "Extraterrestrials? This is confirmed?"

"No, sir," General Mitchell answered sadly. "It's just, as of now, the only thing we can't rule out."

"The whole world's been hit, Mr. President," added General Wong, the Army's highest-ranking officer. "Every superpower and regional power. Unless it's some—I dunno—James Bond-type super-villain."

The others began to smirk but were quickly shut down by the CIA Director.

"It isn't! No individual, corporation or entity of any kind has ever had the ability to accomplish this. That is a certainty."

"So then, it *is* . . . we *are* . . . talking about aliens?" Michael asked.

The brass and their subordinates reluctantly nodded, murmured yes. It had to be that. Nothing else was possible. Right?

"All right," said the Commander in Chief. "Do we know how they pulled it off? And feel free to go sci-fi-crazy on my ass. We're in unchartered territory, I get that."

"We have no idea, sir," said Admiral Effington. "There was no radiation emanating from any of the destroyed facilities so we know it wasn't nuclear."

"We also know they didn't attack from space," added General Mitchell. "Our world was hit *before* the alien vessel appeared in Earth orbit. Their devices— whatever they were—had to have been planted and detonated from inside."

"What are you saying?" asked Michael. "Like a suicide bomber? Are we talking interplanetary terrorism?"

"That's only our best theory, sir," said General Wong.

"But the precision," added the CIA Director. "The timing. Something like this would have taken years to coordinate. Decades."

Gloria shot Raymond a look of daggers. Isn't that precisely what Jean-François had been warning them about? You fool.

"How we coming with that G8 call?" Michael asked his Chief of Staff.

"Forty-five minutes, sir."

"Good," Michael said as he took yet another moment to assess everything.

Aliens. Goddamn aliens. Really?

"Interesting they'd leave us with our communications," he wondered aloud.

"In what regard, sir?" asked General Wong.

"They're obviously trying to take us out," Michael mused. "So why leave us with an ability to mobilize a united Earth front? They destroyed our weapons and soldiers. Why not our phone lines and TV stations too?"

The room was silent for no one had an answer, then NASA administrator Raymond Saticoy plunged himself into the fray.

"Because they want them," he said simply.

"Come again?" Michael asked, as startled as everyone else.

"They want to live here, sir," Raymond said as he rose and proceeded to pace the room. "They want our phones and our TV stations intact for themselves. They love our buildings, our freeways, our bridges, our entire infrastructure."

Jean-François and Gloria exchanged looks. Where was he going with this?

"They love everything about our planet . . . except *us*! And soon they will begin their slow, methodical extermination of the human race."

"Raymond, what are you talking about?!" Jean-François shouted, no longer able to contain himself. "What you say is not supported by any of the data at all."

"There's data?" Michael asked with growing anger. "You knew about this?"

"Well, yes, Mr. President," Raymond answered meekly.

"Then why the hell didn't you tell someone?!"

"Frankly, sir, in order to maximize panic and confusion, we didn't want any of you to know about us until we were completely ready to begin."

"What?" blurted out a confused Gloria.

"We?" Michael demanded. "What are you talking—who's 'we'?"

"Oh my God!" shouted Army General Wong, the first to solve the mystery.

With no hesitation, the General dove in front of Michael as Raymond tore off his human skin to reveal the .44 Magnum he had concealed within his insect body. His first shot caught the General in the chest but that was not the primary target. His next shot nailed President Addison right through the heart. Mission accomplished.

Within seconds, the room was ablaze with thunderous roars of smoke and gunfire. Jean-François dove under the table, weaponless, terrified. "Raymond" retrieved a second concealed .44 with his free arm, then a third and fourth with his two lower arms. He leapt across the room blasting four guns at once toward the stunned Secret Service and military men. In the short few seconds it took them to regain their wits, duck for cover and harness their weapons, half of them were dead.

Raymond ripped one of the giant TV monitors out of the wall to use it as a shield against the onslaught. A Secret Service agent took advantage of the moment and blasted the alien in the leg. His crusty, chitin scale tore open and he roared in pain, but it did not stop him from spinning around to return a battery of fire, killing the agent, killing a Navy ensign, and killing Gloria Ames.

Jean-François watched in horror from under the table as the shoot-out continued. It was one alien against tens of impeccably trained agents and officers, and the alien seemed to have the upper hand. For a brief moment, he locked eyes with the beast he had previously known as his boss. Raymond bared his nail-like teeth and curled his ugly, snarled lips into some sick, alien smile, then turned back to the gunfight as if to taunt Jean-François for his irrelevance, that he'll kill him later when the shoot-out with the real men subsided.

Jean-François watched another agent go down, another military man, another agent. He watched as a Marine colonel fell to his death, his pistol flying out of his hand only to land a mere inch from the terrified scientist's reach.

Jean-François didn't know what to do. He had never fired a gun before—prior to today he had never even seen a real one. He was a pacifist, mon Dieu!

He trembled as he nervously reached for the weapon. His two hands visibly shook as they held the gun pointed at the alien's massive chest, the widest possible target. With sweat raining from his pores, Jean-François squeezed the trigger and fired a bullet right into the center of the alien's head.

It had all taken less than a minute, but virtually everyone was dead. Raymond, Gloria, the President, all gone except for Jean-Françcois and but one of the Joint Chiefs.

General Wong, the first casualty of the gunfight, dragged himself across the room with his last ounce of life. He fumbled as he reached up to a desk to grab hold of a telephone, knocking it over and down to the ground. He turned his head weakly to face the receiver then uttered his final, breathless gasp, "Get the Vice President."

After that, Jean-François was the only survivor, and he cried.

CHAPTER EIGHT

It was a beautiful afternoon on the subtropical paradise of Key West. Situated on the southernmost tip of Florida—hence the southernmost tip of the continental United States—the sleepy island town was an unparalleled blend of natural beauty, cultural diversity and a never-ending warm breeze of romance. The hibiscus-speckled streets with their conch houses crowned with twin roofs and gingerbread trims had once been home to Ernest Hemingway, Robert Frost, Tennessee Williams and Jimmy Buffet—only a few of the rich and famous who had fallen in love with the peaceful tranquility that the picturesque village inspired.

The horrific news of the morning's alien attack had been kept from the press in order to avoid global panic, although in some cases it was a matter of begging the more clever journalists and broadcasters to sit on the information that they had acquired on their own; and the President's assassination was so recent that most of the staffers inside the West Wing didn't even know about it yet, so the Key West locals and tourists went about their day as if it were any other day in Heaven.

Two cyclists cruised along a charming, residential road. Children splashed each other in an inflatable wading pool on their front lawn. A husband and wife sat on deck chairs on their porch, sipping margaritas while browsing their favorite websites on their iPads.

With no warning, the ground shook hard and violently, the equivalent of a six-point-eight earthquake. A giant wormhole that spanned far beyond the road's four lanes appeared from out of nowhere. Ten thousand human-sized, four-armed, biped-insect soldiers jogged out in perfectly coordinated groups of seven (called "swarms") and opened fire the moment they entered our world.

The first swarm took aim upon the cyclists—their massive cannon-like rifles held steadfast in perfect balance by their powerful upper arms. Their lower arms, having been their middle legs in the earliest stages of their insect evolution, were for pressing the series of buttons that unleashed the ferocious negative density energy.

The weapons erupted in deafening explosions as they emitted solid beams of white light that created tiny voids in space and time, cleanly removing from the world anything with which they made contact.

The second swarm gunned down the husband and wife with equal efficiency. The third swarm ended the children. Each victim lay dead on the ground, having received but a single shot per, dying fast with a perfectly circular, one-inch hole in the center of their hearts.

The fourth swarm out of the wormhole jogged into the first house they encountered, the next swarm into the next, the next into the next, and on and on.

And within each house, their mission was simple: find every human and kill them. They did so with mathematical precision.

Men, women and children ran screaming but they were gunned down as they fled. People hid quietly but they were found trembling and shot. If they tried to fight back with their home pistols or shotguns, they were killed. If they begged for mercy, they were killed. If they were innocent little babies asleep in cribs, they were killed.

Not until a swarm-of-seven deemed a home "clean"—and they had the equipment to know with scientific certainty—were they even permitted to move on, at which point they would scrawl a hideous alien symbol upon the front door then jog to the next unmarked structure.

Speed was not a requirement of their mission, only perfection.

The streets were littered with alien swarms-of-seven moving from one home to the next with the rhythmic exactitude of a ballet. They would pause only long enough to peek into the parked cars they passed just in case a human had managed to find refuge. If empty, they would mark the car "clean." If "dirty," they would kill the human within, then mark the car "clean."

Swarm upon swarm continued to spew out of the wormhole in relentless droves, along with giant tanks, roving high-tech cannons and rockets, and sleek, roofless vehicles on which stood alien officers barking out orders in a language reminiscent of a smoker's cough, their soldiers receiving the orders from great distances via two tiny antennas that protruded from the top of their insect skulls.

If a man or woman running down the street in an attempt to find safety had happened to glance into the massive wormhole, now fully exposed in the day's sunlight, they could have seen into the alien world, and they would have seen a vast green meadow in which awaited infinite lines of biped-insect soldiers carrying their inconceivably sophisticated weaponry—and the man or woman would have stopped running because they would have known that their survival was hopeless.

The floors of palatial, luxury hotels were consumed with alien swarms cleansing one room at a time. Guests and workers alike were running, hiding, jumping out of windows. None of it mattered. They were all as good as dead already.

At the marina, men and women raced to their boats to escape on water only to be gunned down by the alien swarms assigned to them. For the very few who were fortunate enough to find sanctuary on their crafts, lucky enough to sneakily steer their way out of their slips and into the channel, the aliens merely fired upon their yachts and cruisers, converting their vessels into giant balls of fire.

In the police precinct, brave men and women in blue fought valiantly against their alien invaders. They held their ground for almost a minute before they, too, inevitably perished. It required only two swarms to complete the task.

An alien swarm was jogging out of a recently cleansed home as one of them accidentally brushed against a table by the front door, knocking over a beautiful, glass vase. The alien in question dropped his weapon in a heartbeat and lunged for the vase just in time to catch it in his lower arms before it crashed upon the floor, attracting dirty looks from the others. All seven breathed deeply—that was close. The alien smiled his hideous alien smile for a moment as he admired the exquisite, subtle beauty of the vase, then gently put it back in its proper place and jogged out with his comrades.

A local news helicopter appeared in the sky to record the massacre. Six of the seven members of a swarm quickly dropped to their knees and took aim, their free lower arm pressed to the ground to secure their balance like a tripod, while their swarm leader raised her unguis (her insect-y hand) to the air. The six remained motionless, having been perfectly trained for just such an encounter. They stood steadfast on their knees, holding their target in scope, waiting patiently for the swarm leader's command, waiting, waiting. Then, for no discernible reason to the human eye, the swarm leader flung down her unguis and coughed out an order. The six fired, and the helicopter and its passengers were no more.

Bringing up the rear of the seemingly endless battalion was the high command vehicle, an alloy flatbed roughly the size of a billionaire's master bedroom. The vehicle hovered just slightly above the ground as it breezed forward as if of its own volition for there was no cabin, taxi, or driver. High-ranking officers huddled around a three-dimensional holographic map of the city—complete with moving representations of their soldiers in action—as they discussed and debated the progress of their onslaught. Other officers stood by the alloy railings with high-powered scopes, coughing out orders to their subordinates on the ground through holographic communication systems that floated in the air beside them. But all showed an unmitigated deference to the most senior among them, who stood over nine feet tall and weighed more than a ton.

The Alien Commander was pleased with the day's events. The destruction of the Earth's military installations had been accomplished without a hitch; the assassination of the planet's leaders had an almost sixty percent success rate (a tad less than he had hoped for but still respectable), his spies were in place all across the globe, and even the exercise transpiring before him—little more than a drill, really—was showing his soldiers to have the same meticulous aptitude they had shown in the simulations. He could barely wait for the real challenge that lay ahead.

He tapped on the symbols on the keypad strapped to his lower forearm. The ground shook violently, and the giant wormhole vanished as if it had never been there at all.

The Commander couldn't believe that he was actually, finally here. It was like a dream. He took a deep breath to soak in the beautiful Earth air—not nearly as clean as the recirculated synthetic variety on his vessel but far sweeter because it was natural, real. After a lifetime on an alloy ship in deep space, natural was good.

He had been born for this mission. Literally. His genes had been spliced and altered while still in embryo to ensure that he would possess all the physical, mental, and psychological attributes of a great leader. Enormous size to garner an immediate, primordial respect from those who would serve under him, a sharp brain designed for strategic thinking with the agile flexibility to adapt to changing circumstances, and an overly competitive spirit with just a hint of insecurity to make defeat wholly unacceptable. Human DNA (less than two percent) had been carefully blended into his genetic makeup while still in the pupal stage to render a small bump on one of the lobes of his brain—a mini-human-lobe, so to speak—giving him natural intuitive insight to the thought patterns of his future enemy, an unexpected byproduct being flabby human flesh surrounding his insect neck and thorax.

His training had begun at the age of one. He had been forced to play every known game until he had mastered them all. By six, he was laughing at recordings of Earth's greatest chess masters and the simplicity of their thinking. By eight, he had devised his first battle plan, complete with footnotes and annotated sources. His proposal was to introduce a certain virus into the Earth's water that would prove fatal to mankind while having no profound effect on the Vessel Dwellers, thereby obliterating the enemy while keeping the planet's infrastructure intact.

His instructors dismissed his work out of hand, explaining that life will always give way to new life and that such a tactic could theoretically produce an unpredictable ripple effect ultimately fatal to their own kind. (In fact, the Dwellers were already in the process of taking measures to cleanse themselves of all microbes foreign to the Earth ecosystem, as well as immunizing themselves against all Earth germs and bacteria.)

His hard work so easily tossed aside by such intellectual inferiors, the pampered young prodigy did not take a tantrum, did not take a fit. He did not lash out at his instructors or at anybody else. He merely hung his little insect head in shame and cried softly because he had missed something so obvious.

He studied every detail of human cultures and civilizations. He led one simulated battle after another—the terrain, climate, and technological conditions constantly changing to keep him on his toes. In a short time, his instructors were unable to come up with new ways to surprise him, so he designed his own simulations, then took medication to induce a temporary amnesia, then battled against his own plan. Sometimes he couldn't conquer himself, and it enraged him.

Upon reaching adolescence, beautiful females would be brought to him upon his request—all volunteers, because what girl wouldn't want to have the great future leader inside her? But he was only permitted to have his way with them in rooms that had been filled with rotting human corpses (brought to the vessel through wormholes) to condition him to grow sexually aroused by the very smell of human death.

On this day, he was very aroused.

CHAPTER NINE

The official term was "undisclosed location." Others referred to it as the "Vice President's bunker" or the "VP's getaway." To Peyton, it felt more like a prison.

It was spacious enough for it was built to house many important people for a very long time. Buried deep beneath one of the plains states, or one of the desert states (can't tell you), it contained comfortable living quarters with full plumbing, a gym, offices, a Situation Room, and a large dining facility—all the comforts of home.

Peyton sat alone in the large mess hall, a glass of Scotch in his hand, a bottle of Chivas Regal on the table. The few members of his staff that had been brought here with him were somewhere or other—he didn't know and he didn't particularly care. They too, patriots all, were rather miffed that they hadn't been allowed to help in this time of global crisis, and Peyton felt as if he had let them down.

Goddamn President, he thought.

He refilled his glass as he realized that he had already consumed close to half the bottle, and it concerned him. "Do we have any more of these?" he asked the young Marine Lieutenant standing by the front door.

"Would you like me to call up for another bottle, sir?" answered the boy whose sole assignment was to remain by the Vice President's side day and night.

"No, I'm just thinking ahead," Peyton answered.

He reached for the remote and turned on the TV on the wall. It was showing the same footage of the Key West massacre that had been playing all day. It was the third time Peyton was seeing it, but it was just as gut-wrenching as the first.

It was an aerial view of the town showing insect-like soldiers gunning down innocent civilians with calculated efficiency and perfect military formation.

"They're killing everyone!" an offscreen reporter shouted over the batabatabata of the helicopter. "People, police, no one can stop them! Where's the government? Where's the Army? Where is *anyone*?! An alien group is pointing their weapons up at—at us!!!!! Get out! Get out! Get –"

Then the screen went to snow, then back to the news studio.

"The final words of WEYW reporter Jim Bannon," said the anchor. "Aptly expressing the fear and loneliness we all share. Where is help? Where is *anyone*?"

Forty years in the service, Peyton thought to himself. Three times decorated in Vietnam. Helped plan the Gulf War—the first one, the good one. Supreme Commander of NATO. Chairman of the Joint Chiefs. And I'm stuck here for the most vital military undertaking in the history of man.

"Goddamn President," the Vice President said aloud as he refilled his drink once more. "I never should have voted for him."

A side door burst open, and two Marine officers entered quickly and officiously. They approached Peyton, then stopped with a snap.

"Sir, you have to come with us," said the first with great haste. "The President has been assassinated."

"Oh geez, that's terrible," Peyton said. "Did I do it?"

"No sir."

"Oh thank God," he exhaled, relieved.

CHAPTER TEN

The ranch hands—black and white alike—were ending their day as the warm August sun set in the distance. They had been anxious to get home to their families ever since they had heard about the travesty in Key West, but the horses and cattle still needed tending. Besides, what could they do once home anyway, other than continue to conceal the sheer terror that they were already hiding?

The breathtaking eighteen-hundred-acre sprawl known as the Long Tooth Ranch was a local treasure and source of pride. The creek for which the nearby town was named ran right through its center, rushing along rolling foothills, wooded forests, and plush green grasslands on which the cattle grazed. Trophy bucks, turkeys, and wild quail ran free, and the owner permitted anyone who wished it to hunt or fish at their leisure.

Cuddled under the shade of a grand old magnolia tree was the main residence. First built in 1795, the Greek Revival-style home exemplified true Southern gentility. The interior was warm and expensive, an elegant mix of modern-day technologies and old-world charm. The exquisite master bedroom with its rich oaks and fine hand-sewn curtains boasted a gold-trimmed, sixty-five-inch flat-screen TV on its wall. If not for the fact that only a very few of the master's most trusted servants were allowed inside, the room could have graced the cover of most decorating magazines.

Also, if not for the shiny walnut coffin that lay in its center.

When the last trickle of the sun's light vanished in the horizon, the casket door slowly crept open and Julius arose, feeling refreshed. He was wearing nothing but a red satin robe, and it took him but a moment to gather his bearings and remember where in the world he was.

Although the original owner of the Long Tooth—as well as the architect of the main residence—Julius had to vacate his home every thirty years or so lest the townspeople grew suspicious of his immortality. He would return forty or so years after that, claiming to be his own son or grandson. He had been back now less than a year, and he was glad for it. He had always loved the New World.

He hopped to his feet and walked to the small table by the window on which sat a tray with orange juice, toast with peach jam, and that morning's edition of the *Atlanta Journal-Constitution*—all which had been placed there only minutes earlier by one of his trusted servants. The orange juice held no nutritional value for him, of course, but he liked the taste and found it a pleasant way to kick off his night.

What adventures lay in store today? he wondered.

He casually skimmed through the nine-hour-old newspaper for something interesting as he used the remote to turn on the flat-screen, and it immediately grabbed his focus.

"They're killing everyone!" shouted the offscreen reporter over the batabatabata of the helicopter. "People, police, no one can stop them!"

Julius watched transfixed as the Key West massacre unfolded before his eyes.

This was far more adventure than he had counted on.

"Where's the government? Where's the Army? Where is *anyone*?! An alien group is pointing their weapons up at—at us!!!!! Get out! Get out! Get —"

Then the screen went to snow, then back to the news studio.

It took Julius only a few moments to process it all, and then he immediately knew his next move.

Leaving the TV on, he walked out onto the terrace and gazed upon the dark splendor of his Georgia home. Like a whip, he thrust out his arms causing his red satin robe to drop to the ground.

"Come to me, my children!" he shouted at the night sky.

His naked body glistened in the moonlight, every muscle perfectly defined, the actual model for da Vinci's *Vitruvian Man*.

"Come to me now!"

The black sky was rendered even blacker as scores of bats emerged from all corners and flew to the vampire. They perched upon his outstretched arms, his head, his shoulders. They lay at his feet, hovered around his impeccable frame. Only once they were settled and all was still did he continue.

"Summon our friends," he commanded. "Summon them all. Summon them to where I shall be."

The bats retreated back into the darkness with the same speed with which they arrived, now on a holy quest to fulfill their master's wishes.

"Fly then, my children!" Julius called after them. "Summon our friends! Fly!"

He returned inside to watch more of the news. Live aerial footage was now showing the alien army marching up Florida's Highway One in perfect formation, seemingly on their way to devastate the next human town.

And Julius proceeded to map out every detail of his plot.

CHAPTER ELEVEN

Not too far away but much later in the evening, four boys stealthily crept into the Heartsoot Creek Cemetery. It was just past midnight and Patrick, one of the two twelve year olds, was wishing he was home in bed.

They were all aware of the recent events that plagued that day's news, the events that had all the grown-ups a'buzzin', but they were too young for the sudden proof of alien existence to be meaningful to them—didn't everyone already know that? The grainy fifteen-second clip that kept playing over and over on all the channels was so short, and it looked kind of fake—not nearly as realistic as any of the Disney-Marvel movies.

Their true concern for the night was the ghosts that they were hoping and dreading to encounter, and they had been planning their adventure for weeks.

If one of the others said this was a bad idea, he would back them up, Patrick told himself. He just couldn't be the first one to cower.

"You sure we should be doing this?" asked Marcus.

Marcus didn't count, Patrick sighed internally. The kid was barely nine, along for the ride only because his big brother Jeb, the largest of the boys and their clear leader, had allowed it. Being the follower of a nine-year-old was just as bad as being the first to wimp out yourself, maybe even worse.

"Don't be such a chicken, Marcus," said Joey, the other twelve year old.

Darn it, thought Patrick. He had been counting on Joey to be the one to say something.

"I'm not chicken, you're chicken!" Marcus shot back.

As they snuck deeper into the graveyard, Patrick wondered if he should have listened to his mother and avoided these boys altogether. Both his parents had gone to college—his father was one of the only two lawyers in all of Heartsoot Creek—and his mom thought it beneath him to be friends with the offspring of ranch hands, truckers, waitresses, and hillbillies. How could he make them see that he was the only kid in school who *wasn't* the offspring of ranchers, truckers, waitresses or hillbillies? And he had no intention of living his life without friends so he had no choice but to prove his mettle.

Besides, other than being a little crazy—like crazy enough to waltz into a graveyard looking for ghosts—these boys were okay, despite what his mother said.

"No, you're a'scared of the ghosts," said Joey, his teasing of little Marcus growing relentless.

"Lay off him, Joey," Patrick said, coming to the tike's rescue. Right is right. "He's just a little kid."

"Butt out, Patrick."

"C'mon. We're all a little scared."

"I ain't scared!" Marcus piped in. "'Cause there ain't no such thing as ghosts!"

Great, thought Patrick. He had said it out loud. Darn that Marcus.

"Is such a thing, though," replied fourteen-year-old Jeb with the quiet wisdom that comes with age. "Ghosts. Yeah, seen 'em with my own eyes. Plenty times. But best not be 'fraid 'cause they feed themselves on our fear."

"Whoa," said the other three in frightened unison.

The boys continued their trek through the darkness, their tiny key-chain flashlights being their only source of illumination, unaware that they were approaching a large, slimy, sticky puddle of green pus that they couldn't possibly see—Mary's alien blood from her encounter with Julius three nights prior.

It was nothing but dumb luck that caused the first three to step right over it, but the luck ran out for poor little Marcus who stepped right into it, tripped on it, and landed face first in the slimy green goo.

Joey and Jeb immediately began to laugh. Only Patrick felt for the poor kid.

"Shut up! It ain't funny!" shouted Marcus.

"It's hysterical," laughed Joey.

"Burn in hell, Joey Thomas!" Marcus shouted as he stood up and flung a handful of the slime into Joey's face.

"Hey!" yelled Joey.

"Come on, guys, take it easy," Patrick cautioned. "You'll get the ghosts mad."

"He'll be a ghost when I'm through with him!"

Joey lunged furiously at Marcus, but big brother Jeb intervened to cut him off. "Calm down, Joey. You ain't laying no finger on *my* li'l brother."

"I sure as hell am!" shouted Joey. "Look what the little retard done to me!"

But Jeb wouldn't have it, and easily held the smaller boy back. But in the struggle, much of the green slime on Joey got smeared onto Jeb. No one thought this particularly meaningful at the time.

"He may be a little retard," Jeb said with authority as he raised a clenched fist aimed at Joey's nose. "But he's my little retard, and you ain't touchin' him. Got it?"

"I'm a retard now?" asked Marcus, more hurt than before.

"I'm protecting you, stupid," Jeb answered.

"That's it. I'm going home. I'm telling Ma."

Marcus turned around and started back out of the cemetery. Jeb quickly shoved Joey aside and raced after his little brother in true fear. Ma would beat the crap out of him if she knew about their little adventure—he'd get it bad for traipsing into the graveyard at night, but he'd get it even worse for having brought little Marcus with him.

"Don't do that, buddy," he begged his kid brother. "C'mon, I brung you with us, dint I? I'm making you one of the big kids. Don't make me wrong fer it."

Marcus had every intention of savoring the moment of big cool Jeb being at his mercy, but suddenly something felt off. "Jeb, I feel funny," he said in a plea for help.

"You know what?" Jeb replied as the same odd sensation began to sweep over him. "I do too a little. Okay, kiddo, let's go home. This was a dumb idea."

"Yeah."

The two brothers walked off, leaving Patrick and Joey to follow along or to continue on the adventure as a twosome.

"Well I ain't going in there with just *you*," Patrick told Joey, feeling fortunate to finally have the out he'd been craving all night.

He was the only one of the four boys who hadn't come into contact with Mary's blood, and he had no idea how fortunate he was.

CHAPTER TWELVE

The cruise ship was somewhere in the mid-Atlantic as the earliest rays of dawn peaked up over the horizon, the sun itself still buried across the sea. Two spectacularly beautiful women leaned on the rail, gazing out upon the marvel with feelings of delight and loss.

"We had better head down," said Prague, an exquisite blonde woman with ocean-blue eyes, milky white skin and a supermodel body. "We must get below deck," she repeated in her ancient Slavic accent when her lover failed to respond.

"He's never summoned us before," said Africa, making no attempt to move.

Her skin was dark as night, her brown eyes rich and seductive. Her curly black hair fell along the back of her perfect hourglass figure and down to her lusciously round buttocks. Her natural smile could captivate the world— and it did for almost every moment of the night and concealed day. She was the fun one, the prankster, bringing warmhearted laughter and smiles to all her kind, her only sadness coming moments before the dawn because she knew she would never again see that most astounding beauty of creation. And with the sun soon to rise, she was sullen once more.

"Do you suppose it is because of the aliens?" she continued to her beloved.

"It must be," Prague answered. "Now, come. We best get below."

Prague started off but Africa remained.

"Don't you wish you could witness it once more?" she asked. "Just once?"

"That's what movies are for."

"I know, but a *real* sunrise. Don't you wish that just once more we could –"

"No, I do not!" Prague said forcefully to stop her ingénue from pursuing such nonsense. "And nor should you, young one. No good derives from such juvenile fantasies. Now come."

Prague extended her hand to lead her lover below deck, but Africa merely turned her head away, clearly hurt by her mentor's tone.

Prague instantly realized that she overdid it—Africa was no longer the innocent that she had rescued in ancient Carthage so long ago. She returned to the railing and leaned over by Africa's side. "Do you regret it?" she asked softly.

"The life?" Africa asked in response. "The life with you? No, not at all, my darling. It's been an exciting, magnificent journey—and I'd be long dead and forgotten otherwise. It's just that sometimes I think about the old days too. Don't you ever?"

"I used to," confessed the older vampire. "Then I met you, Africa."

Africa smiled. She took her mentor's hand, ready at last to go below deck to safety, when two very inebriated men arrived on deck.

"Holy hell!" said the first drunk upon seeing the beautiful vampires. "Look at the two 'a 'you! Just wanna do ya both right now!"

For some reason unbeknownst to anyone, his drunken friend found this very, very funny. "Shut up, dude," he blared through his loud chortles.

"No, I do, bro," said the first drunk. "I mean, hell, look at those tits. Just wanna bury my face in 'em and go aaaaaaaaaaaahhhhhhhhh!!!"

Prague looked at Africa and calmly asked, "Hungry?"

"I could eat," Africa answered with a playful smile.

Then Prague turned to the drunks and said, "Follow me, boys. Today's your lucky day. Meow."

She headed below deck as the drunks followed, exchanging high fives. Africa brought up the rear, doing her best to keep her fangs in check until that perfect, final moment when she could devour the poor, wretched souls.

CHAPTER THIRTEEN

By now, the people of the world knew everything.

They knew about the destruction of the military facilities. They knew about President Addison's assassination, along with the assassination of close to sixty percent of the planet's leaders. They knew about the Key West massacre, the Key Largo massacre, the Florida City and Homestead massacres and every massacre in between, and they knew that the aliens had spread west across the state while still marching north—a massive moving embankment systematically killing every human in their path with no one to stop them.

The panic and confusion that the Alien Commander had sought was in full force across the globe.

Peyton sat behind the large desk in the Oval Office while a young lady applied his makeup. Technicians set up lights and camera as a small fan blew at the Stars and Stripes behind him to make it proudly wave.

He had taken several cold showers and drank several pots of black coffee since learning of Michael's assassination the prior afternoon. He had been whisked back to Washington on Air Force Two whereupon the Chief Justice of the Supreme Court swore him in as the next President of the United States. He had spent the rest of the evening and night conferring and planning and negotiating and strategizing with most of the world's leaders—many of them as new to their jobs as he.

He had spoken extensively with Jean-François early that morning, the

NASA astrophysicist and sole survivor of the Situation Room murders, and the only man alive who had ever actually *known* an alien.

By midmorning, the new President had seized control of all commercial and private airports, commandeered their planes, and issued top secret orders to have manufacturers retrofit the smaller jets as bombers. The crafts would lack the technology of the modern era, and there would be no time for safety inspections. It all had to happen fast, down and dirty, just an airplane with bombs, a pilot and a bombardier. World War II style.

And as soon as his speech was done, he would be meeting with his newly appointed Joint Chiefs—none of whom he thought of highly, the best of the best having all been killed.

His senior staff had spent their time sweating over every word of the critical speech that was soon to be broadcast live to the world. They respected the hell out of their boss, but they knew that public speaking had never been his forte. But if he just stuck to the script he'd be okay.

With only moments to go, the young Marine Lieutenant who had been by Peyton's side since the bunker approached him with a small, silver, whiskey flask.

"Your, uh, medicine, sir," he offered discreetly.

Peyton looked at the flask almost salivating, paying no attention to the worried looks of the others. This was his battle alone.

"No," he said to the boy with bold conviction. "The next drink I take will be after I win this thing, or after I'm dead."

Everyone breathed a quiet sigh of relief, including his staff (who also silently prayed that Peyton didn't word things like that on camera. Just stick to the script, boss.)

"In five, four," began the director. "Three, two."

Cue Peyton.

"My fellow Americans," the General read from the teleprompter. "It is with great sadness that I address you in my new role as your President. As many of you know, extraterrestrial invaders have murdered President Addison. Michael was a good man, a great American, and a dear friend, and he will be missed."

Peyton's Chief of Staff breathed another sigh of relief. Peyton had fought him on calling Michael "a dear friend," but the little white lie was crucial for the world to hear. But he said it nonetheless, and he pulled it off. Only those who already knew it was a lie could feel the insincerity. To everyone else, Peyton just seemed rather stiff—a win under the circumstances.

In homes, offices, bars, restaurants, and institutions of every kind, the world was glued to their sets. They wanted—*needed*—to know that someone was going to do *something*.

"The invaders have destroyed all military bases and facilities across the globe," the President continued. "They have killed over ninety percent of our planet's fighting men and women. Their intention is to create mass panic and to exterminate mankind –"

And with the world on the edge of their seats, the teleprompter went dead.

"Um, their intention is to create mass panic," Peyton mumbled as he tried to recall his next line from memory.

The Chief of Staff began to panic himself. Can he cut off this live broadcast? Right at that point? But can he let Peyton proceed with no script? Which is worse?

He was about to tell the director to shut down the broadcast when Peyton defiantly raised his hand to stop him. He knew what needed to be said—and he didn't need someone else's words to do it. He's got this, his hand gesture clearly indicated.

"To create mass panic and exterminate mankind," he repeated purposely this time, forcefully. "But I—and *you*—will not let them succeed."

Not bad, thought the Chief of Staff. A brief, succinct and powerful line, and one that had not been in the original written speech. Not bad.

Around the world, a few people even smiled—a glimmer of hope?

"We have seized control of the airlines," Peyton continued off book. "If you live in Florida, flee to the nearest airport to be flown to safety. Tickets are not necessary, this one's on us.

"To date, Florida is the only land on which the aliens have appeared, but the other nations of the Earth prepare for their fight, as do we. I have been in close communication with the other world leaders, and we prepare as one.

"American reserves have been called to active duty. Survivors of our armed forces are to report to the nearest recruitment offices for new orders.

"Veterans are urged to volunteer for active duty recall. American military personnel abroad are ordered to support the militaries of their host nations. There is no time for all the nations of the world to deploy their remaining soldiers home, and the chaos that would ensue is exactly what our alien invaders are counting on—and the aliens get what they want no longer.

"But if you're here, if you're nearby, and if you've ever worn a uniform—be it ours or another nation's—we need you.

"For there are no countries anymore. Just us, and them.

"Too many of the world's soldiers are gone, and we need *you*!

"Veterans in prison will be granted full pardons if you fight with us."

In prisons and penitentiaries across the country, former soldiers in orange jumpsuits cheered loudly. Many stood and saluted the screen.

"Civilians, untrained adventurers who have ever fantasized of battle, we will give you the tools you need. Hippies, peaceniks, pacifists of all stripes—this is a war like none before it. If you're willing to take the life of monsters that strive to end you, if you're willing to risk your own life to save humankind, we need your help.

"Burglars, gangsters, organized crime, it's time to do your part," Peyton went on. "Give us your weapons. Donate your guns and pistols and whatnots. You have them, and we need them. It's time to step up, boys."

The Chief of Staff thought that part a little weird but, judging by the looks on the faces of the people in the room, it didn't seem to matter. In both the Oval Office and around the world, the mood was shifting. The General was on a roll.

"My fellow North Americans," Peyton continued to ad-lib as he exponentially grew into the role that had fallen upon him. "Tourists, immigrants legal or otherwise, we can win this, but it will take all of us. For more than ever before, it is clear that we people of the Earth are one family. The rivalries of our past must be forgiven, if not forgotten. For we embark upon the most important battle our world has ever known. The stakes have never been so high, the consequences of defeat never so final. Extermination. Extinction.

"Well, not on my watch!

"We will come together because we must! We will stay together because we are one people, one race, one planet, one family! And we shall be victorious because we are good! Damn those bugs, and God bless the human race!!!!"

In homes, offices, bars, restaurants, institutions of all kind all around the world, people clapped, cheered, whooped and hollered. Many shed a tear or two.

And in one small coffee shop in a sleepy town in South Dakota, Harve shed a tear as well.

PART TWO

WAR

INTERLUDE #2

Three of the Deinonychus eggs had already hatched, but Dinah's focus remained on the one that hadn't. She nudged her giant snout against the egg with concern, hoping the jolt would awaken the life within. Why is this taking so long?

Only a few feet away, the three hatchlings waited impatiently. Let's call them Donald, Daffy and Dizzy—Donald, the first hatched, being the precocious one. They made small, chirpy sounds as they whined at their mother to hurry, brushing softly yet persistently against her large, feathered haunches.

So much to do, so much to learn, come on, Ma! their gestures insisted.

Dinah knew they were right. The last egg would hatch in its own time, when it was ready, whether she watched it or not. It wasn't fair to deny the others the life lessons they so needed and deserved.

She looked down upon them then uttered a soft shriek. "Follow me," it meant. "Single file."

This not being the first lesson, the hatchlings were expected to know what to do. Dizzy, the only daughter, fell in line right behind her mother, with Daffy behind her, and Donald bringing up the rear.

It's a good line, thought Dinah. Straight and ordered with no stragglers.

It was a simple exercise, of course, but a crucial part of a Deinonychus hatchlings' training because the Deinonychus hunted in packs with many complex maneuvers and strategies, each dinosaur utterly reliant on the other. The first lesson of teamwork was to learn to *walk* as a team.

But little Donald didn't like being in the back. He was the oldest by several minutes, and instinctively knew that he should be the one to lead the brigade. He could even lead Ma—boy, wouldn't she be proud to see that!

He stepped out of line and briskly waddled ahead of Daffy, then Dizzy, and then Ma herself. Dinah instantly bit down on the feathery scruff of his neck, picked him up and dropped him back down in the back of the line.

"No!" meant her loud shriek, and Donald got the message loud and clear—at least for most of the day.

For several more hours Dinah led her hatchlings in a perfect formation in a large circle around the nest. When she at last spotted two lizards by a tree several yards ahead, she decided that it was time to ratchet things up a notch.

She breathed a barely perceptible chirp, then crouched down low to demonstrate how to stalk prey. Daffy and Dizzy followed suit, but Donald was confident that he already knew how to kill a lizard, and he was eager to prove it.

With a bolt, he charged out toward the lizards. The lizards heard him easily and whipped off in opposite directions. Donald chose the closer one and leapt straight at it, missing completely, crashing headfirst into a tree.

The dazed little dinosaur stood up in a fog. He took a few staggered steps like a drunken hobo, and then fell down again.

The edges of Dinah's mouth curled upward as she exhaled a series of gaspy squeaks, a repugnant facsimile of fond laughter, a horrid nasal sound to human ears but one that fully conveyed her undying love for her hatchlings.

Little did she know that only a few yards behind them, lurking in the brush near the nest, an adolescent Tyrannosaurus rex was scoping out the unhatched egg. Certain that the Deinonychus mother was preoccupied, the young T. rex made a beeline for the nest, crushed the egg open with his powerful claws, then gobbled up the soon-to-be-born hatchling inside!

Dinah heard it, turned to it, saw it—but only while it was happening and thus too late. She shrieked loudly and charged.

The T. rex tore off in a snap. Claw heard the cries from the woods and bolted to chase after the T. rex as well, but to no avail. Even a teenage T. rex can outrun an adult Deinonychus, and he and his mate both knew it.

Helpless, defeated, the parents howled. They nestled against each other to offer comfort, but there was no comfort to be had.

CHAPTER FOURTEEN

The patrons of the small coffee shop were still clapping, cheering and whistling at the TV the on the wall. The new President had concluded his awe-inspiring speech only moments before, and one could barely hear the cable-news pundits who praised and criticized him. But no one was as moved as Harve who sat at a booth with Frank and Johnny, once again in handcuffs.

They had spent much of the prior day walking to the town. By the time their cell phones had reception there was nobody to call. No one was answering anywhere, which Harve had thought quite strange at the time. He got them a single room in a cheap motel to hole up for the night and figured he'd make more calls in the morning. It was from the motel room TV that the threesome learned about the horrors in Key West, the aliens, the assassinations, the military facilities, everything.

By morning, Harve's plan was for the three of them to simply wait it out in the town until he could figure out what to do next, who to contact, where to go. Be it days, weeks, whatever, the bottom line was that he still had a prisoner to bring in. He just didn't know where to bring him.

So they went to breakfast, and they saw the new President's speech.

"You cryin'?" Frank asked Harve, noticing the tear in his eye.

"No."

"Oh my God," Frank teased. "Harve! You been crying!"

"Shut up."

"Harve is a crybaby," Johnny sang like a schoolkid. "Harve is a crybaby."

"Whatever," Harve replied, having wasted too much time on this particular point already. "Gimme your hands."

"Why?" asked Johnny.

By way of answer, Harve forcefully grabbed hold of Johnny's wrists, then unlocked his handcuffs. "Like the Commander in Chief said, you've been pardoned. Now let's go."

"Where?"

"To get our new orders, obviously," Frank answered on his Sergeant's behalf. "Let's go kick some alien butt!"

"Yeah, right," Johnny laughed. "Count me out, thanks."

"It's the condition of your pardon, moron," Harve said firmly.

"Don't care."

It wasn't so much that Johnny was afraid of the aliens—which he was, everyone was whether they admitted it or not—but fear wasn't what was stopping him. Mission after mission in the Middle East, it never had. This was simply a matter of there being no way in hell that he would ever go to battle for an army capable of the things for which he knew them responsible.

"Buddy," Frank explained softly. "You only get the pardon if you fight."

Johnny turned his hands palms-up and offered them to Harve. "Then take me to jail."

"Wouldn't know what jail to take you to if I wanted to," said Harve. "Which I don't. Now let's go."

"Not a chance."

"Listen, Private," Harve said as he grabbed Johnny by his collar and stared coldly into his eyes. "You're going to fight . . .and possibly die . . . or I'll kill you myself."

"That'd be murder," Johnny stared back. "You'd end up the one in jail."

"I'll be pardoned."

*****

ADELINE MCGIBBONS HAD SPENT the morning glued to her TV. She couldn't tear herself away from the endless replays of Peyton's speech, particularly enjoying the channels that juxtaposed the images from the tragedy in Key West with the sound of the President's promise of victory and a new world order.

She was surprised when she realized that it was almost eleven. She had to be at Alma's Bar & Grill in half an hour to work the lunch shift, but she was also dying to watch one more replay with her sons. She felt a little irresponsible for letting them sleep this late, but it was summer.

"Marcus! Jeb! Rise 'n shine!" shouted the single mom as she butted out her cigarette and marched up the rickety stairs and into their bedroom.

"Up 'n at 'em, boys. President Willis made a speech last night and the whole world's gonna change. You'll be tellin' your grandchil'n 'bout today someday."

But neither of them budged.

"Come on, sleepyheads!" she shouted as she yanked the covers off their shared double bed.

They looked bad. Something was wrong with them. There were blotches on their face. Their teeth were rotted. Their fingernails had grown inches overnight. And their newly opened eyes looked dead.

"Oh my God!" she shouted. "What happened to you?!"

They reached up their arms as if to hug her. She wrapped her arms around them, physically assuring them that their ailments would somehow be mended.

"Awwww, my babies," she said. "It'll be okay."

Marcus slowly reached his hands to her cheeks then chomped down hard on her nose, biting the skin clean off her face, leaving only exposed bone in its stead. Jeb tore his rotted teeth into the back of her neck and gouged out a mound of her flesh. Adeline screamed in shock and pain as she fell to the ground. The young zombies dropped on top of her, gnawing away at her entire body with disgusting drools and ghastly smacks of their lips, ultimately devouring their mother like the starving little cannibals that they had become.

*****

A BEAT-UP OLD Chevrolet Silverado sped along the country road at breakneck speed. Joey's father was at the wheel while Joey's mother sat in the backseat with her son, who looked just as bad as his friends Jeb and Marcus.

"It's okay, sweetheart," Joey's mother said soothingly. "We'll get you to Doc Brady, and he'll fix you right up."

"Almost there," said Joey's dad. "You hang in there, sport."

Joey looked up at his mother with his sad, dead eyes. He sputtered a little sound, trying desperately to speak.

"What is it, snookums?" asked the mom as she leaned in, putting her ear to his mouth to listen closely, then the son bit the ear clean off. She jerked back and screamed in pain, when Joey took hold of her face and began to eat away at that too.

Joey's dad turned to see the horror that was transpiring. He reached back to yank his son from his wife, but Joey merely bit off his finger.

The father screamed. The Silverado careened out of control and crashed full speed into a large sugarberry tree. The hood squashed like an accordion, and no one came out of that car for a very long time.

*****

LAUREL SAT ON THE floor of her bedroom in the East Wing of the White House. She held a framed photograph of the former President, and she was crying.

There was a knock at the door. She put the photo back on the nightstand, sniffled as she grabbed some tissues and quickly wiped away her tears. Only once she felt her old self did she respond.

"Yes? Come in."

Secret Service Agent Denison entered. "Anything I can get you, ma'am?"

"No, thank you. I'm fine," she answered unconvincingly. "Thank you."

"Very good, ma'am," he said as he started back out.

But she needed someone to talk to, and she had known Denison for such a very long time. "He wouldn't have won without me, you know."

"Yes, ma'am."

"Forget the presidency. He wouldn't have made it through the primaries without me."

"That's what the papers and blogs said, yes."

"So I killed him."

Denison sighed. "Don't do this to yourself, ma'am."

"The aliens wanted the president dead," she explained. "If he wasn't the president, he'd be alive. If I hadn't been so damn charming, he'd be alive."

"You weren't that charming, ma'am."

"Flatterer," she said with just a hint of a laugh.

Denison knew that warmth had never been his forte, but his job was to support the slayer any way he could. He had never let her down before, and he wasn't about to start now. He walked to the edge of the bed and sat down on the floor next to her as he took her hand.

"He was a beloved governor with a solid record and a determined mind," said the Guide with as much gentleness as he could muster. "You helped him, true. But make no mistake. He was the one who won."

She took this in, then felt the need to change the subject.

"You still planning to reenlist?"

"I was a US Marine Corps major. Under the circumstances, I think I have to."

"You do," she said with a sigh, missing the big man already. "When?"

"As soon as I get you back into fighting form. I owe that much to the Society." He kissed the top of her head and stood up. "So you got twenty more minutes to grieve, then it's back to work," he added as he headed toward the door.

"I need more time than that."

"I know you do. You just don't have it. They're coming and in big numbers. They see the panic the aliens have caused, and they're coming to retake the town you've denied them these many years."

"I'm the one who told *you* that."

"Yes you did, ma'am. So don't think for a moment that I won't kick your butt to get you ready just because I feel bad for you."

"I would never accuse you of such kindness," she said with a smile.

"Ma'am," the Guide smiled back, then left the room and closed the door behind him.

Laurel reached out for Michael's picture again. She kissed it, then pressed it against her bosom. She looked up to the sky in wonder.

How on Earth could she continue to be what they wanted her to be? How on Earth could she trust her slayer instincts, feeling as she felt?

She didn't think she could.

CHAPTER FIFTEEN

The military blockade at Jacksonville's north and west city lines stretched for miles, rendering access impossible without a fight. Marines with binoculars were positioned along the beaches, scouring the Atlantic for unusual activity, rendering a surprise attack from the east impossible as well. The only way into the city was from the south, where the aliens were, and it too was being watched extensively.

Security stations were set up at half-block intervals to validate each volunteer's true identity. Behind them were upright X-ray machines through which approved soldiers would need to pass to confirm their human-ness. Behind those were formerly retired Navy SEALs with M16s in case anyone tried to crash the line.

In front of each security station was an endless queue of jeeps, trucks, cars, motorcycles, and men and women on foot, all waiting their turn to be confirmed. Most, but not all the men and women, wore uniforms. Most, but not all the uniforms, were American, and most, but not all, didn't fit. The groups included seniors, the obese, the disabled. The organized chaos was akin to US customs at a major airport on Christmas. The call had been answered!

Harve, Frank and Johnny got out of the bus with other volunteers, then made their made to the back of the queue. The scope of the blockade and the thousands of men and women who showed up were nothing less than overwhelming.

"Wow," said an astonished Frank. "Look at all these people."

"It sure is encouraging," Johnny said in reply.

"So you're ready to fight now?" Harve asked him.

"No. But with such a great turnout, I don't think I'll be needed."

Harve whacked him behind his head, grabbed his sleeve, and yanked him to the back of the queue where the three men awaited their turn.

Miles away, at the opposite end of that very same queue, a Canadian Armed Forces Lieutenant and a US Army Captain held charge at one of the security stations. The Lieutenant sat at a makeshift desk on which was a laptop connected to a small metal plate. The Captain, who sported a deep scar that ran from the top of his left temple across his lips and down to the bottom of his chin, stood behind with a clipboard and pen, the overseer of the whole operation. Both wore dark glasses to combat the Florida summer sky.

"Next!" shouted the Lieutenant.

A sickly thin man in his midforties slowly stepped forward on crutches. He wore tattered clothes, had long, greasy hair, and he was missing a leg.

"State your name and rank, then place your hand on the plate," the Lieutenant barked, treating the man like any other applicant.

"Private Roger Hayes," the man said humbly. "Rog."

Rog placed his hand on the metal plate like he was told. It hummed softly as his service record popped up on the screen, along with old driver's licenses, birth certificate, hospital and phone records, high school transcripts, old e-mails and love letters, photos of good times and bad—the entire digital life of a man, compliments of a paranoid government.

"I know I can't do no proper fighting no more," Rog continued apologetically. "But I saw the veep on TV and thought I could, I dunno, pitch in maybe?"

Next in line, sitting atop Harley Davidsons were a Mexican Army Sergeant and her lower-ranking kid brother. The Sergeant was a beautiful woman with short black hair, fierce brown eyes, a fire-breathing dragon tattoo on her left arm, and more attitude than most men could handle.

"Get the lead out, you monkeys!" she shouted.

"Wait your turn, Sergeant!" snapped the Canadian Lieutenant.

Sergeant Sanchez smiled, laughed internally.

"You really think we should start off by insulting the officers?" asked kid brother Miguel, a dashing looking boy in his own right..

"They think we're 'less-than,' *chico*. We gotta show these *pinche gabachos* we're 'more-than,' just so they treat us 'good-as.'" She then turned back to the officers. "Let's go, *pinches*! I got me some bugs to kill!"

"I'm warning you, Sergeant!" shouted the Captain-with-the-scar. "One more word and you're back of the line!"

Sanchez raised up her palms in surrender, mimed zipping her mouth closed, then snapped a sarcastic salute.

"Like that," she told Miguel. "They'll remember me now."

The American Captain and the Canadian Lieutenant shook their heads at the noncom's blatant disrespect, their natural instinct being to dole out punishment on the spot. But their orders were to be inclusive of everyone. Man, woman or child, as long as they could be confirmed as human, if they wanted to fight, they were in.

They turned their attention back to the task at hand and surveyed the onscreen life of the handicapped man before them.

"You seem to have disappeared for some years," said the Lieutenant as he studied the screen. "What have you been doing since the war?"

Rog looked down to the ground in shame. "Well, panhandling mainly."

"Oh yeah, there it is," the Canadian continued as he stared at the screen. "It's all over your police files. Arrested four times, eh?"

"Five," he shamefully corrected. "But two of them were—I was just hungry. I got myself arrested on purpose so they'd feed me."

"He is who he says he is, Captain."

The Captain-with-the-scar leaned in to skim Rog's military service. "Impressive record though. Bronze star, purple heart."

"Yeah," sighed Rog as he awaited the "but" that was sure to follow.

The Captain looked at the Lieutenant for a moment, then came to a decision. "We'll find something for you, soldier," smiled the Captain-with-the-scar.

"Yeah?"

"Welcome to the American Division of the New International Armed Forces."

"Yes sir!" Rog shouted giddily as he saluted with an ear-to-ear grin on his face—clearly his first smile in a very long time—then hobbled through the X-ray machine to confirm his humanity beyond reproach.

*****

THE WELL-DRESSED COUPLE going door-to-door meant well. They were aware that some people found their visits an annoyance but for others it was the first step toward salvation, and it was well worth bearing the brunt of the occasional rude comment in order to help their fellowman find Christ.

They approached a dilapidated old shanty near the swampy part of the creek—people who lived in places like this often needed their guidance most. The door was open, but they rang the bell anyway. When no sound came out, they knocked.

Adeline McGibbons staggered toward them. She looked worse than her sons had earlier that morning for she not only had the same rotted teeth, blotchy skin, extended fingernails and dead eyes, but much of her flesh had been chewed away, leaving large patches of her skeleton exposed. She gazed blankly upon the do-gooders as they began their pitch.

"Hello, neighbor. We can see that you are having a bad day. And with all the horrible events happening in the world, many wonder if God really exists. What are your thoughts on this topic?"

Adeline drooled for a moment, then wrapped her arms around the pious man and proceeded to chomp on his flesh just as her own had been chomped on earlier.

The devout woman screamed and turned to run but there stood zombie-Jeb and zombie-Marcus who flailed their arms upon the unsuspecting do-gooder, knocked her to the ground, and pigged out on her fine sinew and muscle.

*****

ON THE LONELY COUNTRY road, a brand-new, shiny BMW convertible peeled to a stop in front of the totaled Silverado that had crashed into a tree. A yuppie man and woman quickly got out of their car and raced to the wrecked vehicle.

"Are you okay?" shouted the woman. "Is anyone in there?"

"I think they're dead," the man said sadly as he peered into the van. "No, wait! The little boy's breathing!"

The woman whipped out her cell phone to call for help, but there was no signal. The man reached into the open window to pull out Joey, then snapped back his arms as he cried out in pain.

"Damn! The kid bit me!"

"Honey, we don't know what we're doing," said the woman. "Let's hurry to the next town and send help from there."

"We can't just leave them here," said the man, rubbing his bite mark.

"Even if you manage to pull them out, what're we going to do? We won't know what to do. And pulling them out may cause them even more damage than leaving them still. We need to get them professional help."

"All right, all right," said the man as he rubbed the bite on his hand and started to sway. "But you'd better drive. I feel kind of weird."

She took the keys from his hand, they got into the convertible, and the woman peeled out. A moment later, zombie-Joey crawled out of the open window. A moment after that, his parents, zombies both now, crawled out as well.

*****

"NEXT!" SHOUTED THE CANADIAN Lieutenant.

The sun was already down for it had taken Harve, Frank, and Johnny most of the day to make it to the front of the queue. Johnny, the next in line, extended his arm in mock courtesy to allow Harve to cut in.

"Age before beauty."

"Go!" Harve said as he pushed the Private forward.

"Name and rank. Place your hand on the plate," barked the Canadian.

"Private Johnny Kester. And for the record, I'm here under duress."

"No one cares, boy," replied the now weary Lieutenant. "We need bodies."

Johnny's service record popped onto the screen, and the Lieutenant seemed immediately flummoxed. He turned toward the next station where the Captain-with-the-scar was standing, and called out. "Captain!"

"Now what did he do?" Harve smirked to Frank under his breath.

The Captain-with-the-scar approached as the Lieutenant pointed to the screen, "Take a look at this. He checks out otherwise."

The Captain looked at it then turned to Johnny. "Private Johnny Kester?"

"Yes sir," Johnny answered.

"You were a chopper pilot?"

"Busted," Johnny said matter-of-factly.

"You were not," blurted Harve, assuming this to be another one of Johnny's scams. "He wasn't," he said to the officers.

"Was, actually."

"Not a chance."

"Pretty good one, if I do say so myself."

"You have to be at least a lieutenant to be a pilot."

"Was a captain before I—let's not get into it. It's embarrassing."

"Correction, sir," said the Lieutenant. "You *are* a captain."

"What?" blurted Harve.

"What?" blurted Johnny.

"All crimes and infractions have been pardoned by order of the Commander in Chief," explained the Captain-with-the-scar. "And we sure do have a shortage of pilots. An honor to have you with us, Captain."

"Captain," Johnny said back officiously, then turned to Harve. "And you'd better start treating me with some respect, soldier."

"I don't believe this," Harve muttered.

*****

NOT TOO FAR AWAY in the Jacksonville district of Northbank, abandoned skyscrapers loomed along the edge of the St. John's River. The once vibrant hotspot where metropolitan crowds would mill through trendy shops and restaurants, quaint old buildings and giant new ones, central offices of banks and insurance companies, had given way to the hustle 'n bustle of soldiers in a hurried attempt to convert the area into a military-base camp. Makeshift offices were set up in charming old bed-and-breakfasts, clothing-store chains became storage bunkers, fast-food restaurants converted to mess facilities, and luxury hotels turned into soldiers' quarters.

Irish Defense Force Major Sean Shaughnessy walked at a brisk pace as he led Peyton and entourage to their destination, and Peyton's Chief of Staff did not seem pleased.

"I wish you'd reconsider, sir," pleaded the Chief of Staff.

"I'm not going to reconsider," said the President. "I'm going to appoint the most qualified general to run this war, and the most qualified is me. Next?"

"But there are so many other tasks a president needs to perform."

"Like what?"

"Um, well, you need to nominate a new vice president."

"I nominate the Speaker of the House."

The Chief of Staff paused for a moment, unable to speak as he processed this. "Um, sir," he said in awe. "That's kind of brilliant."

"Yeah?"

"Yes, sir. The Speaker is next in the line of succession anyway. And by nominating a member of the opposing party, you'd be showing unparalleled bipartisanship in a time of global crisis. It guarantees a swift confirmation in the Senate while making you a hero to the nation."

"I just never liked the son of a bitch, and it's a crappy job," Peyton admitted "But say it to the press your way."

They arrived at the front door of the towering Wells Fargo Center, which was guarded by four Army Rangers with M16s. Major Shaughnessy barely paused as he began the password sequence. "DiMaggio."

"Gretsky," replied one of the Rangers.

"Jabbar," answered the Major.

Three of the Rangers stepped aside as the fourth opened the door.

Peyton and the others entered and were instantly greeted by Army Colonel William Williams, Peyton's handpicked deputy commander and longtime subordinate, who proceeded to guide them through the massive lobby now converted to a veritable arsenal. Rows upon rows of shelves upon shelves of M16s, AK-47s, Glocks, Beretta M9s, RPGs, grenades, cannons, Uzis, and countless samples of heavy artillery filled the giant space along with enough ammo to overthrow a small country. The good Colonel went on to explain how this was only one of sixteen facilities just like it spread throughout Northbank, and Peyton was quite impressed.

"Where did they all come from?"

"Some were ours, some from local police. Various embassies and consulates. Museums, street gangs, the Mafia. But mostly from survivalists."

"God bless the nutjobs," the President said with a smile.

"Aye, Mr. President," added Major Shaughnessy. "We also have a bleedin' fleet of Hummers given by local car dealerships, armored vans from security companies, and bleedin' helicopters from the news stations. Aye, we're armed as armed can be."

Peyton picked up one of the RPGs and pressed it against his shoulder as if taking aim.

"Any regular citizen can buy one of these?" he asked.

"Yes sir," answered the Colonel.

"Bet those bugs never factored in our messed-up political system."

CHAPTER SIXTEEN

That same night, two lobbyists were walking through Washington's National Mall. They had lived in D.C. for over ten years but had still never tired of visiting the inspiring structures.

They strolled alongside the Reflecting Pool toward the Lincoln Memorial when a handsome young couple in tattered clothes approached them. The couple seemed down on their luck, and the men braced themselves for the handout plea.

"Excuse me," asked the young man. "We're a little lost. Could you help us?"

"Of course," said the lobbyist, relieved that they wouldn't have to dole out any cash. "Where are you trying to get to?"

"Hell!" the young woman shouted with a smile as she hissed and revealed her fangs! The young man followed suit, and the two vampires pounced.

From out of nowhere, Laurel leapt in front of the demons, wooden stakes in hand, and thrust. But in the time it took her to yank her stakes out of their vanquished hearts, three new vampires appeared behind her. She whipped around to face them only to sense five more approaching from the back.

It was a trap, and she had walked right into it.

They formed a circle around her as she quickly sized them up. In a flash, she dove headfirst to the ground and cartwheeled straight at one of them. With her hands on the ground, she wrapped her legs around him, backflipped away and flung him across the circle into three of the others.

She sprung back to her feet as two more charged her from opposite directions, their dastardly fangs unfurled. She jumped straight up into the air, causing them to bash into each other and fall to the ground, then she landed with one foot upon each of their chests, driving the wooden heels of her stilettos into each of their hearts.

Then five more vampires appeared. Then six more after that.

This time they charged as a unit.

She leapt into a spread-eagle position and took out four at once—two with a wooden stake each, two with a designer heel each—but it wasn't enough. The others grabbed her before she could recoil.

Lacking the strength to free herself from their powerful hold, she used their own leverage against them, causing them all to tip over and land in the water of the Reflecting Pool with a mighty splash.

She killed two more as they fell, and two more while underwater, but more kept coming. Ten more, twenty more, thirty.

Laurel fought valiantly as the battle stretched from one end of the Reflecting Pool to the other, but ultimately there were just too many for her. By the time she reached the far side of the pool, fifty of the fiends had her pinned down while Prague and Africa held her face in the water, drowning her.

Trap indeed.

Maybe I was destined to end like this, she thought as she clung to the last drop of air in her lungs. She would be with Michael soon.

She could see the Washington Monument—blurry from her underwater point of view—and then what appeared to be a man standing by the foot of the pool.

"Let her breathe," she thought she heard him say.

Prague and Africa yanked Laurel's head out of the water by her hair. So deep was her gasp for air that she barely felt the pain.

But when she saw the man's face, she couldn't comprehend how this could be the one who saved her. For it was the one vampire she hated most of all, and the only one that she truly feared.

"Hello, slayer," the vampire said with a wry smile.

"Well, well, well. If it isn't my old friend Julius," she said casually, refusing to let any of them see how terrified she actually was. "At last we meet."

"The pleasure is all mine," Julius answered.

"So you finally caught me. And it only took what? A hundred of you? A hundred monsters to beat up a girl—you must be so proud."

"You're probably wondering why we haven't killed you by now."

"We want to, you know," hissed Prague.

"Dying to," hissed Africa with a cold smile.

"I'm here to offer a truce," Julius explained.

"You're what to offer a what?"

"Temporary, of course."

"What are you talking about, monster?"

"You can't beat the aliens, Laurel. They're stronger than you humans and smarter than you too. I know this because they're stronger and smarter than *us*."

"And why do you care so much about human survival all of a sudden?"

Julius took but a moment to answer. "Because the aliens are messing with our food source, and we can't have that!"

Laurel stared at him. It was a good answer for him—utterly selfish and pure evil, hence the only answer she could possibly believe. But how could she believe him at all?

"So what do you want from me?" she asked.

"You must arrange a meeting between the new President and myself. Explain what we are, and vouch for us."

"And how do I know this isn't one of your little monster tricks?"

"Because we're going to let you go, stupid," he told her. "You slayers have been a thorn in our side for eons. Every atom in our bones cries out for us to kill you. But instead," then he turned to Prague. "Let her go."

"Are you certain?" Prague asked, hoping he would change his mind.

"I don't speak otherwise."

Prague turned to Africa and the others. They removed their hands from

Laurel and backed away, disappointed all.

But Laurel refused to get up, refused to be in debt to her arch-nemesis.

"And what if I don't do your bidding, monster?"

"Then both our kinds will be no more, slayer," answered the vampire.

CHAPTER SEVENTEEN

The streets of the sleepy rural town of Heartsoot Creek were littered with mutilated zombies staggering aimlessly about or feeding on the screaming living, soon to be zombies themselves. Marcus, Jeb, Joey, Adeline, Joey's parents and the well-meaning religious couple may have been the first to spread the virus but that gave them no special privilege—they had to find their own prey just like the rest.

Twelve-year-old Patrick Hutchins sat under the kitchen table with his father's hunting rifle perched between his trembling knees, a long-corded telephone receiver clutched in his sweaty hands. The only boy of the prior night's graveyard adventure who had not come into contact with alien blood, he had no idea what had happened to his neighbors, or why he was among the few that had been spared. All he knew was that after waking up late and playing hours of Grand Theft Auto—which he wasn't really supposed to do but his parents were off at work—he looked out his bedroom window to see the zombie hordes gorging on those he once knew, and he had no desire to be eaten himself. So he sat under the kitchen table and frantically dialed, impatiently waiting for someone on the other side to answer.

"Heartsoot Creek sheriff's office," said Deputy Louise Trent at last.

"Please! Send help!" he shouted. "Everyone's turned into zombies!"

"Patrick Hutchins, is that you?" asked the Deputy. "Does your mama know you're making this call? Do you know how much trouble you could get into for –"

The downside of living in a town where everyone knows everyone.

He heard the front door creak open—the door his mom kept slightly ajar in the summer for added ventilation. Why hadn't he locked it? he wondered. Stupid!

He dropped the phone and, with rifle in hand, snuck to the side of the swinging door that led to the living room. As carefully as he could, he pushed it open less than an inch to peak through it.

Oh thank goodness, he thought. It's Dad!

"Daddy!" he shouted as he flung the rifle onto his back and raced toward his father. "What is going –"

He stopped cold the moment he saw it. Dad had been zombified!

"Oh no! They got you!"

The zombie moved toward the boy slowly. Patrick backed away, terrified.

"No, Daddy, don't," he pleaded. "Please. Just remember, I'm your son. Just remember a little bit. Why can't you remember me?!"

But Mr. Hutchins had no ability to remember the life he had once possessed. Patrick was no longer a son to him, just food. He continued to stagger forward as Patrick continued to back away when he hit the wall on the other side of the stairs. He was pinned. There was nowhere to run, and the zombie kept moving at him.

He whipped the rifle off his shoulder and pointed it at his father, praying to God Almighty that he wouldn't have to use it.

"Daddy! Please, don't! I'll shoot! I will!"

But Daddy didn't stop, couldn't stop. He walked straight at the boy until the barrel of the rifle jammed into his chest.

"Stop!" Patrick wailed.

The zombie flailed his arms trying to grab hold of Patrick.

Patrick fired!

The zombie's chest blew wide open as he sailed back across the living room, crashing onto the stairs with a thud.

Patrick dropped to the ground and sobbed.

Outside on the street, the zombies heard the gunshot. They instinctively turned toward its source, staggered toward the house and through the door that zombie-Mr. Hutchins had left wide open.

The boy saw them in an instant. Fired! They flew back, but others kept coming in their place. Fired again. Same deal.

He had to run while he still had the chance, he realized. He bolted up the stairs, leaping over his father's corpse when Mr. Hutchins suddenly opened his dead eyes and grasped for his son. The shock of the thing's cold hands against his jeans caused Patrick to lose his balance and fall, his knee jamming smack down into his father's now brittle skull, crushing it to mere shards.

With the other zombies clamoring and climbing over Mr. Hutchins to nab the boy, now inches within their grasp, Patrick leapt over the bannister and back down to the first floor, then sprinted back into the kitchen and out the back door.

Where there were still more zombies!

He could see his bicycle lying on the grass just a few yards away—if he could get to it, he could ride to safety. As the zombies from inside the house were filing out after him, he realized that he had no choice but to be brave. He ran straight toward his bike, hence straight toward two of them, then faked a move and ran around them. Easy, as it turned out. He did the same with the next two, then deked out three more. It was just like playing touch football—well, life-or-death touch football.

They were slow, he realized. Slow and stupid. That discovery could be the only thing that would save him, he told himself.

There were only two zombies remaining that stood between him and his bike, but they were too close to it for him to grab it. He stopped a few feet before them, waiting for them to come to him, drawing them near.

"Come on," he said to them. "Come get me. C'mon."

But the others were approaching him from behind. This better work!

At last, the zombies in front began to stagger toward him. A quick deke and he was around them, yanking his bike up by its handlebars, jumping on it as he ran.

Terrifying, he thought, but not so difficult. He turned back to check the distance he was putting between himself and his predators, unaware that he was about to ride straight into the clutches of another zombie right in front of him!

He saw the thing at the last second! He swerved aside just as the zombie grasped at him, its decrepit hand instead finding its way in between the bike's spokes, severing it from its skeleton arm.

Another lesson learned, thought the boy.

*****

HE HAD BEEN PEDALING for close to an hour but he still did not feel safe. Although the zombies were far behind him on the lonely country road, they were still following in their slow, relentless pursuit.

Patrick knew that he had to get to the sheriff's office. Even if they didn't believe him at first, it would only be a matter of time till they saw what was going on, and at least he'd have law enforcement to protect him during the wait.

But what he saw next shocked him to his very core. The wood bridge over Keller's Ravine, the bridge that had always been there, the bridge that he had been counting on, was half-gone. It was as if someone had taken an axe or a bomb or something to purposely destroy any access from one side to the other.

He pedaled to the edge of what remained, got off his bike and studied it. It was at least ten feet to the other side over a twenty-foot drop to a rocky gorge below.

And the zombies behind him were coming, still coming.

He considered riding off-road and into the brush, but then he heard noises emanating from it. Maybe they were people who could help him, maybe harmless animals. But as he probed further—no, they were more zombies coming at him from the side.

He looked down into the ravine again. It was crazy to do what he was about to do, but it was even crazier to do nothing and let the zombies get him. He had to try. God help him please, he had to try.

He walked his bike back away from the ravine, then began running with it toward the drop. He jumped on the bike in full motion and pedaled as hard and as fast as he could, harder and faster than he ever had before. A mere half inch before the drop, he jerked up the handlebar in a desperate attempt to alter his trajectory and put gravity on his side.

Then he was in the air. Sailing upward over the gorge with his eyes closed, then downward again.

He opened his eyes just in time to see that he wasn't going to make it! He could see it. Just a few feet short!

At the last second, he pushed his feet down hard upon his pedals and lunged himself up over the handlebars, flipping over them and landing on his back on the ground on the other side of the drop.

He could hear his bicycle crashing on the rocks below, splintering into a million pieces. Could've been me, he thought.

He lay on the ground, panting. He smiled as he realized just how lucky he had been.

Then from out of nowhere, the business end of a sawed-off shotgun was shoved against his nose. A seven-year-old, blonde-haired, blue-eyed pixie of a girl wearing tattered denim overalls and messy streaks of mud on her face angrily held her cute little finger against the trigger.

"Who the poop are you?!" she yelled at him.

CHAPTER EIGHTEEN

He was just one of fifty managers in the United States who had been charged with the top secret mission of converting private airplanes into bombers, and at this moment he could not have been more proud to have been given the assignment.

He gazed out over the rail to watch his workers below tearing out seats and cutting holes in their crafts' fuselages, constructing ordinance bays in their place, and loading payloads into the newly retrofitted mechanisms. It was all going swimmingly.

It seemed that his whole life had led to this moment. His service in the Air Force, his experience as an intelligence officer and consequent vetting for the high security clearance he would require for this task, and his long tenure at Boeing. He wondered how many of his old friends were currently managing factories like this one across the country, around the world for that matter. It was of no consequence though. They only needed one of them on the inside, and each factory would have at least ten. He already recognized a few of the workers on the assembly line from the large space vessel on which he had been born.

He had originally hoped to be chosen as one of the moles assigned to the destruction of the Earth's military facilities because that task was an absolute, this one merely a fail-safe. He was crushed when he had learned that he hadn't made the cut, but the Commander explained that this assignment was just as crucial to the cause and had a ninety-six percent probability of coming to fruition.

"The Earth people will absolutely try to convert their peacetime aircraft into weapons because it's the smart thing to do," he had told the hundreds who had been assigned the same task that magnificent morning so long ago when they had been wormholed to Earth. "It's the only thing they *can* do. It's what I would do. If they don't think of it, they're even dumber than I thought, and this enterprise will take even less time than planned."

As usual, the Commander was right. He was always right.

The manager knew that he would die in glory—it had been the Commander's promise, and the Commander never lied.

Songs would be written about him. His descendants would be showered with wealth and honors. And he himself would live forever as One-with-All-Matter.

He looked at his watch. It was almost time.

He caught the eye of one of his old vessel compatriots. They smiled a subtle, bittersweet smile to one another. It was time. Mission accomplished.

Songs would be written about them.

Three, two, one . . .

The manager flipped a switch.

And at that precise moment across the nation, all across the planet, factories just like this one ignited into giant balls of fire, ultimately reduced to mere piles of ash and scrap metal.

No human aircraft was to be converted into weapons, and mankind would have no aerial support in the coming battle. The Alien Commander had decided that long ago.

CHAPTER NINETEEN

Upon hearing the news, Peyton was utterly silent—so silent that it concerned some of the others. Had the man cracked? Was he thinking about drinking again?

He sat at the head of a conference table in the boardroom on the mezzanine of Northbank's luxurious Omni Hotel, surrounded by a bevy of political aids and his newly handpicked commanders. They silently waited for him to speak, but he merely rubbed his chin pensively and stared at the three-dimensional map of the city that had been set up across the room.

He had chosen to wage his final stand in Jacksonville in the northernmost part of the state in order to buy himself some days to organize his new army while still keeping the enemy landlocked with seas on both sides, and also to drum up a strategy to defeat them. But with the bugs expected to enter the city the following morning, and lacking any kind of Air Force, he still had no ideas.

"We have other factories ready to gear up, Mr. President," said the Chief of Staff. "We can still have the bombers you wanted. Just give the word and we're a go."

"No," was all Peyton said in reply as he continued to rub his chin.

"It'd only put us a few days behind schedule, sir," added Colonel Williams.

"This was all top secret, right?" Peyton asked rhetorically.

"Of course, Mr. President," answered the Colonel.

"And we have no idea how the aliens found out about it?"

"We're still working on that, sir," said the Captain-with-the-scar.

"Then however the damn bugs did what they did, they'd just do the same damn thing all over again," he said with certainty. "Mission failed. Onto the next."

(The Alien Commander had ascribed only a twenty-three percent likelihood that the tenacious Earth leaders would make this correct decision. Had Peyton ordered new factories to try again, alien moles would have once again blown them to bits, along with the hundreds of human people who worked there.)

How the hell do I play this? Peyton wondered.

He knew that the alien forces slightly outnumbered his own, but not by enough for it to be consequential if he could come up with the right strategy. His civilian volunteer rate had been outstanding as even dovish antiwar protesters of conflicts past showed up to help the cause, but unable to spare even one able-bodied soldier to train them, the task had fallen to veterans of World War II and Korea. The sight of eighty- and ninety-year-old drill sergeants screaming their abuses while leaning on walkers would have been comical if there hadn't been so much at stake. Peyton didn't assume that the new recruits would be ready for battle any time soon.

So how do I play this? the General asked himself again.

He had learned long ago that the best way to defeat an enemy is to figure out how they think. Every move the aliens had made so far had been precise, deliberate, and impeccably planned, which told him much about their character.

After mowing down every living soul on the Keys to arrive on the mainland, the bugs had spread their troops across the state as they continued their systematic killing spree north. But once the Florida evacuation had been completed, the bugs reconvened into one single, immense fighting force and headed straight toward the human camp in Jacksonville. This told Peyton much about their strategy and goals.

There are two basic approaches to battle, Peyton knew, be it a world war or a drunken bar fight or anything in between. The first, the most common, is to attack your enemy's weakness to gain a quick and early advantage. The second, far less common yet extolled by many mythical martial-arts guru-priests, is to attack your enemy's strength. Riskier perhaps, more time consuming definitely—but once you've taken away your enemy's strength, the rest is a cakewalk. It was clear to Peyton that this was the tactic his new enemy had chosen.

But that was all he had. The autopsy of the alien spy who had killed Michael turned up nothing of military usefulness, although the biologists gleefully reported that they'd be filling the annals of scientific journals for years to come.

And those assigned to study the aliens' human-skin costume didn't even know where to start. Based on all science, practical or theoretical, it was impossible—yet there it was before them. A marvel of technology beyond anything they had ever seen, they claimed it a perfect synthesis of biology and electronics. Despite the vast difference between the human frame and the insect exoskeleton, the skin seamlessly wrapped around its subject, stretching or contracting wherever needed, filling in every insect cavity while creating every human contour. On a molecular level, it was completely human down to the last cell, fat deposit and zit. It breathed, lived, and even aged whether the subject was wearing it or not. And most startling of all, it somehow masked the insect interior under scrutiny of X-ray, MRI, or CT scan, displaying instead a perfectly accurate image of human anatomy (the health of which being dependent on the character of the wearer.)

Of course, none of this helped Peyton one lick.

There was so much the former general still didn't understand about his new enemy. It was obvious why they had denied him air-strike capability, but he couldn't for the life of him fathom why they had no warplanes of their own, given their obvious technological superiority. A handful of strategic bombers could take out his entire army within days, so why were the damn bugs doing it the hard way?

Then a thought occurred to him, something Jean-François had mentioned to him when they had first met, something that seemed so trivial at the time.

He turned to the astrophysicist who he had been keeping by his side as the resident expert on all things alien—a role in which Jean-François did not feel at all comfortable. "You said they want to keep all our infrastructure intact, didn't you?"

"Well, that's what Raymond—er—the alien who killed the President—er—the other President—President Addison—said. That they want them intact, yes sir."

"And if that's true," Peyton continued slowly, rubbing his chin as he hatched his plan. "And given their m.o. so far there's no reason to believe it isn't—then they won't attack us by air either. If you attack by air, you destroy infrastructure. It's unavoidable." Another brief silence followed, then Peyton sprung up from his chair smiling ear-to-ear and clapped his hands once.

"Okay, boys and girls, we got ourselves a ground war!"

"Yes sir!"

"Or do we?" said the Commander in Chief with a mischievous grin as he crossed to the three-dimensional map.

"Sir?"

Peyton picked up the pointer and laid it all out for them.

"Right down here in Southpoint, in and around this intersection of Southpoint Parkway and Bellfort Road. I want thirty snipers on top of buildings here, here, and here, with enough supplies and explosives to last a month—I'm talking the heavy-duty stuff—cannons, mortar, artillery—and I want the artillery rigged to fire downward not up. Can artillery be rigged like that?"

"In theory, sir, aye," said Major Shaughnessy. "But it'll take weeks."

"You got twelve hours," Peyton insisted, then returned to the map. "Then we do the same thing in this area, this area, this one, and here. As the enemy advances, our snipers lay low, quiet, unseen. We let the enemy march right on past them, a good quarter mile. Meanwhile, the bulk of our troops are positioned along this street, this street, and this one, then here, here, and here. We draw those bugs right to us, right into the ground war they've been begging us for, the ground war they've been forcing us into since the day they got here. We give them *exactly* what they expect with our ground troops blasting at them from the front—and then we rain the wrath of God down upon their scaly butts from the rear. And if we need to destroy a high-rise or two in the process, let's do it just to tick the buggers off. Any questions?"

It was all very clear, and very clever. Everyone shook their heads quietly as they did their best to suppress their smiles. Their General was back.

"Good," said Peyton. "Now let's get this party started."

CHAPTER TWENTY

By early the next morning before the crack of dawn, the specific missions had been worked out and orders had been issued down through the ranks. Weapons had been dispersed, command posts established, and the troops were marching across the Main Street Bridge to Southpoint. The enemy was estimated at two hours away.

They may not have been the best-trained, best-conditioned or best-equipped military that the United States had ever sent into battle, but this motley crew of thousands was by far the most motivated. For every soldier knew to the depths of their souls that they weren't fighting for a mere piece of land, a political ideology or even an abstract God that they took on faith, they were fighting for the very survival of their species.

Even Johnny was catching the gung ho fever. He sat in the pilot's seat of the Bell 407 that had been assigned him—one of the many helicopters that the Army had commandeered from local TV stations, each one gutted of its equipment and seats (save the pilot's) to create additional cargo space, the doors on both sides removed for weight. Having memorized the emergency-procedures checklist earlier that morning, he continued to study the overheard and main instrument panels to better familiarize himself with his new aircraft. But the energy and activity that whizzed all around was not lost on him, and he couldn't help but be inspired.

The incident be damned, he thought. It's a new world—maybe it's a new army too—and he wanted to be a part of it.

It seemed that it wasn't only his rank that had been returned to him with his pardon, he was realizing, but his belief in his fellow man as well.

His mission was to transport more than three months' worth of supplies and ammo that the rooftop snipers would need for what was expected to be a long, drawn-out battle—this next drop being his ninth of nine, his last for the day. The thinking was that once the fighting started it would be difficult to get any air support close enough to restock anything—the aliens having proven themselves quite adept at shooting down helicopters in the sky.

Although most of the snipers had begun their march across the city while it was still dark, a few had been ordered to remain back and help with the loading and unloading. Harve and Frank had been assigned to Johnny's aircraft, as were Sergeant Sanchez and her kid brother.

"We don't have to be in the same squad all the time, Anita," said the eighteen-year-old as the siblings shoved wooden crates into the helicopter's newly enlarged cargo space. "I don't want the others to think I need my big sister to take care of me."

"But it's my job to take care of you, *chico*," she told him with a smile. "Before we left, Mama made me promise to keep you safe."

"Well, she made me promise to keep *you* safe."

"But unlike you, I always keep my promises to Mama."

Johnny laughed. He was glad that Sanchez had been assigned to him. Although they hadn't officially met yet, he couldn't help overhearing her conversation with her brother and found her to have a sharp wit, a good heart, attitude up the wazoo, and above all, she was ridiculously hot.

Harve he could have done without.

"All right, we're at max takeoff weight!" the Sergeant shouted. "Start 'er up!"

Johnny whipped through the pre-start, twisted the throttle to idle, and hit the starter switch. The 407 fired right up, and he was reminded for the ninth time that day how much he had always loved the sound. Batabatabata. He was home.

Harve quickly ushered the other three into the aircraft. First Frank, then Miguel, then Sanchez.

"Heya gorgeous!" Johnny shouted over the whirring rotors. "Need a ride?"

"Yes sir!" Sanchez shouted back, ignoring the blatant come-on, merely looking forward to kicking some alien ass.

"You can call me Johnny."

"Oh for Pete's sake!" Harve shouted as he made his way inside. "We gotta get these supplies moving! Fly, you imbecile!"

"That's 'fly you imbecile, *sir*'!" Johnny corrected.

And with that, he steadied the cyclic and pulled up on the collective, easing the 407 up to the sky and then south into history.

*****

EVERY MONITOR ON EVERY wall in the WTLV control room showed a different part of Southpoint where the pending battle was to take place. Army and Navy officers sat at the consoles switching cameras and adjusting angles and zoom while the screens displayed Major Shaughnessy's battalions moving south, and the alien army marching north directly towards them.

"We live in a very 'camera'd' time, Mr. President," Lance explained as he led Peyton through the small Northbank television studio. "Banks, small businesses, hotels, all have their own security systems inside and out. It was just a matter of figuring out how to hack into them all and render them one cohesive system."

"Who are you again?" Peyton asked the young man.

"I'm Lance," he answered then gestured to Jean-François. "I'm with him."

"You told me to put together my team, Mr. President," Jean-François explained. "Lance is my team. He is one of the most brilliant computer programmers alive today. He may not seem it, but he's very smart."

"I seem smart," Lance muttered, hurt.

"Well good work, son," Peyton said, adding with a chuckle. "I've never led a war from a TV studio before."

"Mr. President," interrupted the Canadian Lieutenant at the console. "The soldiers have arrived at their locations and are moving into position."

"This is getting exciting," Peyton said as he jumped into the director's seat.

And just as the snipers headed into the stairwells and elevators of their assigned buildings, all the monitors blinked twice then faded to black.

"This is impossible," Lance said in nervous dismay. "My systems don't crash."

*****

THE ALIEN COMMANDER DID not feel bad for the genocide that he had begun. It was the correct, logical, even "humane" thing to do.

As he led his ten thousand troops north toward battle, he reflected upon the millennia in which his species had had to live inside their metallic vessel in space. He imagined the original ancestors who began the journey shortly before their home planet's sun went nova, and how proud they would be that he fulfilled their dream.

Era upon era, ancestors had scoured the galaxy to find a life-sustainable planet, but it was a difficult, often hope-crushing endeavor. There was no science behind it, no patterns to follow—it was simply a matter of trial and error, a one-planet-at-a-time search, a terribly frustrating process for the ultra-logical insects.

But in time, not too long before the Commander's birth, three prospects were discovered. Each one had a dominant life form that would have to be exterminated, but there was something particularly special about Earth.

It was already built up. It was, in the parlance of its own people, "move-in ready." The dominant life forms on the other life-sustaining planets were still in a primitive phase, their continents lacking anything resembling a city. It would take decades for the Vessel Dwellers to cover those planets with homes and offices, bridges and roads and airports—all the things that make a world comfortable enough to live on—decades during which the bulk of them would need to remain on their vessel in space. And it would take thousands of years more for any of those new constructions to achieve the romance that comes with decay—like the Earth's own Parthenon and Coliseum that the Commander was looking forward to visiting.

Consequently, the Vessel Dweller's ultra-powerful weapons would need to be modified for battle on Earth. Time-space armaments, with their infinite range and perpetual velocity, would be highly inefficient on a planet whose structures one wants to preserve, as well as dangerous for the Dweller soldiers themselves. A soldier in Florida could, hypothetically, fire a beam into and through his human enemy that could continue onward into his own Dweller comrade miles away, through him and onward to blast through the Liberty Bell in Philadelphia, onward from there to destroy the Empire State Building in New York, onward to cause an avalanche in the Arctic Circle, and then off into space to do who knows what. So it was decided that their weapons would be redesigned with a maximum range of one kilometer if unobstructed, and would stop cold upon contact with anything thirteen centimeters in depth—roughly the size of the average adult human chest.

Of course, the notion of peaceful coexistence with these highly skilled builders of buildings had been discussed—the Commander himself as a young teen in training had aptly broached the very topic with his instructors (his liberal phase). If nothing else, he had told them, it would be much easier.

But as he continued his studies, he came to see that humans are a naturally fearful and suspicious species. Even amongst their own kind they are distrustful of all those they view as different, while possessing a deep-seated need to consider themselves superior to their brothers. Any attempts at peaceful immigration could render only one of two possible outcomes: (1) the Vessel Dwellers would be greeted with immediate hostility and violence, resulting in a war for which they had not prepared, or (2) the Earth leaders would greet them with open arms and full immigration, but the Earth people would never truly accept them. In a short time, the Vessel Dwellers would find themselves in a kind of second-class citizenry, if not full-out slavery. It would be a status they would never accept, the result being a messy, disorganized civil war that would take decades upon decades to resolve, with much death on both sides and massive damage to all those beautiful buildings.

ZOMBIES vs ALIENS vs VAMPIRES vs DINOSAURS

All Earth movies, television, literature and art pointed to war, and not one of the thousands of spies he had sent to Earth ever found evidence to deny it.

Far better to take the time to plan carefully, move in swiftly in an efficient, organized manner, and rid the planet of them all within eighteen months.

Besides, with what the Earth people were doing to their atmosphere, the planet would be unlivable for them in less than a century anyway.

He was doing them a favor.

*****

HARVE ALWAYS GREW A little sullen before battle, and it was no different this time as he was flown over the breathtaking sprawl of the city of Jacksonville. It was just his way. Not a Chatty Cathy to begin with, his mind was drawn to his God, his parents, his high school football team, a future life with a handsome woman and many children—all the things for which he'd be fighting and possibly dying.

He knew that others had different ways of preparing themselves for the dangers ahead. His good buddy Frank would mumble the multiplication table over and over, like a prayer or mantra, and often incorrectly. "Six times eight is forty-six, six times nine is forty-six." It was weird and a little sad, true, but Frank had more than proven himself to be a good soldier and loyal friend, so what did it matter?

"Don't worry, *chico*," Sanchez told her younger brother. "I'll be right by your side the whole time. I won't let Mama down."

"Will you stop?!" Miguel told his big sister in his loudest possible whisper.

Poor kid, thought Harve as he chuckled internally. How embarrassing.

"So you got any plans for after the battle?" Johnny asked the Latina Sergeant.

"Yeah," she shot back. "Going to bed till they send me into the next one."

"Good thinking. Want some company?"

"Hey! *Pinche!*" Miguel shouted. "She's my sister!"

Harve hadn't made up his mind up about Johnny—the Captain—what a joke. After induction they had been separated into different units, and Harve was certain that Johnny would go AWOL, but he didn't. The guy seemed competent enough to fly the machine, and he didn't seem phased about heading into a danger zone, but there was just something about the brash Californian that rubbed him the wrong way.

He was glad that Johnny would be flying back to base after this last drop and that a Marine lieutenant would be leading them. The thought of Johnny as CO was too ludicrous to fathom. The Lieutenant and the other twenty-five snipers would be in position by now, and Harve was looking forward to being led by a real soldier.

The helicopter descended into a perfect, gentle set-down on their assigned rooftop, close to the wood crates of weapons and ammo that they had been unloading throughout the morning. All but Johnny disembarked to unload the new drop but there appeared to be not another soul around.

Strange, Harve thought. They should have been here by now.

"You sure we been hittin' the right roof all morning, Cap'n?" he asked with more than a twinge of sarcasm on the word "*Cap'n*".

"Was that a joke?" Johnny replied unfazed. "Hey, everyone! Stop what you're doing! Harve tried to make a funny!"

"I'm just saying, 'cause the rest of them should've been here by –"

"INCOMING!!!!!" Sergeant Sanchez yelled at the top of her lungs.

For charging straight at them were seven swarms of alien soldiers, their weapons poised, the fingers of their lower arms pressed to the trigger-buttons.

And the roars of their blasts were deafening!

Harve and his team leapt out of the way not a moment too soon as white beams of time-space void whizzed right where they had been standing. Johnny dove out of his pilot's seat and hit the ground. He tried to crawl to safety, but where was that? All he could see from his vantage point were deadly white beams and insect legs. A hand came down from above and yanked him up by the back of his shirt.

"Come on!" shouted Harve.

Harve ran and Johnny blindly followed. When the Sergeant dove behind a large air- conditioner condenser, the Captain did the same—an alien blast grazing across the top of his floppy brown hair.

Johnny hit the ground behind the condenser to find his other three passengers there as well. They had removed their sidearms and were shooting back at the aliens—popping up from the condenser just long enough to get off a single shot or two, then dropping right back down to safety.

"Thanks," he told Harve.

"Whatever," Harve grunted, then drew his pistol and joined in the shooting.

But what Johnny saw next shook him to his very bones.

For scattered along the far side of the rooftop, in front of the other giant air-conditioner condenser, behind the elevator and stairwell and every other spot that could be used as cover, lay the Marine Lieutenant and his twenty-five snipers, all dead with perfectly round one-inch voids in the center of their hearts.

CHAPTER TWENTY-ONE

"So you killed your daddy?" asked the little blonde pixie girl in the tattered overalls. Her name was Rhiannon (pronounced "Ree-ANN-in" like the Fleetwood Mac song after which she was named).

They were sitting on the beat-up sofa on which Patrick had spent the night, in her daddy's dilapidated cabin deep in the southeast Georgia woods, the sawed-off shotgun and a large shovel laying by the little girl's feet. The front door swung breezily from one hinge having clearly been shot up sometime earlier. The floor was littered with wrappers of Cheetos, Ding Dongs and Mars bars from which they had gorged, as well as cans of Pepsi and Mountain Dew. Patrick had to admit that although the little girl was the epitome of what his mother would call "white trash," she had been quite an excellent hostess.

"Yeah," Patrick shamefully answered her question. "I mean, I think I did."

"Well ya did or ya dint," Rhiannon said matter of factly.

"Well I shot him in the chest and he *seemed* dead," the boy explained. "But then he got up and tried to bite me. Then somehow I ended up crushing his skull, and he seemed dead again. So who knows?"

"You killed him," the pixie said with authority. "Not the first time but the second. Who else you kill?"

"Um, only him, I think, maybe some neighbors. Mostly I was just running. How about you?"

"Let's see. Ma and Pa. Irene—she's my big sister. And Uncle Ferd, who ain't really my uncle just a second cousin who was havin' sex with Ma behind Pa's back."

"You don't seem sad about any of it," said Patrick.

"Well it's the virus what's *really* killed who they was."

"What do you mean?"

"It's like this," Rhiannon said as she proudly launched into her zombie tutorial. "Picture a picture of a brain. It's got all this bright red pulsatin' stuff here and yonder. That's our feelin's, our memories, our idears—the stuff that makes us us. But when you catch the virus it all goes different. So now picture a picture where only a teeny-weeny part of the brain is lit, and it's all just a dull pinkish, barely pulsatin' at all. That's them. No feelin's nor memories nor nuthin. No longer who they ever was. Just a peein', poopin', killin' machine.

"And if they bite ya, or scratch ya, or heck, if they merely drool into your mouth—if they get any part of them into any part of you, then you become just like them. Dead—but not dead—but dead."

"Wow," said the boy, impressed and terrified. "How do you know all this?"

"Pa was swipin' the cable from the neighbor so I'd watch *Walkin' Dead* when he was passed out drunk. Hey! Want some hooch?" she asked as she made her way to a cracked wood cabinet alongside the wall. "I know where he keeps it, kept it."

"You're too young to drink liquor," Patrick told her. "*I'm* too young to drink liquor."

She pulled out a half-empty, unmarked bottle of something brown and headed back to the boy. "Way this zombie thing's spreadin', we ain't gonna live long enough to be old enough. What's your name?"

"Patrick. Patrick Hutchins."

"Rhiannon Montadel," she said, then raised the bottle in a toast. "Nice to know ya, Patrick."

She took a giant swig of the brown liquid then grimaced. "Ugh!" she cried out. "That's herrible! Ich! Want some?"

"Um, okay," said Patrick as he reached for the bottle—no way being outdone by a seven-year-old girl.

"Got smokes too, if you want 'em," she said, referring to a pack of Kools and a Zippo lighter on the coffee table. "Me, I don't get it, just makes ya cough, but knock yourself out."

Patrick took a deep breath as he prepared himself for whatever the brown liquid held in store, but before he could put the bottle to his lips, the front door creaked the rest of the way open. Rhiannon put her finger to her mouth to hush him.

A zombie had just entered the cabin.

CHAPTER TWENTY-TWO

"How the hell did they know?!" Peyton shouted as he watched the monitors.

It had taken less than an hour for Lance to discover that his surveillance system had been sabotaged, even less time than that to get it up and running again, and even less time than that to realize that he needed to set up some kind of backup HQ in case a future form of sabotage turned out irreparable. But he knew better than to bring that up now because the leader of the free world was pissed.

"Look at that!" the President shouted. "The damn bugs are on every rooftop we're on! How could they have possibly known?!"

Peyton had already warned the ground troops that they would have to proceed without sniper cover, and he despised telling them that. He had already given the order for the snipers to evacuate, but they had all left their communication devices inside the helicopters from which they had fled, so none of them heard the order, and that only served to make him angrier.

"Spies? We got spies right inside us?" he yelled to the room in general then turned to the Captain-with-the-scar. "You were supposed to check everyone out!"

"We absolutely did, sir," answered the Captain. "And our methods and technologies were impeccable. Every single person on this base, soldier and civilian alike, has been thoroughly examined and reexamined for a human past—their service records, employment records, prison, hospital, even high school records in some cases. There is no way that a nonhuman could have slipped through."

"The alien plan runs deep, sir," Jean-François cautioned. "I worked for Raymond for fifteen years, and he was at NASA for ten years before that."

"Maybe they anticipated our plan, Mr. President," the Captain offered as an alternative. "Maybe we did what they would have done so –"

"This is more than anticipating," Peyton told him. "Even if they assumed I'd take a high-ground strategy, look at the screens. The bugs are on every single rooftop we're on, and *only* on the ones we're on. How could they possibly have known the precise rooftops I'd choose other than through spies?"

"There is a third possibility, Mr. President," proposed the Canadian Lieutenant. "If the aliens can travel through time like the physicist says, maybe they knew what we were going to do because they had already seen us do it."

"*Non*, they cannot change their past," Jean-François explained.

"But wouldn't this be changing their present?"

"Imagine the following scenario," began the astrophysicist. "We succeeded at taking the rooftops, which led to us winning the day. To alter that, the aliens would have to send someone back to a time before our soldiers got on the rooftops to warn themselves of their defeat—the scenario we'd allegedly be in now. And let's suppose that enables the aliens to win instead. Why then would they send someone back in time to warn themselves of a defeat they hadn't experienced? Why would they take measures to stop us from holding rooftops that we never held? They wouldn't. They couldn't. Therefore, they didn't."

Peyton merely stared at the physicist for a moment, then muttered to himself. "What a week to stop drinking."

*****

"SO WHAT'S THE PLAN?" Harve asked Johnny as he loaded a new clip.

They hadn't been there long but it felt like forever—pinned behind the large air-conditioner condenser, popping up to fire a shot or two then dropping back down for cover as white beams whizzed all around them. They were heavily outnumbered and outgunned, their pistols no match against the aliens' high-tech-whatever-they-were. And although they had winged a few bugs, they had not been able to fire off a single kill. They may as well have been fighting with slingshots.

"So what's the plan?" Harve repeated.

"What're you asking me for?" Johnny replied.

"Because you're the highest-ranking, you idiot."

"I'm a pilot," the Californian said, as if the most obvious thing in the world. "I don't know anything about tactics. I haven't shot a gun since basic."

"You gotta be kidding me."

"Okay. As senior-ranking, I'll delegate. Sergeant, take the lead."

"Oh for crying out loud," Harve groaned as he popped up, fired off another round, then dropped back down.

"I don't get it, Sarge," said Frank as he ducked back down beside Harve after firing off two rounds of his own, one ripping a bug in its lower arm. "Why aren't they exploding the chopper? They're just leaving it right there in the open. It's like they're giving us a way out."

"Because there's enough explosives in that bird and the crates around it to blow the top three stories of this building to kingdom come," answered Harve. "And themselves along with it."

"And they wouldn't let us get near it anyway," Sanchez added.

"Maybe," said Harve as a thought began to form. "On the other hand, maybe it's our only hope."

"What're you getting at, Sarge?"

"It's a long shot, but we're not going to win this thing with our Berettas. But if one of us can get close to that bird, those bugs won't risk taking a shot at him."

"Or her," added Sanchez.

"Or her. So if he—or she—can get close, then he-she can get inside where we got our M16s, RPGs, everything we need. He-she grabs hold of one of them, then can sit out in the open blasting bugs all the livelong day without a trace of return fire. He-she gives the rest of us the cover we need to hightail it over there, then Johnny, you fly us off this hellhole."

"You get me in that bird, I'll get us off this roof," Johnny vowed.

"It sounds like a suicide mission," said Sanchez.

"So is staying here," Frank said. "At least it's a chance."

"But what's to stop the bugs from shooting down the chopper once we're ten, fifteen, twenty yards off the roof?" she asked.

"You get me in that bird, I'll get us home," Johnny repeated with intensity.

"Enough talk," Harve barked. "This is the plan."

"Hey, *chico*, you don't outrank me!" Sanchez said defiantly. "We're both sergeants, we both have the same three stripes. Just because you're white –"

"Don't go there, girlfriend," Harve barked at her. "The Captain put me in command, I'm taking command. That's all."

Just then, on another rooftop across the way, human soldiers in another helicopter managed to make their getaway. But just as Sanchez predicted, the aliens merely waited for a safe distance to accrue between the roof and the chopper, then fired their rifle-like weapons into its fuel tank. The machine erupted into a giant ball of flame in the sky, leaving only chunks of scrap metal and human bone to drop like bombs to the battlefield below.

Sanchez turned to Johnny. "Think their pilot mighta made the same promise you did, *chico*?"

Johnny merely looked deep into her eyes and answered, simply, "Trust me."

It was a strange moment between them because, for some reason, she did.

"Okay," she said softly.

"So unless anyone's got anything better," Harve announced. "This is the plan."

"I'll do it," volunteered Miguel. "I'll go."

"No!" snapped his big sister. "Miguel, you don't have to."

"Yes I do!"

Sanchez turned to Harve with sheer determination and said, "*I'll* do it."

"No! I will!"

"We don't have time for this!" Harve shouted, then turned to Miguel. "Okay, kid, you volunteered first, you're up. Stay low. Don't let 'em see you. We'll provide distraction and cover. Remember, you only have to get close. Once you're close, you're in. Then grab a weapon and start blasting."

"Got it," said Miguel.

"I'll take decoy," Frank volunteered.

"Good," said Harve. "Go!"

Frank bolted out and sprinted across the roof in the opposite direction of the helicopter. "Hey! Bugs! Look at me!" he shouted, drawing the aliens' fire, diving for cover behind the elevator structure that protruded up from the floor below. At the same time, Miguel hit the dirt and slithered along the ground as fast as he could toward the chopper, concealed only by the gun smoke of battle overhead and the element of surprise.

*****

"FIRE!" COUGHED OUT THE Alien Commander.

In less than a second, the deafening explosions of the alien weapons erupted through the streets of Southpoint. White beams of void rocketed toward their human targets. Giant alien cannons fired Buick-sized globules of time-space nothingness eradicating ten humans at a time. Bulletproof alien tanks rolled effortlessly forward to crush the human barricades that blocked the roads.

But the humans fought back. Flame and smoke exploded from their M16s and RPGs as they fired from behind the barricades that they had constructed; they fired out through the open windows of modern apartments and office buildings; fired down from the giant oak trees that populated the boulevards' medians and roadsides; fired up from the sewers in which they stood, only the barrels of their M16s and the tip-tops of their helmets exposed; and the human artillery units positioned a quarter mile back rained infernos upon the alien tanks, blowing them to bits long before they could get close to touching the humans' barricades.

The once charming roads were enveloped in smoke, fire, flames, white beams and globules—the integrity of the human structures kept intact thanks only to the pinpoint accuracy of the alien soldiers and their Commander's severe orders. Red and green blood gushed and spewed everywhere. The screams of the dying could not be heard over the thunderous ruckus of battle. Humans were dropping like flies. Bugs were dying like people. Human medics dragged their casualties onto stretchers by the hundreds, then into ambulances to be driven north to hospitals, while dead and wounded aliens were engulfed in wormholes and whisked back home. In terms of calculating the deceased, it seemed an almost equal battle except for one terrifying fact.

Every time an alien could fight no more, be it from death or injury, the ground shook, a wormhole opened and a replacement insect soldier ran into our world to blast away in his stead!

The alien forces could not be lessened.

CHAPTER TWENTY-THREE

The zombie staggered its way into the dilapidated cabin without a goal or purpose—it just happened to have found its way there.

Rhiannon motioned to Patrick to hide. She picked up the large shovel that was almost as big as she was, then moved toward the coat closet that was directly along the zombie's jagged path. She opened the closet door and hid behind it, knowing full well that the zombie had already seen her, yet confident that the oblivious creature wouldn't remember something that had happened almost five seconds earlier. She grunted as she raised the large shovel over her shoulder and waited to strike.

The zombie staggered aimlessly past her, then the little girl bashed the metal blade across the back of its skull. The zombie went down fast, but Rhiannon had been through enough to know that it didn't mean the thing was in fact dead. So she bashed the shovel down upon its head again, and again, and again.

She was panting hard because the shovel was so heavy for her. The thwack of each strike was so loud that she couldn't hear the second zombie stagger into the cabin, and with her back to the front door, she couldn't see it either.

The zombie wobbled straight toward her, salivating over its next feed. She remained unaware as it reached out its skeleton hands to grab hold of her.

BAM!

The zombie flew back and away from the little girl with several bullet holes sprayed across its chest. Patrick stood on the far side of the room holding the smoking shotgun. He smiled at the girl, proud that he saved her.

"You idiot!" she yelled at him.

"What? I just saved your life."

"First, you only shoot 'em in the head," she explained as if it were the most obvious thing in the world, then proceeded to bash in the new zombie's head with the shovel. "Second, you don't shoot 'em at all."

"Why not?"

She gestured toward the window. "That's why not," she scolded as Patrick looked outside to see dozens more zombies turning toward the cabin and heading their way. "They's attracted to big noises. Don't you know anything? Now what do we do?!"

"How the heck would I know?"

"You're the older one. Come up with something!"

Patrick tried hard to process everything he had learned on this very strange day. She was clearly right about the zombies liking loud noises—he had witnessed that very thing firsthand when he had shot his father and more zombies came into his house, he just hadn't realized at the time that he himself had been the cause.

He needed to create a loud noise behind the approaching zombies so they'd turn around and go the other way. But how does one do that?

Then he had a wild thought. He had seen it in a bunch of movies, he just wasn't sure if it was true, if it would work in reality. But with no better options, he raced back to the coffee table and picked up the bottle of moonshine.

"Now? You're boozing it up *now*?" Rhiannon asked. "You're just gonna up 'n quit just like that? Okay, gimme some too."

"No one's quitting anything," Patrick said hurriedly. "I'm trying something."

He ripped a piece of fabric off the dilapidated sofa and shoved it into the bottle, then grabbed the Zippo lighter off the coffee table and raced back to the broken front door.

"Oh, I see where you're goin' with this," she said. "It's crazy but it just might work."

"Let's hope," Patrick said as he lit the sofa fabric that hung from inside the bottle. He waited just a moment for the rag to ignite into a good solid flame then flung the bottle over the zombies' heads where it landed on a rock behind them, igniting in a perfectly loud explosion.

Like a herd, the zombies turned toward the sound of the blast and staggered away from the cabin.

"Sweet," said Rhiannon as she raised her hand for a high five.

Patrick slapped her hand then embraced the command position worthy of his years. "Okay. You got backpacks? Let's pack up every liquor bottle your father had and tear up more rags from the couch—this trick might come in handy again. And let's pack up some rocks and pebbles 'cause those might be enough to fake out one or two if we're in close range. And let's get some water in canteens or jars or whatever you got. I'll hang onto this," he said as he put the Zippo in his pocket.

"What's the water for?"

"We might get thirsty," Patrick answered simply. "Now, you got any bikes?"

*****

THEIR PREPARATION WAS COMPLETE. Rhiannon sat on her little bicycle in her father's dilapidated shed next to his dilapidated cabin, her two feet touching the ground by her tippy-tippy-toes. She wore a large backpack overstuffed with supplies, and the shotgun was strapped across her shoulder. Patrick stood next to her on her older sister's bike, wearing an even larger overstuffed backpack from which the shaft of the big shovel jutted out.

"We got to get to the sheriff's office," he explained. "They're the only ones who can help us, and they're not going to believe this stuff till they see it. The zombies have probably forgotten about our exploding liquor bottle by now and are just staggering around stupidly again, so they may spot us and try to follow us, but they're slow, and it won't be hard for us to keep ahead. You just gotta tell me about any more bridges that you took out or roads that are –"

He stopped short as he noticed a huge smile growing on Rhiannon's face, along with an occasional flare of little-girl giggles.

"What's so darn funny?" he asked.

"You're on a girl's bike!" she laughed.

Patrick sighed. Really?

But he decided not to engage the child on this point and said, simply, "Ready?"

"Lock 'n load!"

They quietly nudged their front wheels into the shed's double doors to push them open, then peddled their way out along the dirt road toward the safety of the sheriff's office.

CHAPTER TWENTY-FOUR

Miguel slithered unnoticed along the rooftop floor toward the helicopter as Frank zigzagged at full speed out in the open, drawing the aliens' attention.

"Catch me if ya can, ya scaly varmints!" he shouted, diving from one safe haven to the next, dodging white beams with what could only have been sheer luck while Harve, Sanchez and Johnny—two of the three of them being crack shots—fired their pistols to provide him with cover. When an alien popped out from behind a chimney top to fire at him, Sanchez leapt up and plugged a bullet between its eyes.

It was their first kill.

"Hooah!" she shouted.

Meanwhile, Miguel's belly ached and burned as it scraped against the rooftop's gravel floor. With only yards remaining, he jumped to his feet to sprint the rest of the way, putting all his faith in the notion that he was too close to the explosives for the bugs to risk taking a shot at him.

And he was right! The Yankee Sergeant's plan was right! By the time the bugs saw him racing to the chopper they were powerless to do a damn thing about it.

But no one could have foreseen that the ground would begin to shake, that a wormhole would appear directly in front of him, that an alien soldier would ascend into our world to replace the one that his sister had killed, and that it would blast a perfectly round one-inch void through the center of Miguel's heart.

*****

"HOW MANY DAMN BUGS are on that damn ship?!" Peyton roared as he and his team watched the devastation on the monitors from inside the WTLV control room.

As bad as things were on the rooftops, the situation on the ground was even worse. Human forces continued to dwindle while the size and strength of the enemy remained a dismal constant. And as the disparity between the two forces grew, the swarms were at last able to get clean shots at the human artillery, blowing them out en masse. Without artillery, the human soldiers could not prevent the alien tanks from mowing down their barricades, leaving those who weren't crushed no option but to flee for refuge inside the nearest buildings. The few soldiers who had dropped their weapons and raised their arms in surrender were gunned down immediately.

"It's impossible to answer that accurately, Mr. President," said Lance as he banged on his laptop. "But judging by the size of the alien vessel relative to the mean size of the alien, there could be upward of ten billion bugs living up there."

"Billion?" Peyton asked. "With a b? That's more than our whole damn planet!"

"But if we factor in that three-quarters of our planet is water," Jean-François piped in, "discount the Antarctic and the North Pole where no one lives, most of Russia and Canada, much of the United States and China —"

"Okay, okay, I get it," Peyton cut him off. "We don't live everywhere, but still. You guys said their ship was about the size of Rhode Island."

"In length and width, yes sir," Lance explained. "But more than half that in height. They'd have multiple levels. It would be akin to thousands of Rhode Islands stacked one on top of the other."

"Jesus Christmas," Peyton exhaled.

The young Lieutenant, Peyton's aide since the bunker, burst into the studio with a mild pant. "Mr. President, the First Lady is asking to see you."

"My wife died three years ago," snapped the President. "Pancreatic cancer. It was very sad. Thanks for bringing it up."

"No, sir," the boy went on. "I meant the former First Lady. President

Addison's wife. She says that you *must* hear what she has to tell you. She actually said the word 'must' like it was in italics."

"I'm kinda busy here, you know," Peyton told him, then sighed. "Tell her I'll get to her as soon as I can." Then he focused his attention back on the monitors.

The roads were now clear for the enemy to advance, which would be their next logical move—take out your enemy's high command, force a surrender, and win the war—but they weren't doing that.

Because the aliens weren't waging a war—Peyton had known that from the start—they were executing an extermination. They had known Peyton would have to bring all that remained of his fighting force to a single spot to stop them, and they were going to stay right where they were until every last one of them was dead—because once the fighting force was gone, exterminating the civilians would be easy.

Peyton kicked himself for underestimating the depth of his enemy's spy system, but how could he have ever predicted this wormhole business? He barely understood it now, even though the physicist had explained it to him several times.

"Get me the other world leaders on the phone," he told a young political aid, the Chief of Staff being back in Washington. "They need to be briefed on this."

"Right away, Mr. President," said the staffer. "But, sir, since we're the only part of the world under attack, wouldn't this be the time to ask our overseas allies to deploy their troops here to help us?"

"No, son. The bugs'd just start the easy part of their extermination over there. In fact, unless I miss my guess, that's *exactly* what they expect us to do—and I am goddamn sick and tired of doing exactly what they expect me to do!"

"Colonel, instruct Major Shaughnessy that the enemy won't advance as long as he and his men are alive. He's got to dig in and hold the bugs in place. We need time to come up with a new plan. In other words, his orders are to not die!

"And we've got to deal with this spy business, got to ferret the bugger out once and for all. Captain, do any of our soldiers have military-police experience?"

"I'm your head of base security, Mr. President," answered the Captain-with-the-scar. "I'd be honored to lead the investigation personally."

Peyton paused for a moment as he sized the man up. "No, I'm going to need you by my side, overseeing the overview. Who else you got?"

"Sir, I'm by far the most qualified."

"I said who else you got?"

"Let me check, Mr. President."

*****

"HOW . . . HOW IS THAT possible?" asked Harve as he tried to process the impossible events that led to poor Miguel's death.

Not a one of them could comprehend what they had just seen.

"It . . . it isn't," answered a horrified Johnny. "It's not possible at all."

As for Sanchez, she simply lost it.

"*Hijo de tu chingada madre!*" she screamed as she ran out from behind the safety of the air-conditioner condenser in a blind vengeful rage, blasting her pistol at her brother's killer, her misses coming dangerously close to piercing the explosive helicopter and ending them all.

"Get back here!" Harve shouted at her.

But she was too far gone to hear him. Her next shot nailed the bug right between the eyes, killing it instantly, but that wasn't enough for her. She flung herself on top of the corpse, pinned her knees upon its shoulders, and discharged her weapon into the dead insect at close range. She was too close to the chopper for anyone to take a shot at her, so all Harve and the others could do was sit back and watch for what would happen next.

"*Por mi hermano!*" Sanchez cried out as she fired a bullet into the mouth of her brother's dead killer. "*Por mi mamá!*" she screamed as she fired a shot into its heart. "*Por mi hermano! Por mi mamá! Por mi hermano!*"

Green blood exploded from the bug's head and thorax with each blast, dousing the girl but not stopping her. When she ran out of bullets, she bashed her pistol into the dead bug's face. When she saw a swarm charging at her, she yanked the dead bug up from the ground to use him as a shield, then grabbed his insect-rifle and fired their own white beams of void back at them.

She's good, thought Harve.

The half-crazed Latina took down one bug after another, blindly moving about with no strategy or thought, until she inadvertently found herself far enough from the helicopter that the aliens could once again open fire upon her. White beams of void riddled the body of her insect-shield, but she just kept shooting.

Then Harve had another brainstorm. "Cover me!" he told Johnny.

"Me?"

With all bug eyes now on Sanchez, Harve raced out from behind the condenser and made a beeline for the chopper to try his plan a second time.

He ran faster than he ever had in his life, and it looked like he was going to make it. He was only a step or two away from the helicopter when a wormhole appeared right before him, cutting him off.

But he didn't stop running. Instead, he blasted his pistol repeatedly into the black void before it was even open. By the time it did, the insect inside was welcomed into our world with a bullet to its throat.

Yet the wormhole itself was still blocking his way, and he had no desire to run into the meadow on the other side. Without breaking stride, he leapt up onto a crate of Uzis and used it as a springboard to hurl himself up and over the terrifying portal, crouched into a roll position while airborne, hit the ground with his head between his legs, and somersaulted straight into the chopper where he grabbed a submachine gun from an open crate and whipped around blasting.

*****

BACK AT THE CONTROL room, Peyton and his officers watched it on the monitor.

"He's military police," said the Captain-with-the-scar.

"He'll do," said Peyton, impressed. "He'll do just fine."

*****

"LET'S GO!" HARVE SHOUTED to his crew. "Come on!"

Johnny and Frank left the protection of their respective hiding spots and raced to the helicopter. As much as Sanchez wanted to keep blasting the enemy to death, her blind fury was waning as it became obvious that for every bug she killed a new one popped up to replace it—and her dead-bug-shield was by now so filled with holes that its time as a useful defense was running out. She slowly backed away toward the helicopter as she continued to fire, just to keep 'em honest. When she was close, she threw her insect-shield to the ground, bashed her boot into its face one last time for good measure, whipped the bug-rifle over her shoulder, then joined her fellow soldiers as they sprinted the final steps toward the chopper.

All the while, Harve blasted his submachine gun at the bugs to keep them from taking a shot at his compatriots while still maintaining a vigilant, panoramic view of his surroundings—anything could still happen, he knew. It was a lesson that had cost Miguel his life.

"Get us outta here, Captain!" he shouted as his soldiers got closer.

"With pleasure!"

They filed into the helicopter as Johnny plopped himself into the pilot's seat. "Now watch me do something I'm good at," he said cockily as he fired up the engine in a flurry of motion.

He lifted the bird into a three-foot hover then slowly pushed it toward and over the rooftop edge. As they moved further from the building, the alien swarms came out of hiding and moved into position, preparing to fire the moment they deemed the helicopter sufficiently far away.

"You sure you know what you're doing?" Harve asked him nervously.

"I'd better be, right?" Johnny answered with a twinkle.

"What the hell happened to 'trust me'?!" yelled Sanchez.

"I got this," the pilot said cockily. "But you should all probably grab hold of something." He turned to Sanchez and smiled, "You can grab hold of me."

She forced a fake smile then latched onto a cargo tie-down, as did Harve and Frank.

Then the aliens fired, and Johnny cut the power!

"Have you gone mental?!"

The helicopter plummeted to the ground as it ducked under the aliens' blasts. The bugs moved closer to the roof's edge and pointed their weapons down at the plunging bird when Johnny fired the power back up, yanked on the collective, pointed the bird to the sky and soared up in a diagonal to the left. The aliens missed again. He sideslipped and dove to the right, and they missed once more. White beams of nothingness whizzed all around as Johnny rode the 407 back to the left, another miss, to the right, missed, another plummet, missed, another steep climb, missed, left, right, up, down, all the while riding the machine like a rocket further and further away from the building.

And at long last, the aliens' white beams began to fall short, disintegrating into transparent vapors before reaching the helicopter.

They had made it!

Harve, Frank and Sanchez took a deep breath as they let go of the tie-downs and let themselves fall back in exhaustion.

"So that didn't go so well, did it?" said Johnny.

CHAPTER TWENTY-FIVE

Patrick and Rhiannon sat on their bikes atop a small grassy hillside looking down on Main Street, the coveted sheriff's office being just on the other side of the road. A herd of zombies a quarter mile back moved toward them, but they were too slow and far away to pose any serious threat, and the spattering of zombies roaming the streets below posed even less, as long as the kids were careful.

They nodded to each other then kicked off to begin the final leg of their trek. They pedaled down the small slope and across the road, drawing the attention of the street-zombies who turned out to be even easier to avoid than expected—or maybe the kids were just getting better at it. They dumped their bikes on the grassy lawn in front of the small structure then raced toward the door.

"Help!" Patrick shouted as he burst inside, then instantly realized his mistake.

There on the ground before him were six zombies in deputy uniforms gnawing on the dead Sheriff's body. Upon hearing the boy, the creatures left the skeletal carcass and headed toward the new fresh meat.

"Jiminy Cricket!" he shouted.

He flung off his backpack to yank out the large shovel, but it was stuck on something inside. With no time to struggle with it, he swung the backpack in front of him in a semicircular motion, back and forth and back and forth again, knocking the zombies away from him but sadly allowing them to remain undead.

Rhiannon, who had by now slunk off to the side, whipped her shotgun off her shoulder and took aim.

"What are you doing?!" Patrick shouted at her. "You're just going to attract more of them!"

"No choice now," said the pixie as she aimed her shotgun right at the boy.

"What are you doing?! Stop!!"

She fired! The spray whizzed over Patrick's shoulder and into the zombie's face, one of the fragments cracking straight through its dull left eye.

"He almost had you," she told him, then turned and fired at the other deputy-zombies who, having been attracted to the sound of her gunshot, were now heading right at her. Patrick raced to the wall and grabbed the first weapon he could reach, a pump-action shotgun, then began firing upon the zombies as well.

The zombies on the streets, scattered across many different roads, heard the gunshots and began to limp toward the building en masse.

The children's aim was good but not flawless, and they both knew that only perfect shots to a tiny part of the brain would kill these creatures—anything else just knocked them back for a moment, after which they'd come at them again—so they scurried about to maintain a safe distance as they blasted their shotguns like deranged little psycho-killers. Pump! Bang! Pump! Bang! Pump! Bang! Bang!

Patrick was by now standing on a deputy's desk blasting away like a madman. Rhiannon was not far off as she fired her spray into the right cheek of the last of the deputies. The zombie went down, crashing into the open front door, but there was no way to know if it was actually dead so she went to it and rammed the butt of her weapon into its skull.

"No!" Patrick shouted.

The street-zombies were heading into the building right behind her—and Patrick couldn't fire at them because there was too much risk he'd accidentally clip the girl with his shotgun's spray. He leapt off the desk and raced to the door, charging into it shoulder first, slamming it shut as he hit the ground, the wood door knocking the zombies back and severing a rotted hand off one of them. The boy jumped up fast and dead-bolted the door then took a deep, relieved breath.

"Windows!" Rhiannon shouted.

PatrickPatrick Patrick turned fast to see clumps of the creatures worming their way inside through the open windows. He raced to one while Rhiannon raced to the other. They used the butt of their weapons to knock the creatures back, then slammed the cell-like bars closed and dead-bolted them secure.

The children scoured the room to make sure they hadn't missed anything.

The zombie-deputies and Sheriff lay on the ground motionless, their heads shot up or crushed to bits, sufficiently dead. The zombies on the other side of the windows howled pathetically as they reached through the bars to grasp at the children, but the bars would hold firm. The zombies on the other side of the door whimpered and scratched and clawed and pounded, but they clearly lacked the strength to ever break through.

Patrick and Rhiannon were safe.

But they were also trapped.

Then Rhiannon ran into the twelve-year-old boy's arms, wrapped her own arms around him, and sobbed like the seven-year-old girl that she was. "I hate this!"

CHAPTER TWENTY-SIX

Of all the sniper units on all the rooftops, only eight had managed to make it into their respective helicopters and up to the sky, and only one of the eight had been able to make a complete and actual getaway.

The mood inside the chopper was grim as the gang flew home. They were exhausted, beaten, and humiliated. Even Johnny had ceased trying to lighten the mood. There had been far too much loss for anyone to smile.

The harsh silence was finally broken when Sanchez turned to Harve and offered with a trace of a sniffle, "I don't blame you, Sergeant. Miguel volunteered."

"Blame me if you need to, Sergeant," he said softly. "Doesn't matter to me. Just remember your brother was a good man, and he died bravely and with honor."

"*Sí*," she said sadly. "He did. He was."

She took a towel from one of the supply packs and wiped her face, removing the green alien pus that had yet to harden. "You know, I don't even blame the *pinche* bugs who did it. They were soldiers just like us, following their orders, just like us."

"That's true," Frank said as he considered such a novel idea.

"But I'll tell you one thing," she went on. "Whatever *bavoso* is in charge of those cockroaches, I am going to find him and take him down. Personally! And this I swear on the heavenly soul of my brother. Their leader will die by my hands."

"Well look at you," Johnny said with a smile. "Even after everything you've been through, you're still a firecracker."

"Honey, you got no idea."

*****

IT WAS LATE AFTERNOON when the Bell 407 set gently down upon the helipad. Harve, Frank and Sanchez disembarked to find the Canadian Lieutenant waiting.

"Sergeant Sedar!" snapped the officer.

"Yes sir," Harve said as he and the other weary grunts snapped a salute.

"The President wants to see you, Sergeant."

"Me?"

"Way to go, Sarge!" shouted Frank as he slapped his friend on the back. "He's probably gonna give you a medal for what you did back there!"

"Not now, Frank," Harve hushed then turned back to the Lieutenant. "Should I clean up first, sir?" Harve asked. "I mean, he's the President of the United States. And even if he wasn't, he's a great man. Look at me, I'm filthy."

"The Commander in Chief didn't specify now or later, soldier, so let's assume he doesn't want to be kept waiting. Let's go."

"Yes sir."

"Wait, sir!" Sanchez interrupted, then handed the Lieutenant the alien-rifle that hung from her shoulder. "I brought this back from battle. Maybe someone can find it useful or helpful or something."

"Nice work, Sergeant," said the Canadian as he flung the weapon over his own shoulder, then turned back to Harve. "Sergeant."

The Lieutenant moved off and Harve followed. Frank and Sanchez mumbled good-byes then headed off in opposite directions toward their respective quarters. Johnny, having put his bird to bed for the night, raced out and followed after Sanchez. He couldn't help notice that she seemed to be wobbling as she walked.

"Hey, are you okay?" he asked sympathetically as he strolled alongside her.

"*Si*," she answered, and Johnny could tell that she was lying.

"Listen, if you need someone to talk to –"

"I'm fine, Captain."

"Johnny."

"Captain," she insisted.

"Captain Johnny?" he offered with his charming smile.

"*Dios mio*," she exclaimed as she came to an abrupt halt. "Are you still hitting on me? Even now?"

"No, I promise," he said sincerely. "I was when the day started, I admit it, but this is a genuine offer to lend an ear, nothing more. Scout's honor. Although to be perfectly honest, I'll probably take another shot at you once you're done mourning."

She glared at him, then couldn't stop herself from laughing. "You know, for someone who tries so hard to come off like a jackass, you can be kind of sweet."

"A bit of a mixed message, but thank you."

"How's this?" she began. "For now I just want to be alone, but gimme some –"

Then she collapsed into his arms, unconscious.

"Even more of a mixed message," he said to himself as he held her.

*****

NORTHBANK'S ST. VINCENT'S MEDICAL Center was the largest hospital in all of Jacksonville, and it was packed beyond capacity. The lobby itself had become a mere extension of the intensive care unit that no longer had space for the critically wounded. Soldiers lay moaning and screaming on gurneys, their bodies ripped open and bleeding as they awaited someone, *anyone*, to provide treatment. The understaffed civilian medical team raced from one casualty to the next to determine which of the critically wounded was the most dire, and it was a constant, heartrending decision for them to make.

"Yet one must wonder why only America has been targeted," said the anchorman on the TV on the wall. "And where the aliens will attack next."

This was the chaos into which Johnny ran as he carried the unconscious

Sergeant Sanchez in his arms.

"Somebody! Help!" he shouted.

"In Europe," the anchorman continued, "The public responded negatively to their nations' reenactment of the draft. Protests abound in Germany and England while the French have turned to riots."

"Anybody?" Johnny continued. "Please!"

A haggard young doctor approached quickly, removing a pair of plastic gloves and throwing them into a bin marked hazard without breaking stride.

"I got this one!" he yelled to his coworkers as he put on a fresh pair of gloves.

"We were walking back together," Johnny explained. "Some might say I was harassing her but I believe she liked it—then all of a sudden she just passes out."

The doctor took a quick look at Sanchez and groaned. "Not again. Orderly!"

"What's wrong with her?" Johnny asked.

Two orderlies arrived with a stretcher—the hospital's stash of gurneys having been depleted long before. Johnny gently laid Sanchez upon it, and the young doctor noticed that some of the green blood had rubbed onto his shirt.

"Oh damn," said the doctor who immediately proceeded to examine the pilot's exposed skin—face, ears, hands.

"What're you doing?" Johnny said. "I'm fine."

"We've had a lot of soldiers coming in with these same fatigue issues," the frazzled doctor told him. "Fainting spells, loss of consciousness, complaints of feeling weird or strange—and all splatted with alien blood like your friend here."

"What is it?"

"We don't know. An allergy, a virus maybe. But look around. We don't have the manpower to deal with it so we're putting anyone who's had direct contact into quarantine." He ripped open Johnny's shirt to examine his chest to see if any of the green pus had seeped through. "I think someone sent a sample to the CDC in Atlanta to find out—I hope they did, I don't know, I got my work cut out for me here. Okay, you're clean." He carefully removed Johnny's shirt from his back and tossed it into the hazard bin, then realized that the orderlies were still there, awaiting his instructions regarding Sanchez. "Oh right, you guys. Yeah. Get her into quarantine with the rest of them."

The orderlies hustled off Sanchez in one direction while the doctor darted off in the other toward another wounded warrior, and the TV anchorman droned on.

"But nowhere is it worse than in China where a historically subjugated people take to the streets against a government in lack of an army to protect them."

"Her name is Anita Sanchez!" Johnny shouted at the orderlies. "Take good care of her! There's something special about that one!"

CHAPTER TWENTY-SEVEN

"Vampires?" Peyton asked incredulously.

He stood in the living room of his new quarters, the posh penthouse suite of Jacksonville's Omni Hotel, and he could not believe what he was hearing, nor understand why he was hearing it.

"Yes, vampires," insisted former First Lady Laurel Addison.

"Come on."

Despite his ill feelings toward her late husband, Peyton had always been fond of the woman, his only friend during his lonely tenure as vice president, and he had always sensed that there was a depth to her that most others just missed. So what was all this about? Had the loss of her husband caused her to snap? Had the revelation of alien invaders been too much for her? Was it something else entirely? Whatever it was, he felt obliged to humor her—he owed her that much.

"They're real, Peyton," Laurel went on. "I should know, I've been killing them since I hit puberty."

"A second ago you said they couldn't be killed."

"Well, only by me," she explained. "Well, people like me. Seventh daughter of a seventh daughter of a—it's complicated. The point is that they exist, and they want to help us. And you more than anyone know that we need help."

"Is this because I didn't make it to Michael's funeral? I'm really sorry, but I've got this extermination-of-mankind thing to deal with and –"

His well-meaning condescension was interrupted by a knock at the door. "Come!" he barked.

Harve entered timidly, straight from the helipad, still grimy and sweat-drenched from battle. "You wanted to see me, Mr. President?"

"Yes, Sergeant. Come in."

But Laurel wasn't ready to give up. "What will it take to convince you, Peyton? You want to meet one?"

"Oh sure, why not?" groaned the Commander in Chief. "It's not like I've got something more important to do."

"Bring him in!" Laurel shouted through the open doorway then turned to Harve. "Sergeant, would you mind getting the drapes? Not the inner, sheer ones but the outer, thick ones." She reached into her purse and tossed him a roll of duct tape. "And then seal them tight please. Very tight."

"Um, yes ma'am," answered Harve who still had no idea why he was there.

Secret Service Agent Denison, now in his Marine major fatigues, wheeled in a cart on which laid an elegant walnut casket.

"Okay, let's see that vampire," Peyton said as he looked at his watch.

"Wait for the Sergeant to finish please," Laurel replied.

Not another word was spoken as they waited for Harve to complete his task. "It's done, ma'am," said the Sergeant as he put the tape on the coffee table. Laurel nodded to Denison. Denison knocked thrice on the casket, then took a step back.

The casket top creaked open. A moment later, Julius sat up so slowly that one could almost hear the Gothic organ music that wasn't playing in the background. He remained sitting, silent and motionless, a stunning specimen of a man in his denim jacket and dungarees, then ominously turned to Peyton.

"Hello," he said.

"Um, howdy?" Peyton replied.

The President didn't even see the man hop out of the coffin but there he was, standing right before him, grasping and shaking his hand.

"My name is Julius, and it is a tremendous privilege to meet you,

General," he began enthusiastically. "And when I address you as 'General' it is not to be disrespectful. It is merely because as a politician you are crude and inept, but as a military leader you are in the league of Charlemagne, Hannibal and Alexander."

All awaited Peyton's response as he rubbed his chin and tried to make sense of the bizarre theater being played out before him.

"So he's good looking and sleeps in a coffin. Doesn't prove anything," the President said at last.

"Touché, sir," the vampire said with a smile.

"Tell him, you monster," Laurel urged.

"No words could convince him."

"Then why'd you have me—then what are we doing here?"

"That is to say it can only be shown," Julius said as he turned to Harve. "My good Staff Sergeant, if you'd be so kind, draw your sidearm and point it toward me."

Harve had fulfilled the First Lady's request to seal the drapes only because it had been the polite thing to do—but there was no chance that he was going to obey this strange fellow. There were only two people in the room who could give him orders—the Marine Major and the great man himself—so he turned to the President for guidance. Peyton merely shrugged and nodded, seemingly at a loss himself, so Harve drew his pistol and pointed it at Julius.

"I will now attack you, Staff Sergeant," the vampire began. "And you must defend yourself. If you don't attempt to kill me, I will most certainly kill you."

Once again, Harve looked to his Commander in Chief.

"Fine, I dunno, kill him. Is this going to take much longer?"

"Please, General, indulge me but a moment more," Julius said, then looked behind him to be certain that no one was there. "Are we ready, Sergeant?"

Harve unlocked the safety and cocked his weapon. "Sure."

With dramatic flare, Julius raised his arms up and outward as if a bat. He hissed and revealed his long, pointed fangs, then transformed to mist and flew straight toward Harve. The startled noncom discharged his weapon but the bullets whizzed through the mist only to riddle the wall behind it with holes.

Before anyone could see it, too fast for the human eye to even comprehend, Julius was behind Harve, his powerful arms wrapped around the big man to keep him in place, his fangs a mere inch from the Sergeant's neck vein.

The vampire waited but a moment to allow the point of his demonstration to sink in, then he released the Sergeant from his clutches with a proud and confident smile. He patted Harve on the shoulder to commend him on a job well done, retracted his fangs and straightened his denim jacket. "Et voilà!"

All eyes turned to Peyton as they awaited his response once more.

"That is really cool," chuckled the President.

"I, and thousands just like me, are at your beckoning, my liege," said the vampire with a flamboyant bow.

Peyton smiled as he rubbed his chin, a new plan playing itself out to perfection in his mind's eye. He knew that the vampire would have some ideas of his own, and the General couldn't wait to hear them. The bugs would never expect this. Couldn't possibly.

"Um, permission to speak freely, Mr. President?" Harve asked timidly.

"Granted, Sergeant."

"He's a vampire!" Harve belted, unable to contain himself. "The undead! In league with the devil! Which would make *us* in league with the devil! How can we hope to win this war if we turn our back on God and partner with Satan himself?!"

"Actually, most of us are Catholic," Julius matter-of-factly corrected.

"Good enough for me!" roared a gleeful Commander in Chief as he grabbed the vampire's hand and shook it profusely. "Welcome aboard, Mr. Julius!

"Laurel, if this thing plays out the way I think it will, you will have done a great service for your country, for your planet, for your species. But now, I really must get you to a safe location."

"Oh, no, no," said the former First Lady. "I have to stay."

"Why?"

"Because I'm the only one who can control them," she explained. "And I do not trust them at all. At all."

PART THREE

THE CAVALRY UNDEAD

INTERLUDE #3

The adolescent Tyrannosaurus rex strolled through the woods with the demeanor of a young prince. The Deinonychus eggshells were still stuck to his lips, but he didn't mind—they reminded him of the tasty little snack he had nabbrf and the prowess with which he had nabbed it.

He could nab anything he wanted.

He looked off into the distance toward the clearing in which hundreds of herbivores grazed. Eating stuff from out of the ground, he thought. How disgusting. Perhaps he'll nab one of their eggs too, he considered, but then reconsidered. Why stop there? Why not just nab one of *them*?

Yes, far tastier and far more rewarding. Perhaps he could find a good Bronto or Steg or Triceratops child to eat—not only hearty and delicious, but good practice for when he's fully grown and taking on the giant adult brutes themselves.

He was the master of all he surveyed. Only Father and Mother were greater than he, but they were so devoted to him that they would never deny him anything. He was the ruler of his universe, and it was only going to get better as he got bigger.

Then, without warning, Dinah, Claw, and two other Deinonychus couples leapt out of the trees shrieking and pounced upon the spoiled young prince! The T. rex was bigger than they, but he didn't know what had hit him, couldn't possibly fathom that anyone would ever dare attack *him*, and the Deinonychus teamwork was impeccable. With military precision, each one gouged at a predetermined section of the adolescent's hide. They sliced at him with deadly claws. They ripped at his flesh with razor-sharp teeth, piercing beyond muscle and fat and through to vital organs so that his very guts spilled out of his soon-to-be-dead carcass.

No longer the warm, loving creatures they were while fulfilling their parental duties, the Deinonychus were now soldiers in a war they were intent on winning, with no empathy or mercy to be doled out.

All the young T. rex could do was writhe and howl in pain, jump and buck to rid his assailants from his back, twirl and spin in desperate futility until he at last dropped to the ground, dead.

The herbivores in the clearing could hear the ruckus, could have seen the incident from where they stood if they had only bothered to look, but they didn't. It was none of their business. They didn't care for either breed, didn't care for any carnivores for that matter. Far better the cruel ones kill each other off and leave the peaceful ones in peace. Even the large herbivores like the Brontosaurus, Stegosaurus and Triceratops that could engage in victorious battle when necessary didn't like it. No tears were ever to be shed for a dead carnivore.

Five of the Deinonychus stepped back from the T. rex corpse, but Dinah remained hovering over the child, looking down upon him with her big, round eyes. She swallowed hard, mustered up a big gob of saliva, then spat upon the dead beast. She turned her back to him, dug her claw deep into the earth and kicked a clump of it onto the corpse's face.

Claw stepped forward to be beside her. She cooed as she put her giant head on his massive shoulder. He leaned his own head on hers and cooed back. It was done.

Claw gave his mate another moment to revel in the vengeance, then at last shrieked out a command. The six Deinonychus, Dinah included, moved efficiently toward the corpse and latched onto a specific part of its dead body as if they had done this a million times before. On Claw's next command, they lifted the beast in unison and began to effortlessly carry it back to their dwellings for the pack to eat.

What had begun as revenge had ended in groceries.

CHAPTER TWENTY-EIGHT

Barely an hour after the President and the vampire shook hands, a fleet of eighteen-wheelers was pulling up to the Omni Hotel. Enlisted trainees and civilians alike opened the backs of the trucks to remove an endless array of coffins, ranging in style from the ostentatiously ornate to the cheap and simple, then carried them inside. Other trucks were opened to reveal herds of livestock which civilian farmers from northern Florida and Georgia corralled out to the back of the building. Inside, civilian carpenters nailed sheets of plywood over every window and glass doorway.

A block away, Harve sat on a little kiddie swing in a little kiddie park, lost in thought. He was still grimy from battle but he couldn't bring himself to head back to his assigned quarters where shower and bed awaited. It would be too quiet, he thought. Most of the other soldiers that had been assigned there were now dead, and he simply wasn't ready to feel their ghosts.

What a strange day, he thought as he swung lazily on the tiny swing. What a strange week.

"Think fast!" shouted Frank, appearing from out of nowhere and tossing his Sarge a can of Bud.

Harve caught it with ease but he didn't seem happy about it. "Where'd you get this? Orders are no booze, we're on active call."

"You look like you need it, buddy," the Corporal said good-naturedly as he took a seat at the picnic table across from the swings and opened a can of his own.

"Get rid of it," Harve ordered, then he flipped open the can in his hand and proceeded to pour the contents onto the ground.

"C'mon, Sarge. Who'll know?"

"Orders are orders. Now, Frank!"

"Okay, okay, easy, mi amigo," Frank said then proceeded to dump out his beer as well. "What are you doing here anyway? I've been looking all over for you. You all right?"

"There're certain things I can't tell you. Very strange, very bad things."

"Hey it's me. You can tell me anything, buddy."

"I've been ordered not to tell *anyone*. But what I *can* tell you is –" then he trailed off, almost wishing he hadn't dumped out his beer.

"It's about those coffins they're unloading down the street, isn't it? Are those boxes for us? Not very encouraging, is it? Downright insulting is what it is."

"It's not about the coffins, Frank, it's—you know we got a spy, right?"

"Yeah, sure. Everyone knows that by now. That's how the bugs knew about the rooftops, right?"

"Well guess who they picked to ferret him out?"

"You?" Frank smiled, proud for his friend.

"Yeah, me. And they gave me these because of it," Harve grumbled, tilting his head toward the shiny new lieutenant bars on his shoulders. "They felt it would be unseemly for an enlisted man to question an officer, so they made me an officer—and I've been given free reign to question *everyone*."

"Lieutenant? Wow! Congratulations, Sarge. I mean, sir!" then he jumped to his feet and merrily saluted.

Harve shot an unenthusiastic salute back to him. "I got nothing, Frank. No evidence, no leads, no theories to follow. I'm not trained for this."

"You're one of the best MPs I ever saw."

"It's one thing to go into a town and bust up a brawl or take in some drunken soldier who got a bit unruly, but this is actual detective work. I don't know squat about that. I told 'em they should find some ex-cop or something, you know, like a real sleuth. We must have a bunch of those in our ranks, don't you think?"

"Makes sense. What'd they say?"

"The President—yeah, the Commander in Chief himself—said that he has no idea who the spy is so he doesn't know who to trust. But after seeing all the bugs I killed on the roof, he knows I couldn't possibly be one of them. Then he cited my MP credentials and said that I should have more confidence in myself, and then he called me 'son'—which was, you know, nice."

"Must've been awesome."

"But I don't even know how to start."

"Can I help?"

"If you got anything, I'll take it. I got diddly."

"Cool," Frank said as he furrowed his brows and tightened his lips in an attempt to think. After a brief moment, his eyes lit up and he smiled. "It's the pilot," he said with total certainty.

"Frank, this isn't a guessing game."

"No, no, no, wait, wait, wait. Think about it. All those helicopters on all those rooftops, and *Johnny's* is the only one that makes it home?"

"He did do some pretty fancy flying."

"Or, maybe the bugs missed us on purpose 'cause they didn't want to kill their inside man."

"Look, I don't like the guy much either, but it doesn't fit."

"The thing is, I do like the guy. He's a total crack-up. Wait. Can aliens be funny? I don't think aliens can be funny. Never mind, I retract. Stupid theory."

But the die had been cast. "But, it doesn't *not* fit, you know?" Harve said as the wheels in his head began to turn. "I mean, what do we know about the guy?"

"That he's a crack-up?"

"And that he's been arrested a whole bunch of times, and that he must've done some terrible thing once to get bumped down from captain."

"It can't be him, Sarge—I mean, sir. Aliens just aren't funny—especially creepy, spooky, insect aliens—they wouldn't know how to be funny. Unless they're played by Robin Williams or the voice of Seth Rogen, but Robin's dead and Seth's working all the time, one movie after another."

"What are you talking about?"

"I dunno," Frank shrugged amiably. "Except that Johnny can't be the spy. I mean, the guy didn't even want to come here. We had to force him, remember?"

"Or, he *knew* we'd force him. And you know what else occurs to me? He didn't kill one single bug the entire time we were up on that rooftop."

"He must've."

"I don't think so."

"I did, you did, the girl did. Even the kid winged a few before they got him. Johnny must've."

"If he did, I didn't see it, and I was crouched right next to him through most of it."

"Even so. He's a chopper pilot. They're not trained for shooting."

"That's what I thought at the time too. Or, maybe he's an expert shot, and he didn't want to take down any of his buddies."

"Or maybe he just sucks."

"Maybe."

"There you go. So let's keep going. Who do we know that has no sense of humor? I mean, other than you. 'Cause Johnny was cracking wise even when we were bringing him in for booking, back before everything blew up."

"Oh heck. I had completely forgotten about that. That bet he made you! You know, it always seemed a little off to me."

"What bet?"

"You remember. We were bringing him in, and he goes, like out of nowhere, 'Ten bucks I don't do any time on that base.' Then boom. The whole base blows. How could he have known that? Then every base on the planet blows—and it's all right after the guy's been MIA for fourteen hours."

"I totally forgot about that, too," said Frank.

"Johnny, eh?"

CHAPTER TWENTY-NINE

Private Roger Hayes darted about the reception area of his Captain's office in his shiny new electric wheelchair with the vitality of a man reborn, his countless years of street living lingering in his mind like a terrible nightmare that he couldn't shake. The irony that his newfound dignity was a direct result of the greatest threat to mankind was not lost on Rog, but he tried not to think of it in those terms. Instead, he laid all his gratitude at the feet of the Captain-with-the-scar who had taken him in when society as a whole had cast him aside, with the Captain who had given him a job, a uniform, the respect that even the lowest-ranked soldier receives, with the Captain who had given him a reason to live. Rog would do anything for the man.

His duties were primarily secretarial, which was A-okay by him. As much as he wished he had the ability to risk his life in battle with his fellow soldiers, that privilege was reserved for those with two working legs—it was Rog's duty to do everything else, everything he could, anything they'd let him. He loved it when his Captain ordered him to deliver a note or memo or stack of papers or whatnot to another building or part of town with no regard for his handicap, as if he were any other private, any other man. He didn't even mind the few times he had been chewed out, only for minor mistakes, but always with no pity or regard for his handicap, as if he were any other soldier.

He was whole again—if not physically, then at least emotionally and spiritually, and that was plenty. The Captain-with-the-scar had made him whole again, and Rog would never ever forget it.

He was filing printouts of soldiers' background checks. It was a boring task, but he was nonetheless proud to do it, honored that his Captain had entrusted him with the personal files of virtually everyone on the base. One of the Captain's primary responsibilities as head of base security had been to validate the backgrounds and records of all the soldiers who had volunteered, denying entry to anyone who lacked the records to prove a human-born existence beyond a shadow of a doubt. Those for whom even a tiny question had arisen were denied entry—a ninety-nine percent certainty simply not being good enough—and all those refused left screaming and yelling and cursing and promising a lawsuit.

Rog's mind wandered as he performed his boring task and a new irony occurred to him. From an alien perspective, his Captain's position would be the perfect cover for their spy. For one, who had checked *him* out? Presumably, he checked himself out and deemed himself a pass. If he was in fact the spy, he could let in as many other spies as he wanted while refusing any human soldier he deemed a threat to the bug cause—and Rog had noticed some dubious judgments on his Captain's part in that regard. Why had this soldier been allowed in while that one had been refused?

If it were true, Rog wondered, if the Captain-with-the-scar was indeed the alien spy, where would his own loyalties lie? With the man who had restored his dignity and self-respect, the man who had given him purpose and meaning, the man who had given him life anew, or with the species that had thrown him away like a piece of garbage in the first place?

CHAPTER THIRTY

Johnny had no idea that he was the sole suspect in the most heinous crime ever perpetrated upon mankind. He stood near the front of the long queue outside the Omni Hotel with all the other officers who had been summoned.

"Any idea what this is about?" he asked the Canadian Lieutenant who walked beside him. The Lieutenant shrugged, equally in the dark (almost all the officers were in the dark). The queue began to move, and the two officers walked inside.

The spacious, elegant lobby had been converted into a massive briefing auditorium. Hundreds of folding chairs had been set up facing a podium in front, behind which a large map of Southpoint was tacked to the wall. The former First Lady and a Marine Major that Johnny didn't recognize stood by the map, seemingly discussing new tactics and strategies.

That part made little enough sense, but what Johnny couldn't understand at all was why the windows had been boarded so that not a drop of sunlight could enter. Officers he recognized from the past few days milled about along with hundreds more that he didn't. The new soldiers had no rank insignia on their fatigue sleeves, only the letter *V*. But the oddest thing of all was that each and every one of the new soldiers was a very handsome man or a very pretty woman.

"Looks like we got some new recruits," said the Canadian Lieutenant to answer Johnny's earlier question.

Johnny spotted Prague and Africa across the room, and smiled. "I always loved new recruits. In fact, I think I'm going to go do some recruiting of my own."

And with that, he was off.

*****

"I HAVE A VERY bad feeling about this, Julius," Prague told the most senior of their breed. "I don't trust humans." Then she gestured toward Laurel and added, "Especially that one."

"Such is fine, my dove," Julius said soothingly. "She doesn't trust us either."

But his attention was suddenly drawn across the room where an impetuous little vampire named Plato—mid-teens by appearance but far older in reality— stood behind the Captain-with-the-scar who was engaged in a heated debate with Colonel Williams, and the Captain had no idea that there was a vampire behind him who gazed salivating upon his neck.

"But, Colonel, as head of base security, I *must* oversee the investigation of the alien mole. Given my experience and background, I should be the one leading the probe . . . at the very least, the Lieutenant should report directly to me."

"The President does things the way he does them."

"He doesn't trust me? Then I should resign. If I'm not entrusted to do my –"

"Stop it, Captain. You're not going to resign. But there is something you should know. I was assigned to the great man as a fresh-faced lieutenant straight out of West Point. He was just a major then, and I've been directly under his command ever since. He trusts me more than he trusts anyone. It's why he chose me as his second-in-command ahead of a long line of generals who by all rights should be here in my place. And do you know what today's briefing is about?"

"No, sir. Not really."

"Me neither. So stop taking it personally!"

Plato had little interest in their words. As their conversation continued, he hissed softly, sprouted his fangs, then inched toward the Captain's neck-vein when suddenly, from across the room, Julius thrust out his open palm as if striking someone in the forehead! Plato's head snapped back as if he had just been struck.

"Keep an open eye, Prague," Julius cautioned his trusted secondary. "This truce must not be broken. Our survival depends on it." Then he belted indignantly across the large space, "Plato!"

Julius was on the other side of the lobby in an instant, towering over the vampire who looked shamefully down at the exquisite marble floor, awaiting the scolding he knew was to come.

"What did I tell you?" Julius admonished. "What did I tell you?!"

"But I was hungry."

"The humans have provided us with plenty of other mammals with which we may eat our fill."

"But I don't like eating other mammals."

"Then you shall remain hungry. Understood?"

Plato looked to the marble floor once again and silently nodded his consent.

"I said, 'understood'?!"

"Yes, Julius," the little vampire answered meekly. "I understand."

*****

LAUREL AND DENISON SAW the drama from the podium, and they knew it was grave cause for concern. Even if Julius was on the level—and that was still a big "if"—would he be able to control the colonies if they didn't share his long-term view?

"This alliance does not feel right to me, ma'am," Denison told her. "Not by a long shot. Are you sure it's a good idea?"

"Not by a long shot," she replied. "But I suppose we'll find out soon enough."

*****

"HEYA ROOKIES," JOHNNY SAID pleasantly as he approached Prague and

Africa. "Welcome to my army."

"*Your* army?" asked an amused Africa.

"Well, technically, it's the President's army. I'm more like the morale leader. And you ladies are creating quite the dilemma for me."

"Is that so," responded a thoroughly unimpressed Prague.

Johnny smiled as he continued to engage the women, unaware that Harve, now showered and shaved and seated in one of the folding chairs, was watching every move the pilot made, writing his findings in a small notepad.

Why is he talking to the vampires? What does he know? What is he trying to know? This isn't proof of anything yet, the new Lieutenant reminded himself, they're just questions. But it was becoming apparent that the more he examined Johnny, the more questions he seemed to have about him.

"And what is the nature of your dilemma?" Africa lightheartedly asked the oblivious suspect.

"Well, it's like this," Johnny affably began. "I'm basically a one-woman-guy. And you're both so—oh, what's the word? 'Radiant.' You're both so radiant that I don't know which one of you I should make a move on."

"You fancy yourself some kind of badass, do you?" Prague asked coldly.

"Well . . ." Johnny replied with comically glaring false modesty.

"Caesar was a badass," snapped the blonde vampire. "Mao was a badass. You are but a little human hustler who'd be dead-dead-dead if he tried this monkeyshine on any other day than today. Am I clear?"

"Crystal clear," Johnny answered then turned to Africa. "*You're* the one I should make a move on."

Africa giggled.

"Don't encourage him," Prague cautioned.

"Soldiers! Take your seats!" Colonel Williams barked from the podium.

"Catch you ladies later," Johnny told the vampires, then leaned toward Africa and whispered in her ear. "And try to ditch your nasty friend."

Johnny moved off, and the girls headed to their chairs behind the podium.

"It eludes me why you must encourage them so, Africa," said Prague.

"You're just jealous."

"I most certainly am not."

"Then my attempt to make you jealous has resulted in a dismal failure," Africa said as she smiled mischievously, and Prague didn't like it one bit. "But fear not, my love. I could never be truly interested in a boy like that," Africa assured her mentor as they watched Johnny take the open seat next to Harve.

"I know you couldn't, my gem."

"I much prefer his manly friend."

Prague merely groaned, which caused Africa to giggle once more.

*****

"WELL LOOK AT YOU, dude!" Johnny shouted as he noticed the gold bars on the former Sergeant's shoulders. "Lieutenant! Way to go! Way to be!"

"Thank you," Harve replied, cold and poker faced.

"So, details, man. How'd it happen?"

"They put me in charge of finding the alien mole," the new Lieutenant answered as he began his fishing expedition. "You know anything about that?"

"Um, I guess. Same as you."

"Oh yeah? What do *I* know?"

"What do *you* know? Um, God is good?"

"I'm going to have to question you."

"My life is an open book—except for the parts that I won't tell you."

"Officers," announced Colonel Williams from the podium. "Your Commander in Chief, the President of the United States."

All snapped to attention as Peyton entered. Colonel Williams moved to the open seat behind the podium among Laurel, Denison, Julius, Prague and Africa.

"Be seated, officers," Peyton said as he took center stage then stoically waited for his order to be carried out.

"As you all know, there is a spy among us. So I will be purposely vague with you as we discuss our next move, and you are ordered to be even more vague when you pass this information onto your squads.

"Behind me sit the ranking officers of what we're calling 'V-Company.' They will report directly to Major Denison, who will in turn report to the former First Lady and myself.

"The members of V-Company have a very unique ability that you will only discover once on the battlefield. I cannot emphasize enough just how unique but, well, pretty darn unique. When their abilities become known, it will cause panic and confusion among the enemy. It must not cause panic and confusion among us. You and your soldiers are expected to be ready to witness the impossible, accept it, and roll with it. Even though it will most assuredly blow your minds.

"Many of you, upon seeing what you will see, will still not comprehend it. This is fine—you only need to fight and kill, not understand. But for those who do recognize what stands before you, you are not permitted to utter a word of it aloud. Remember, the man on your right may be the enemy spy, so let's let the damn bugs figure it out on their own." (Coincidentally, Johnny was seated to Harve's right.)

"Now on to the fun part. Tactics."

Johnny couldn't help notice that Harve was quietly shaking his head in his personal contempt for the plan. "You know what they are, don't you?" Johnny asked.

Harve said nothing, but his face was scowled with distaste, his eyes locked with Africa's.

"Come on, man. What are they?"

He had no intention of telling his prime suspect what he had just been ordered not to tell anyone, but the answer clamored through his brain.

They are evil incarnate.

CHAPTER THIRTY-ONE

"I beg you," Jean-François pleaded in the overcrowded lobby of the St. Vincent Medical Center. "I must speak with Sergeant Sanchez immediately. The outcome of the war may depend on it!"

"No can do, mac," answered the hefty triage nurse, as she placed a red tag on one bleeding, screaming soldier, then moved on to examine the next.

Jean-François followed her, utterly perplexed. He had the complete backing of Colonel Williams, which meant he had the full backing of the President himself. He had the world's greatest scientists on their way to Florida to assist him with his project, and he was perched to be the world's new Oppenheimer. Yet somehow this trivial, self-important woman was able to thwart his ability to move forward.

He had been absolutely overjoyed earlier that day when the Canadian Lieutenant had brought him the alien weapon to study and analyze—overjoyed and terrified. It was so beyond anything he had ever seen, anything he had ever read or heard about, and he dared not press a button.

Human weaponry had always been based on the notion of thrusting foreign objects *into* the bodies of their enemies—metal blades, flying projectiles, germs—but the alien weapon *removed* portions of their enemies' bodies, leaving not a trace. Given that, and given the aliens' wormhole capabilities, Jean-François was working on the assumption that the technology was based on some kind of space-time-quantum theory. If that were the case—and he had no real certainty that it was—the weapon could theoretically possess an infinite range and a perpetual velocity. But the battles he had watched on the WTLV monitors showed otherwise. The weapons' range seemed less than that of a standard M16, and the velocity too weak to break through a mere foot of steel.

Why would a warmongering people devise weapons *less* powerful than their theoretical maximum? Could there be some setting switches to adjust velocity and range? He saw many buttons that *could* be, but he dared not touch them.

And why did they emit such deafening charges? Theoretically, they should make no sound at all. Was the noise a mere ploy to achieve some psychological advantage in battle? (It was.) Or was Jean-François just barking up the wrong tree altogether? (He wasn't.)

But if the gun did in fact possess infinite range and perpetual velocity, and if Jean-François and the team he had assembled could decipher the science behind it, it would mean that a human soldier could theoretically shoot down the alien craft that orbited above them in space. The enemy would have no more soldiers to replace their fallen. America's overseas allies would be freed to send their forces to Florida to help slay the last of the bugs. And the war would be over.

On the other hand, if used incorrectly, the weapon could render all of Earth into oblivion. Jean-François dared not touch the thing.

But one human already had—and she had used the weapon with deft proficiency. Whether she had intuitively known something or she had just been lucky, whatever the Latina had done she had done right. Jean-François simply needed to get her back to his lab where the precious weapon remained under lock and key—it being far too powerful and mysterious for him to risk brandishing it about. But this annoying little woman stood in his way.

"You don't understand," he reiterated. "Our very survival as a species may well depend on the knowledge that Sergeant Sanchez alone possesses."

"No, *you* don't understand," the fat nurse replied as she placed a yellow tag on the next wounded soldier, then moved on again. "No one knows what kind of virus Sanchez has or how it spreads, so no one goes into that quarantine until the doctors get direction from Atlanta. I'm trying to save our species too, mac."

"I'll take this straight to the President."

"Good for you," said the nurse. "I don't work for the President." Then she moved off, down the hallway and away from him for good.

Jean-François sighed, then left the hospital to head back to his new lab.

The early evening air was thick and humid, and the Northbank roads were a flurry of activity. A big meeting had just broken up at the Omni Hotel where some new military strategy had been adopted, and soldiers were hurriedly running from hither to yon as they prepared to head into battle.

But the astrophysicist barely noticed them as he planned his next call to the Colonel. He had no doubt he would receive the support he needed— and if for any reason he didn't, he would sneak into the quarantine area to speak with Sanchez anyway, bug-gun in tow. Virus be damned. Even if it rivaled the Black Plague, which was unlikely, humanity did manage to survive that horror. Without knowledgeable use of the weapon, it didn't look like we could ever survive this one. Beyond that, the scientific benefits this new technology could wield were unfathomable. And even beyond that, he just had to know! How does the damn thing work?

He arrived at his lab to find the door unlocked, even though he knew with certainty that he had locked it before leaving. He went inside and was startled to find someone removing the precious weapon from the now-open safe. The physicist recognized the man and couldn't comprehend why he would be so reckless.

"Are you crazy?!" yelled the Frenchman. "Put that down right now! Do you know how dangerous that is?"

"We can't let you have this," the man said as he pointed the weapon at the scientist's chest. "You know that, don't you?"

Jean-François understood in an instant. "You're the spy."

"I am indeed."

"Are you going to kill me?"

"You can out me now. I have no choice."

Jean-François sighed. There was no escape for him. There was nowhere to run, and he knew that no amount of begging or crying would make a difference to a bug. *"Je comprend,"* he said stoically as he bravely accepted his fate.

"Don't feel too bad, little human. It was only a matter of days till you'd be dead anyway."

"May I ask one small favor before you end my life?"

"You can ask."

"How does it work?" beseeched the Frenchman. "What is the science upon which it is based? Please. I must know."

"Monsieur, je suis un espion, pas un scientist. Je ne sais pas comment ça marche."

And with that, the spy blasted a one-inch void through the center of Jean-François's heart. The weapon emitted no sound at all.

The spy then peeled open the human skin that covered his head and thorax. He set free his lower arms, which had been concealed within his costume, stretching them outward to the sky like an early morning yawn. During this, he used his upper left arm to tap upon the keypad that was strapped to his upper right.

The floor shook slightly when a small wormhole, roughly the size of a duffel bag, appeared in the air, hovering by the spy's midsection. He placed the alien weapon inside, removed a small scroll of parchment and read his new orders, then grabbed two pens from Jean-François' desk. While holding the parchment with his two left ungues, he used his two right ones to draft his new report—writing top-down with his upper unguis to describe the new information he had gathered since his last communiqué, writing bottom-up with his lower to offer new insights and suggestions. When the two reports met in the middle, he was done.

He rolled the parchment back into a scroll and placed it in the wormhole next to the rifle, then tapped upon his keypad. The floor shook slightly, and the wormhole snapped shut and vanished. The spy tucked his lower arms back between his thorax and abdomen, sealed up his human skin, and ran off.

Jean-François's dead body would not be found for nearly twenty-four hours.

CHAPTER THIRTY-TWO

"Request permission to retreat!" Major Shaughnessy shouted through his gas mask and into his wrist-mike.

He was crouched under a window in an office on the fourth floor of some building—he didn't even know which one at this point. The place was filled with the gray tear gas that the aliens had fired into every building in which they suspected human soldiers hid. Although the bugs seemed quite dedicated to preserving every structure, they had no qualms about crashing windows or breaking doors.

White beams whizzed everywhere, and their deafening roars boomed. Shaughnessy knew he had been lucky to receive one of the gas masks—it hadn't been due to his rank, he was merely in the right building when the supply runners snuck south. Those less fortunate had the choice of choking to death inside or running out into the streets for air to be gunned down in cold-insect blood.

He was at his wit's end. He had managed to keep the bugs in Southpoint as he had been ordered, yes, but at a great cost. The morning had begun with close to ten thousands troops under his command. Now, with the sun having set in the West, the final hues of light just peaking over the horizon, it was less than two thousand.

He and his men had tried everything. They had snuck from one building to another to blast a few rounds from open windows to make the enemy think the human numbers were greater than they were. They had attached automatic timers to M16s, then balanced the guns in the arms of mannequins, forcing the enemy to waste time searching empty buildings. One little trick after another, but in the long run, none of it seemed to matter much.

"Permission denied, Major," Colonel William's staticky voice bellowed through the Major's earpiece. "We need you to hold your position."

"We cannot, sir!" Shaughnessy pleaded. "It's a bleedin' suicide mission!"

"Major, this is President Willis," came a reassuring voice. "You've done an outstanding job, son, under impossible circumstances, and we're all proud of you. But I need you to hold just a little bit longer. Reinforcements are on the way."

"Reinforcements?" asked the Major, as much to himself as the President. He had been involved in all stages of the early planning. He knew well the total numbers of their volunteers, and that they had shot their wad on this one battle.

He grabbed the binoculars strapped to his neck and looked north to see thousands of new soldiers miles away, advancing toward him like armed angels.

"Where the bloody hell did they come from?"

*****

THE ALIEN COMMANDER WAS asking the very same thing.

He had thus far been quite impressed with Peyton. Long before the battle began, every possible human decision had been anticipated, and Peyton consistently made the right ones—often the low-probability ones. He had declined to weaponize his planes a second time, which would have been the typical, emotional, cocky human response, and he had kept his overseas troops overseas, which prevented the Dwellers from sweeping easily through Afro-Eurasia. That decision alone had added months to his master plan, yet still he was enjoying the chess game. But this?

He watched the human advance through his scopes from the rear of his infinite battalion, wondering who these new soldiers could be. He knew that Peyton had been training civilian volunteers, but it would be foolhardy to send them into battle with so little preparation—and Peyton had proven to be anything but foolish.

But the larger question was why? Given the overwhelming strength of the Dweller forces, it was sheer folly for Peyton to send his soldiers straight at them. There were but two possibilities: (1) the humans had some new secret weapon that had been overlooked by his spies, which was highly unlikely. The Commander had received the report about a new secret strategy but that did not imply a secret weapon, and this reckless move was no strategy at all, or (2) Peyton realized he could never win and was just trying to get the whole sordid mess over quickly, but that was also unlikely given what the Commander knew about humans.

The move was utterly unanticipated—but even the unanticipated had been anticipated. He coughed an order to his Sub-Commander who in turn coughed the order down the ranks. On a dime, the Dweller soldiers altered their movements and ceased the extermination. With efficient perfection, the swarms took new strategic positions on roads and rooftops, every bug having known in advance precisely where he or she should be. Then they waited to see what came next.

*****

"Look at him!" Peyton shouted merrily from his director's seat in the WTLV control room. Although most monitors displayed the various locations of the battle to come, Peyton's eyes were glued to the one that showed a close-up of the Alien Commander. "He doesn't know what the hell I'm doing, and it's making him nuts!"

"Has the old man lost his marbles?" Peyton asked as if he were the Alien Commander, then answered his own question. "Yes, I have, you ugly son of a bitch!"

He smiled at Laurel who stood on the side of the room, watching the monitors as well. "You may have just single-handedly saved mankind, ma'am."

Laurel forced a confident smile back. "Let's hope so."

The truth was, she was a nervous wreck. She had put all her faith in a species that she had despised for as long as she could remember. She knew they were lying, deceitful, self-absorbed monsters, and that their leader possessed those qualities more than any other. There was a better-than-not chance this was one big trick, that the vampires had worked out some kind of deal with the aliens, or that they were so arrogant that they sought to take out the aliens and humans combined to gain the planet for themselves—there was no telling what these fiends could have up their sleeve. Single-handedly saved mankind? She may have single-handedly destroyed it.

Why did she do it? she asked herself as she watched Julius on the monitor. Why did she bring him here in the first place? Why did she convince Peyton to bring the monster into the fold? Why did she insist they put that giant clock on the wall to count down the hours, minutes, and seconds till dawn to protect the vampires from sunlight? To "protect" the vampires? What was she thinking? Why did she do this?

Because, she answered herself, something deep within had told her that Julius was on the level, that Julius could be trusted—that Julius was, in fact, good!

But she also remembered thinking that she needed more time to grieve for Michael and that all her instincts were off.

"You better not be messing with me, monster," she whispered to the monitor.

*****

"YOU'D BETTER NOT BE messing with us," Major Denison told the senior vampire as he led the forces to battle.

Julius maintained a mere half step behind Denison to confirm the soldier's military seniority—that had been part of the agreement, and Julius felt it a small concession under the circumstances. Right behind him walked Prague and Africa, behind them thousands more of their kind, behind them a few hundred remaining human soldiers, and above them the military's sole surviving helicopter.

"I was against this from the start," Denison continued. "And I still am. But my Mistress takes you at your word, and I take her at hers. But if you double-cross us, I will dedicate my life to destroying you. No, not vampires anymore, only you."

"It will be what it will be," Julius replied with a smile.

"That's not very reassuring."

"My dear Denison," the vampire went on. "If I told you that you need not worry, you would worry nonetheless. Therefore, 'it will be what it will be' is the only truth of our moment. *Qué será será.*"

Denison only grunted, and they walked the next few minutes in silence as the Major sized up the specific positions of the alien swarms. They were already close enough for the bugs to open fire, but they didn't, just as the President had predicted.

"Be ready," Denison told the senior vampire as he raised his arm to the sky.

"*Parate bellum!*" Julius shouted to his ranks behind him. The legions of vampires hissed and extended their arms to mimic the wings of a bat.

The Alien Commander watched through his scopes. They were so close that he wondered if he should open fire—but that would be an emotional response, a human response. Or was that Peyton's plan? Was this all a bluff to get his soldiers close? No matter. If things devolved into a mere gunfight, the Dwellers would win. He merely had to be patient and see what the humans had in store.

Major Shaughnessy watched it all from his window. What the bloody hell was going on?

Peyton watched from the control room, leaning forward in his director's chair, giddy over the victory that he knew was to come.

Laurel watched from the side. What have I done? What have I done?"

"Wait for it," said Denison slowly. "Wait . . . wait . . . wait." Then with a snap he flung down his arm. "Now!"

"*Invadite!!!!!*" Julius cried out.

In a flash, the thousands of vampires transformed to mist and soared across the space that separated them from their enemy, sprouting their pointed fangs midflight. The Alien Sub-Commander, following his superior's lead, coughed out orders, and the bugs opened fire. But their

161

white beams whizzed through the mist to no effect, like punching a cloud. The vampires descended upon their enemy, wrapping themselves around the bipedal insects like vaporous boa constrictors, sucking out just enough blood to kill them before moving on to devour the next. Julius had warned the colonies about the tart, acidic taste—unlike human blood, which was sweet and creamy—so having been prepared for it, most of them found the feasting pleasurable. And oh what a feast it was.

The vampires were gluttonous, ferocious, fierce, and none more than Julius.

The human soldiers in the rear dropped to their knees and blasted M16s into the pandemonium with no concern for harming their vampire allies in front of them, their bullets merely whizzing through the mist and into the hideous bugs.

"*What are those things*?!" the Alien Commander bellowed in his smoker's-cough language. He tapped on the symbols on the keypad strapped to his lower forearm. The ground shook as a garage-sized wormhole opened behind him and his officers. The command vehicle slowly backed into the meadow within, stopping at the portal's edge where the upper brass watched the debacle from the safety of their home, the Commander keeping his unguis perched upon his keypad to shut the wormhole down in an instant should these creatures get too close. "*What are they*?!"

"*Facite impetum!*" Julius cried out once again. Thousands upon thousands of bats suddenly emerged to blacken the already black sky, crashing upon alien soldiers five, six at a time, pecking out their eyes, gnawing into their insect throats.

The sole remaining helicopter glided forward from the rear to hover above the fray as Harve and Frank rained down grenades from RPGs—the bugs so consumed by what was around them that they could pay no heed to what hovered overhead.

"That's what they are? Really?" laughed Johnny.

"And we'll all burn in hell because of them," said Harve as he blasted away.

"Maybe, but they're so darn cute!"

"Yeah, baby!" shouted Peyton as he leapt up from his director's chair like a little boy on Christmas morning. "This is the funnest battle I ever fought!"

Laurel watched Julius at work on the monitor with a relieved, exhausted smile. "You were telling me the truth," she said as if to her nemesis, welling up in a giant flurry of mixed emotions. "The whole time you told me the truth. My instinct about you was right. Go get 'em, you beautiful monster."

"Fire at will, Major!" Colonel Williams barked into the microphone.

"What the bloody hell is going on, sir?!" Shaughnessy was heard over the loudspeaker.

"No time for that, Major. Fire at will."

"But it's too chaotic! We might hit the—whatever those bleedin' things are!"

"Don't worry about them, Major," shouted Peyton with a smile. "You can't hurt them. Just gun down as many of those son of a bitch bugs as you can!"

"Aye sir!"

The pandemonium on the ground hit a fevered pitch as bats and vampires devoured their alien foes like a Thanksgiving dinner. The swarms continued to blast their weapons only to have their white beams whiz through the mist to kill their own kind. Wormhole upon wormhole opened to bring alien replacements, but the humans shot the new bugs dead before they could even enter our world.

Even Julius was coming to enjoy the sharp taste of the green blood. Perhaps he had gagged on Mary's (the girl in the graveyard) so many days ago because he simply hadn't been expecting the sublime harshness, like guzzling down a can of Coke when you expect a vanilla milkshake. The alien blood also seemed somehow lighter to him, for even after devouring hundreds, he didn't feel close to satiated.

The Alien Commander, having been genetically engineered to find defeat unacceptable, grew in insurmountable rage as he watched the fiasco through his scope from the safety of the inside edge of the wormhole. He had relied on the fact that Peyton wouldn't send any of these new "soldiers" through the portal for fear it was some kind of trap. It wasn't, and the

Commander was relieved that his counterpart had fallen for the bluff. (The truth was that taking out the enemy high command had been a primary part of Peyton's plan, but a sun was shining in that meadow. Prior to this battle, no one had ever considered whether vampires were vulnerable to all suns or only that of the Earth, but no vampire was willing to risk the horrid, painful death to find out.)

"*What are those things?!*" the Commander continued to furiously cough. "*Those are not human! How did I not know about them?! What are they?!*"

Then he wrapped his giant ungues around his Sub-Commander's insect-throat and squeezed as he icily coughed.

"*I want one.*"

CHAPTER THIRTY-THREE

"As America asks, why are the bugs only attacking us?" droned the TV anchor on the wall. "In Russia, rebel forces have seized the Kremlin, while in India –"

Patrick turned it off with the remote—it was just background noise by now anyway. Blah blah blah aliens blah blah blah war, but nothing at all about zombies.

He sat at one of the deputy's desks, deeply concerned. Why wasn't the news saying anything about zombies?

Hours earlier, he and Rhiannon had climbed the strange ladder bolted to the wall that led to a trap door in the ceiling that led to the building's rooftop, and they had seen the thousands and thousands of zombies that circled the building in which they were trapped, and countless more staggering toward it. It seemed that the whole town had gone zombie, and they were all congregating around the building to share in their one final meal.

This was typical for them, according to Rhiannon. "Zombies move in packs," she had explained. "They follow each other even though none of them ever knows where they're going no how. I'd say it makes 'em feel safer but they don't feel nothin' at all."

"Then why?" he had asked.

"Dunno. *Walkin' Dead* never 'splained us that part."

She had also described how a virus spreads quickly in our modern era, from city to city and around the world in a matter of days, using *Rise of the Planet of the Apes* as her primary source material for that particular point. But again, then why wasn't the news reporting any of it? Could she be wrong? She was only seven after all, and the *Apes* movie was just a remake. Could it be that Heartsoot Creek was in fact the only infected spot in the world? Because if that were the case, no one would ever believe them enough to send help. And if it weren't the case, no one would be *able* to send help. It looked like they would never get out of there.

And even if they could, he continued, where would they go? The zombies would just follow them, and they'd end up infecting a whole new town, then another and another. He and Rhiannon would be the ones responsible for spreading the worldwide virus, and that was a responsibility he wouldn't accept. They were stuck.

To make matters worse, their food supply was running low as evidenced by the many candy wrappers, empty soda cans and broken glass that littered the front of the vending machine they had smashed open hours before. Patrick had suggested they ration their supplies because they didn't know how long they would be stuck there. Rhiannon agreed in theory but didn't listen at all in practice, and just ate to her heart's content.

What could he do? Hit her? She was just a little girl. Better to simply match her binging so as not to be left without any sustenance at all.

And so he sat at the deputy's desk, munching on the very last Milky Way bar when he noticed certain words on the deputy's telephone display. He brightened slightly. It was worth a try.

*****

THE TUMULTUOUS SOUNDS OF the Southpoint battle thundered even throughout Northbank miles away. Private Roger Hayes motored across the reception area on his shiny electric wheelchair to answer the ringing phone. He had stopped trying to figure out whether the Captain-with-the-scar was the alien mole some time ago, because he realized that it didn't matter. He would serve his benefactor loyally, whatever he was. If it turned out that he was the spy, and the aliens won the war, perhaps his Captain would keep him around like some beloved pet or something—it was certainly more than the humans would do once they no longer needed him, and that Rog knew from experience.

"Base. Security. Captain's office."

"Thank God!" said the little boy on the other end. Rog noticed the caller ID and groaned—his Captain had been getting crank calls from this number all day. "My name is Patrick Hutchins! I'm twelve years old from Heartsoot Creek, Georgia! Zombies have overtaken our town! Please send help!"

"You again?" Rog said impatiently, ultraprotective of his Captain's precious time. "What, aliens and vampires aren't crazy enough for you wackos, you gotta have zombies too? How'd you get this number anyway?"

"It was at the top of recent calls," the boy answered innocently.

"I meant the first time."

"This *is* the first time! From me, I mean. The other calls would have been from the Sheriff or a deputy or something. But they've all turned!"

"Listen to this, boy," Rog barked then held the phone toward the open window. "It's the sound of war. Good men and women are dying so that you and I can live, and none of us got time for your little games! Got it? Don't call this number again!"

He slammed the receiver down hard with a bang as the Captain-with-the-scar came out of his office carrying a large manila envelope. "What was that all about?"

"Nothing to waste your time with, sir."

"Good," said the Captain-with-the-scar as he handed Rog the envelope. "Get this to the control room, pronto. Hand-deliver it to Colonel Williams personally."

"To the Colonel personally. Yes sir!"

The Captain-with-the-scar briskly turned his back on Rog to return to his office, as he would have with any other private. Rog wheeled himself out the front door as ordered, shaking his head with a wry smirk.

"Zombies. Sheesh. As if."

*****

SERGEANT SANCHEZ HAD REMAINED unconscious since she had collapsed in Johnny's arms hours earlier, but the thunderous roars of battle stirred her awake at last.

She sat up in her hospital bed. Her once beautiful skin was now covered with ugly gray blotches, her teeth were rotted, her fingernails were four inches long, and her open eyes may as well have been closed because they revealed no soul within.

Her head, not her eyes, darted about the room to survey her surroundings, but she lacked the mental capacity to comprehend anything she saw. If she could have understood, she would have assessed that she was in a very large hospital ward. The walls were glass, but the curtains were drawn closed so that no one from the outside could see in, or vice versa. Hundreds of beds lay empty, with only a few containing unconscious soldiers who looked somewhat like her, their zombie-virus having yet to fully gestate. The other two hundred former soldiers, now zombies all, staggered into the glass wall desperate to reach the source of the powerful sounds they adored, bounced off the wall, then staggered right back into it again.

Sanchez was enamored with the ruckus as well. She lacked the capacity for words, the capacity to think even, but if she hadn't been so lacking, her thoughts would have been these:

"Pretty boom."

She lugged herself out of the hospital bed and staggered toward the wall to join those of her new kind. She walked into the glass wall like the others, bounced backward, then staggered back into it again, and again, and again.

"Pretty boom," she would have said if she had words. "Pretty pretty boom boom."

CHAPTER THIRTY-FOUR

The combined vampire-human forces had been kicking extraterrestrial-butt all night. The livid Alien Commander had adopted one new strategy after another, each one leading only to greater death and defeat. Most of his replacements weren't even able to make it through the portals before being gunned down, and his soldiers on the ground had been diminished by more than half while there had not been a single human casualty since the V reinforcements had arrived so many hours ago.

The special V clock on the wall in the WTLV control room read zero hours, fifty-two minutes, and there's no point in mentioning the seconds because they kept ticking down to dawn.

"You'd better bring them back," said Laurel.

"Not yet," Peyton answered, his eyes glued to the monitor that displayed the enemy Commander. "We've got the bugs on the run."

"It's less than an hour to sunrise, and they still have to make it across town."

"Look at him," Peyton said, transfixed on his counterpart. "He's thinking retreat. C'mon, you bastard, just say it. 'Retreat.' Shout it out for your men. 'Retreat.' You know you want to. C'mon, say it for Papa."

The truth was that Peyton couldn't understand why his counterpart hadn't called for retreat long before, and it was great cause for concern. With human victory so close at hand, it would raise too many questions if Peyton were the one to suddenly bring his soldiers home, and it would reveal the one giant flaw, the great kryptonite that had lied at the heart of his plan all along.

Vampires can't fight in the daytime.

He had known from the start that he needed a victory so immediate and decisive that the bugs would deem Earth more trouble than it's worth and fly off to find some other planet to conquer—or at the very least, regroup to return at a later date, hopefully at night. The problem was that he had achieved the exact kind of victory for which he had hoped and the damn bugs weren't going anywhere.

And the seconds to sunrise were ticking, ticking, ticking down.

"Retreat, you son of a bitch! Your people are dying all over the place! Show a little compassion for the troops, man. What kind of general are you?"

Just then, for no reason discernible to man or vampire, the furious Alien Commander coughed out an order. He tapped on the symbols on his keypad causing the ground to shake violently, akin to a six-point-eight earthquake. The garage-sized wormhole from which the high command had watched the battle widened, spreading out far beyond the width of the great boulevards and parkways on which the fighting had taken place, and the swarms fled full speed toward it.

"And blackjack," Peyton smiled then turned to Colonel Williams. "Let 'em go."

The Colonel conveyed the order down through the ranks. The weary human soldiers lowered their weapons. The vampires returned to their human form panting, spent, stuffed. Some held their cramped bellies, swollen from over binging. Some threw up. But all noticed the earliest rays of dawn emerging in the distance.

As the last bug ran into the wormhole and onto the grassy meadow within, the Alien Commander tapped on his keypad again to cause another great quake. The giant wormhole snapped shut and vanished as if it had never existed at all.

It was done.

"Rot in hell you scaly bastards!!!" Major Shaughnessy shouted, which led to an eruption of cheers, laughter, whoops and hollers, pats on the backs and high fives.

In the control room, the same celebratory sentiments abounded albeit handshakes being more prevalent than high fives.

Laurel watched Julius on the monitor with moist eyes. She was so proud of him, and so confused that she *could* be proud of him. He was a monster, a tool in a war for survival after which he would return to his evil ways. He had said so himself, a "temporary truce" he had called it. But as hard as she tried to hold onto her hatred, she couldn't help but smile and fondly whisper to her nemesis, "You did it."

"Colonel, get those covered trucks out there now and get the Vs out of the light," Peyton instructed. "Leave a third of the men where they stand, and have the others rotate in to replace them on three-hour shifts till the bugs come back—because they will. Then let's get another thousand troops out there, fresh faces, ones the aliens haven't seen, and put "V" insignias on their sleeves. I want those bugs to see V-Company marching out in broad daylight."

"With all due respect, sir," began Colonel Williams, "Why leave the men *there*? The bugs can wormhole anywhere they want, including right into our camp."

"They can," Peyton explained professorially, "but they won't. Don't think of this as a war because the enemy doesn't—and you don't exterminate your hornets by jumping past a massive clump of the nastiest of them. No, this enemy will show up wherever our fighting force stands, and the other side of town is fine by me."

"Um, sir?" the Canadian Lieutenant began tentatively. "Regarding the extra thousand troops—we don't *have* extra troops. We've been all-in from the get-go."

"We have the civilian trainees."

"They're not close to ready for battle, sir. Most of them can't even fire a gun."

"That's all right, son," Peyton assured him. "V-Company doesn't use guns."

*****

THE SOLDIERS WERE HALFWAY to base when they caught up with the trucks that had been sent back for them. Although the sun was not yet visible, the light over the horizon was getting brighter. The humans were exhausted, and the vampires weak from the burgeoning dawn as well as their all-night binging—but you wouldn't know it from their boisterous spirits as they filed into the covered transports.

Julius was furthest from the trucks for he had led the charge. He walked with a group of human soldiers—his new admirers—when Denison approached him.

"Julius, I owe you an apology," said the slayer Guide. "I was certain that you would betray us, but you prevailed in the highest of form. I was wrong about you, sir, and I thank you for proving me so." Then he put out his hand.

Julius looked at the hand with suspicion at first, but despite centuries of warfare with the likes of Denison, he was moved by the gesture. He smiled and clasped Denison's hand with both of his own. "You are most welcome, my friend."

Just a little bit ahead walked Prague and Africa, the two next-eldest vampires, Julius's second- and third-in-command. Africa delighted in teasing her best friend and lover, playfully taunting her into submission. "So? So? Nothing more to say?"

"Okay, it was fun," Prague granted. "I concede it. Exhilarating, delicious."

"And humans?"

"Well, perhaps they're not *all* bad."

"That's monumental growth for you, my treasure," she said with a smile.

Just a bit ahead walked a squad of human infantry, laughing and joking, with Plato only steps behind, his eyes locked on the back of a soldier's neck. The vampire licked his lips and hissed softly, sprouted his fangs and moved in for the kill. Prague saw it not a moment too soon and jerked out her arm in a palm-heel strike. She touched nothing, but Plato fell to the ground as if he had been punched in the head.

"What did Julius tell you?!" Prague shouted as she moved toward the boy.

Suddenly, the ground shook. Four ninety-feet-tall, cylindrical wormholes shot straight up from the ground, each one enveloping one of the four vampires who had yet to make it into the covered trucks, along with the human soldiers around them.

It was nothing like Julius had ever seen. The center of the cylinder remained Jacksonville—the Bellfort Road pavement still under his feet, the traffic light ahead, the fire hydrant on the curb—but five yards beyond him in every direction was the alien world, the sunny, grassy meadow from which the bugs had come and gone.

Before anyone could process what had happened, two alien swarms emerged to blast every human who had had the misfortune of walking by the vampire's side. Denison was the first to die, followed by everyone else. The bugs then harnessed their rifles over their shoulders and approached the vampire with alloy spears, ingot ropes and electronic metallic nets. Julius deduced that they had been ordered to take him alive, but he had ideas of his own. He turned to mist and charged.

*****

THE HUMANS OUTSIDE THE cylinders drew their M16s to rescue their new allies as they gaped at the giant pillars in stunned awe. What the hell were these?

Major Shaughnessy cautiously reached out his arm to touch the black wall, but he felt nothing. He slowly moved his hand into the pillar, only to see his arm protrude out the opposite end ten yards away, his forearm seemingly detached from his elbow like a cheesy magic trick. He peeked inside to take a look, only to find his head appearing ten yards away as if detached from his neck. He took a single step into the wormhole, then was instantly exiting the other side—those watching did not lose sight of him for an instant. It was as if the wormhole wasn't there at all.

*****

"DID THOSE BUGS JUST steal my Vs?!" Peyton screamed as he leapt from his seat. "They're *my* goddamn Vs! Let 'em get their own goddamn Vs!"

*****

INSIDE THE CYLINDER, JULIUS fought valiantly but soon came to realize that the effort was futile. The all-night gorging had exhausted him, and the opening at the mouth of the cylinder ninety feet above showed the Earth sky growing ever brighter.

The alien ropes and nets merely passed through his mist-self, but he knew that wouldn't last long. He was finding it difficult to focus, difficult to remain as mist, his human form popping in and out. And for every enemy soldier he managed to kill, a new one emerged to take its place.

He made a quick assessment. The Earth sun should still be below the horizon, while the alien sun seemed to be at its noon-strongest. Even if he was wrong, he thought, he'd still rather suffer the excruciating death-by-sun on his own planet.

He focused every last bit of his intellect on remaining mist, then soared straight up ninety feet to the mouth of the cylinder. As he had thought, the sun had yet to appear but it was close, too close. The moment he rose above the edge of the cylinder's opening, he was blasted in face and chest with the sun's agonizing rays.

He screamed in mortal pain as he was reverted to human form against his will, losing his ability to fly. He summoned his last bit of strength to make one final lunge forward before gravity took hold and heaved himself over the edge of the cylinder wall, freed from the alien world, whereupon he crashed down on the concrete road ninety feet below.

The ground shook, the cylinder vanished and Julius lay face down on the ground as the light burned fire through his pores. It was only a matter of time till the sun would reveal itself, and he knew his end was near. But giant oak trees offered shade just on the side of the road, only two car-lengths away. He knew they wouldn't save him, but they could at least offer some temporary relief from his agony. He lacked the strength to stand so he crawled like the little baby he had been almost three millennia ago, the two-car-length distance feeling like a thousand miles.

You had a good run, ole boy, he told himself. Longer than most. Well done.

*****

THE CYLINDER IN WHICH Africa had been trapped held the same underlying properties as the one that had contained Julius—five yards of Jacksonville on all sides of her that were impossibly surrounded by the alien world. She had made the same basic decisions as her leader—an initial instinct toward combat in which she slaughtered one alien soldier after another, followed by the awareness of her exhaustion and limitations, followed by the calculated risk of flight. (Plato had jumped straight to the flight instinct and hadn't bothered to fight at all.)

She flew straight up the ninety feet to the mouth of the cylinder just as Julius had, and was also blasted in face and chest with the sun's agonizing rays. She too screamed in mortal pain and was reverted to human form. But unlike Julius, she was unable to make that final lunge over the edge, and when she crashed down to the ground she was still within the cylinder borders, surrounded by alien soldiers intent on capturing her, her paranormal abilities gone.

Before she could rise to her feet, two bugs tossed their electronic metallic net upon her. The net immediately began to wrap itself around her as if possessing a mind of its own. Africa struggled to free herself but the more she did so, the tighter the net became, as if fighting back of its own volition.

The alien soldiers took half a step away to watch from a safe distance as they laughed at their once ferocious foe, knowing she would soon have no struggle left. One of them looked back toward the meadow and coughed loudly. "*We caught one!*"

The others rubbed their ungues together in a hideous parody of applause.

*****

THE GREAT OAK TREES were only yards away, but Julius was too weak to crawl even an inch more. The sun would soon be visible, but by now the vampire welcomed it—a quick, stinging death being far preferable to this slow, tortuous one.

Through the haze of his blurred vision, he could see a Harley Davidson careen toward him. The bike peeled to a halt by his side, and a woman jumped off.

"Julius!" she shouted.

He recognized Laurel's voice and deemed it a fitting end—far more dignified to be done in by a mighty slayer than to have been caught in the sun, a rookie error.

But to his surprise, Laurel made no attempt to kill him. Instead, she slid her hands under his armpits and dragged him the rest of the way to the great oaks.

"A hearse with your casket is on its way, so you hang in there!" he heard her muffled voice as his backside dragged against the gravelly pavement.

"It won't get here in time," he muttered through his agony.

"It will! And I came back here to keep you safe till it does. So don't you dare give up on me, monster! This war ain't over yet, and we still need you!"

*****

AFRICA LAY ON THE ground, fully restrained by the electronic net. With her arms squeezed against her sides and her legs squeezed against each other, the aliens were moving in to take her away. Still unwilling to surrender, she snapped her mouth open and closed repeatedly until two aliens, standing feet away from her on opposite sides, jammed an alloy rod in between her fangs to stop her. She now had nothing left with which to fight so she closed her eyes to pray.

The swarm moved in to lift her when she suddenly heard the loud bra-tat-tat of a submachine gun coming from above. She opened her eyes to see the thorax-chests of her captors rip open from the blasts as they each fell dead to the ground. A rescue harness dropped down from the sky next to her but she had no free limbs to grab hold. A powerful human arm yanked the alloy rod out of her mouth then scooped her up like a small child and clipped her onto the harness, net and all, and then she felt herself ascending up toward the mouth of the cylinder.

New aliens ran into the cylinder to blast their rifles up at her and the human, but Harve, her most unlikely hero, gunned them down before they had a chance to fire. Up, up, up soared the vampire and her vampire-hating savior until they cleared the mouth of the cylinder and were whisked off to the side where no bug could aim.

And then she screamed in mortal agony!

The sun had still yet to rise, but the now bright rays above the horizon seared into her soul. Harve used his body to shield her from direct contact as best he could, but the harness was twisting in the air as it ascended toward the helicopter above.

"Hurry!" Harve shouted into his wrist-mike over Africa's howls of misery.

"The pulley is already set on high!" he heard Frank through his earpiece.

"It's not fast enough! The poor kid's burning to death! Let's go!"

Small pockets of flame began to flare up on Africa's arms and legs. Harve used his hands to pat them out, scalding his own flesh on behalf of the demon. When they finally reached the chopper door, Harve untethered her as Frank yanked her into the bird then straight into an open coffin and slammed its lid shut.

Harve pulled himself into the chopper, then dropped to the floor exhausted.

"That was fun," said Johnny from the pilot's seat. "Let's do it again."

*****

PRAGUE'S FIRST INSTINCT UPON finding herself trapped in the cylinder had been to attack. But unlike Julius and Africa, her flight instinct never took hold. She had not felt bloated by the prior night's battle nor weakened by the early rays of sunlight, so she had seen no reason to run from these insects that she had been devouring all night with ease. Fueled by the fury over their gall at daring to capture her, the mightiest of all female vampires reveled in tearing these bugs to shreds. (Only Julius was more powerful, which was why she was next in line to assume leadership.)

But as the sky above the mouth of the cylinder grew brighter, as the bugs kept coming and coming, her mistake grew rapidly apparent. She was no longer able to remain mist for more than a few seconds at a time now, rendering her ability to fly murky at best, and certainly not ninety feet straight up.

But ever defiant, ever superior, she was unwilling to quit—even if she had to fight as a human. When one alien lassoed its alloy rope upon her arm, she jerked the rope right toward her, pummeling her vampire knee into the bug's head, crushing its insect skull. When two others threw an electronic metallic net toward her, she dropped to the ground and rolled under it, tore her fangs into one of the bug's calves, and rammed her fist up into the groin of the other, penetrating its crusty scales and yanking vital digestive organs clean out of its insect body.

She stealthily circled the ground, fangs out, hissing, menacingly swiping her luscious fingernails at the air like a crazed mountain lion. The bugs, having been ordered to bring her in unharmed, were terrified of getting too close and the badass vampire took full advantage of it. She'd attack, withdraw, attack, withdraw, bite, claw, scratch, gorge, all the while wondering how long she'd be able to keep it up.

A third swarm of bugs ran onto the road with their rifles drawn. Were the bugs changing strategy? Prague wondered. Had they now been ordered to kill her? Had they not learned that their puny weapons were useless against her?

But the bugs aimed their rifles upward toward the mouth of the cylinder and began to fire. Prague realized that a helicopter hovered above, and the fact that she hadn't sensed it, hadn't even heard it, was great cause for concern. How many of her other abilities were gone?

Johnny worked his helicopter wizardry as he dodged the alien blasts that whizzed all around his aircraft. Frank clipped Harve to the harness but there were too many white beams for the new Lieutenant to safely descend from the bird.

"I can't get out!" Harve screamed. "Get us to a safe angle!"

"You won't be able to drop in from a safe angle!" Johnny shouted back.

"I can't drop in this way either!"

"Then throw the harness down without you! Frank, unclip him!"

"What good will that do?!" shouted Frank.

"Let's at least give the girl a fighting chance!"

"That's crazy! We'll get blasted ourselves!"

"Do what the Captain says, Frank!" shouted Harve. "Now!"

Prague continued to keep her predators at bay as she watched the rescue harness fall toward her. She recognized the precarious situation of her human rescuers and how wrong she had been about these creatures, risking their own fragile lives to save hers. They were noble allies indeed. The harness dropped into the cylinder, and Prague immediately grabbed onto the line and started to climb.

"She's got it!" Harve shouted. "Bring her up!"

Frank flipped the switch on the pulley while Johnny shot the bird skyward. Two bugs leapt toward the harness and grabbed hold of Prague's legs. The beautiful blonde vampire kicked the closer one in the head who fell back into the second one. Both fell to the ground as she rocketed upward, her escape imminent. She cleared the top of the cylinder only to suddenly find herself face-to-face with the sun itself, the tippy-tippy-tip-top of its scalp shining violently upon her face.

Despite the wretched agony that consumed her, she knew that she had no time to scream. With only a second of life remaining, she rang out her final thought.

Africa, my eternal love, the sunrise is as beautiful as you remember it, as beautiful as you. Live happily, my cherished one.

Then she burst into fire and fell backward into the cylinder. Four alien soldiers tried to catch her in a synthetic blanket to keep her unharmed by the fall, but by the time she landed she was nothing but ash.

Africa, safe within her casket, received her lover's message with perfect clarity, and tears rolled down her cheeks.

*****

THE HEARSE SEEMED A tiny dot miles down the road, and whether it would arrive in time was anybody's guess. The sun was fully visible over the horizon, and their tiny island of shade was rapidly shrinking.

Laurel sat on the ground with her back leaning against the giant oak,

Julius seated in front with his back pressed against hers. Her bare, toned arms were wrapped tightly around him so that the weakened vampire wouldn't tip over into the light, and the perfect, yellow sun shone brightly behind them. The only sounds were the chirping birds and the soft breeze brushing through the leaves. In any other context, it would have seemed a very romantic image, and they both knew it.

"How long have you yearned for this moment, Laurel?"

"What moment?" she asked, offended by his presumption.

"Watching me die."

"Oh, that moment. Most of my life, actually. But you're not going to die. Not unless I'm the one who kills you, monster." He laughed slightly at this, and she liked the feel of it, and she didn't like that she liked it. "Thank you, by the way," she added.

"You're thanking *me*?" he smiled. "For what?"

"For joining forces with us. For envisioning a truce and bringing it to fruition. You fellows were pretty fierce out there."

"It's easy when we're not at odds with one trained to slay us. You should have been out there with us."

"Slaying aliens isn't exactly what I've been trained for," she said with a smile.

There was an awkward silence. They had never spoken to each other this way before—even when they had made their truce it had been with deep suspicion and distrust. It was unsettling for them both, but especially for her.

"I have never felt ill toward you, Laurel," said the vampire. "Many of my kind hate you, but –"

"They have no cause to hate me. I'm a defender of man, no more no less."

"And how would you like it if every time you went to your market for a fine roast beef, you were stabbed in the chest by some magical cow?"

Laurel suppressed a laugh. "Okay, I can see why they may not be fans."

"But never have I hated you. You have been a most worthy foe."

"Stop talking like you're dying."

"But I am dying," he admitted. "Dying in the loving embrace of my mortal enemy. If that's not a kick in the pants, I don't know what is."

"This is not a loving embrace," she said emphatically.

He looked deep into her naked eyes. She was being kind to him, tender, and he to her. Their bodies were so sensually comfortable pressed against the other, and he knew that she knew it. Why did humans feel the need to deny the obvious?

And her only thought as she fell lost in his gaze was what an extraordinary looking man he was—but it was quickly interrupted by a second thought. No! Michael, Michael.

"Okay," was the vampire's only reply.

"And never have I admired *you*, by the way," she went on. "You are a monster and a fiend, and never have I felt anything but hatred and contempt toward you."

"Until today," he answered. "Today you felt gratitude. That is what you said."

"Yes, all right. Today I felt gratitude."

"And all that hatred and contempt and the passion which fueled it for a lifetime had nowhere to turn. And here I am now in your loving embrace."

"It's not a loving embrace!"

"Okay."

"It's not! When this war ends, we shall be enemies once more—like the US and Russia after World War Two. Once Germany was defeated, they returned to their mutual hatred." Julius only smiled. "What's so darn funny?" she demanded.

"I was just imagining Roosevelt and Stalin in a loving embrace."

This time, she couldn't stop a tiny laugh from taking hold. "Shut up, monster."

"As you wish, slayer."

The words hung awkwardly yet sensually in the air when the hearse screeched to a stop yards before them.

"We made it," sighed a relieved Laurel as four soldiers bolted out of the vehicle to retrieve the vampire's ornate casket, then sprinted it toward them.

Without warning, the ground shook. A wormhole opened behind them, and a swarm of aliens emerged to gun down the four soldiers. Six of the seven jogged out to retrieve the casket while the smallest positioned herself in front of the tree to study Julius.

"Like, what's wrong with him?" she asked the former First Lady.

Laurel was startled by the insect's use of English, surprised by the female voice, but hoped that it might imply some degree of compassion. "He's been shot!" she lied. "He needs urgent medical attention! Please let me get him back home!"

"Nah," the alien said pensively. "I think it's probably the sunlight."

Her voice seemed familiar to Julius, hauntingly so, and he needed to confirm whether he had lost his faculties once and for all. "Do I know you?" he inquired of the apparent swarm-leader.

"How can you even ask me that, Julius?" the lady bug answered. "It's only been like a few days for you since we were together in that graveyard."

"Mary," he sighed with a bemused smile. "You lost the accent."

"Told you I would. 'Course it's been like five years for me so, you know, not really all that impressive, right?"

The other aliens set the vampire's casket on the ground beside him. They wrapped him in a synthetic cloth to shield him from the sunlight then lifted him into the box, all while Mary prattled on.

"And sorry we gotta kidnap you and torture you and stuff, but we gotta figure out what makes you guys die, you know? Decades of studying humans, and vampires trip us up. Go figure, right?" She sealed the casket closed as she summed it up. "Okay, so we'll like chat later, 'kay? Have a good one."

The bugs carried the coffin into the wormhole as one of them coughed out some sort of reminder to Mary.

"Fine, whatever," she snippily responded, then she turned to Laurel with what appeared to be genuine sadness in her eyes. She removed the time-space weapon that hung over her thorax, and took aim. Laurel gasped at first, then closed her eyes as she prepared to be with Michael once more.

Mary fired. The blasts from her weapon were deafening as white beams whizzed at the tree. Only once the noise subsided did Laurel realize that she was still alive, and that one-inch voids in the giant oak tree surrounded her like a chalk outline.

"I admired your husband," Mary whispered confidentially. "Woulda voted for him if I'd been a citizen."

She winked her bulging bug eye then crossed back into the wormhole to join her brethren, then tapped on the keypad that was strapped to her lower forearm. The ground shook, the wormhole snapped shut and vanished, and the mightiest vampire of all was gone from our world.

PART FOUR

EXTERMINATION COMPLETE

INTERLUDE #4

Dinah lounged in the shade as her hatchlings gnawed the meat off the adolescent T. rex's carcass. Dizzy had the best spot by the large upper ribs, while eldest-born Donald was by the smaller ones, and the big brother didn't like the arrangement at all. He head-butted his little sister to shove her aside when Dinah eeked out a soft shriek. Little Donald dropped his eyes to the ground then returned to his original spot.

From out of nowhere, a cacophony of rapid, heavy footsteps was heard. Dinah looked up to see two enormous Tyrannosaurus rexes charging toward her at full speed. It didn't take much for the highly intelligent Deinonychus to deduce that the fourteen feet tall, forty feet long beasts were the parents of the adolescent on which her pack had been feeding and that they were now seeking a vengeance of their own. Let's call them Rex and Tyrene.

Dinah instantly grabbed her hatchlings in her mouth and scurried up the nearest tree as fast as she could, but the dreaded T. rexes were fast upon her. Rex opened his giant jaw and snapped it down hard over Dinah's backside, his knife-like teeth catching only a few of the Deinonychus mother's butt feathers.

Dinah and hatchlings made it to the top of the tree, but it was only a few yards taller than the T. rex parents themselves. She yelped out an ear-piercing shriek, a cry for help, as Tyrene leaned her massive body against the trunk, causing the tree to bend sideways and the top to tilt lower toward Rex's gaping mouth.

Dinah covered her hatchlings like a blanket to shield them from her predator's wrath, sacrificing herself as the first to go. She could feel Rex's stinky, hot breath upon her. There was no escape, no hope. The T. rex male readied himself to chomp down when fifty shrieking Deinonychus suddenly leapt out of the trees! Half of them landed on Tyrene, the other half on Rex, each one cutting and slicing with their razor sharp claws, all with flawless precision and teamwork.

Claw wrapped himself around Tyrene's head, slashing at her eyes and ears. The female T. rex lurched back in pain and let go of the tree causing it to whip out in the opposite direction, sending Dinah and her hatchlings flying. The hatchlings landed in the soft brush unharmed, but Dinah's head hit a rock, rendering her unconscious.

The fifty Deinonychus sliced at their enemies' throats and underbellies, gouging thick chunks of hide from their leathery frames. The T. rex couple smashed themselves against trees and boulders as they crushed their assailants to bits.

Then all of a sudden, the ground shook violently—the equivalent of an eight-point-two earthquake. The dinosaurs stopped dead in their tracks to look toward the source of the shaking, and they were utterly confounded by what they saw. Even the highly intelligent Deinonychus could not make heads or tails of it.

CHAPTER THIRTY-FIVE

Julius had no sense of how long he had been asleep, nor did he have any idea where he was. There was so much to process all at once that he had to consciously slow down his racing brain and work things through one at a time, even though it only took him a matter of seconds to do it.

He quickly deduced that he must have had quite a long rest because the wounds that had been inflicted upon him by the sunrays were gone, his vision and hearing were clear, his thoughts lucid, and his determination to survive intense.

He lay naked on a gurney bound by leather ties, with wireless electrodes taped to his body. The gurney was in the center of a large space with clean, white, cracked walls, suggesting that he was in a building a hundred or so years old—the kind you'd find in a northeastern city like New York or Boston. Metallic carts on wheels sported all sorts of surgical tools, as well as human weapons both modern and archaic. Two bugs in white lab coats moved about with purpose, and holographic images of his skeleton and organs hovered in the air. A third alien, also in a lab coat, sat at a holographic keyboard, manipulating the angles of his hovering innards.

A fourth alien, this one an armed soldier, stood by a window with stylish synthetic blinds pulled a quarter of the way down. Julius could see the endless multitude of shining stars, more brilliant and infinite than he had ever seen on the darkest night on Earth, as well as the sun itself shining directly upon him.

Why it hadn't scorched him into nonexistence he could not decipher, but the rest was obvious. Despite the Earth-like feel of the place, he was in a medical operating room on the alien vessel, and he was soon to be tortured.

"Morning, sunshine," Mary said brightly as she entered the room wearing her human skin under a white lab coat with a stethoscope around her neck. She tapped on a keypad next to the door, and Julius could hear seven dead bolts lock in place.

He immediately tried to transform to mist, but it didn't take. When that failed, he tried to tear through the leather straps but he couldn't do that either.

"Don't bother, boo," she said affectionately. "The sun's shining right on you."

"Then how am I alive?"

"Special filter on the window," she explained as she crossed to the sink to wash her hands. "We actually designed it for ourselves long ago 'cause, like, moving through space, sometimes we're really far from a sun and sometimes like really close, and too much sun isn't good for anyone, so it's got all these different intensities. Right now it's set to let in just enough UV to keep you weak, but not enough to like totally kill you. It's a teensy brighter than we normally like it, but we can't have you flying all over the place wreaking havoc, you know?"

She pulled up a round stool, grabbed a tongue depressor and flashlight from a cart, and proceeded to examine him. He could see on her face the five years that had passed for her since their last encounter days ago. Still beautiful, she had gone from bashful teenager to confident young woman. He found the change alluring, even though he knew he would have to find a way to kill her before she killed him.

"I actually kinda owe you," she said sweetly as she shoved a tongue depressor into his mouth. "I was originally sent to Earth to be an observer spy—like, our bottom level. I was to keep a low profile, find out what people were up to a few days pre-invasion, then report it back to five years ago and let our planners plan. But after you tried to kill me that night— which seriously hurt my feelings 'cause I was so into you—still am, actually—I get home all beat-up, and everyone asks what happened so I tell them I was attacked by a vampire. And they're like, 'The vampire is of human fiction. Such things do not exist.' And I'm like, 'Yeah they do. One just attacked me.' And they're like, 'No they don't." And I'm like, 'Yeah, they do.'

"They thought I lost it. They wouldn't let me work on anything. So just to prove my point, I scoped out everything I could find on you guys—every book, tome, scroll, movie, TV series, but no one cared—they figured that if humans didn't believe in you, then you couldn't be real. I also watched a ton of *Hannah Montana* and *Gossip Girl* to like make my English awesome. Oh, and baseball too. Wow, that was random." And with her stethoscope now upon his chest, she added, "Cough please."

Julius complied so as not to disrupt her train of thought—despite her incoherent rambling, she might divulge some useful information to help his escape.

"Anyhoo, cut to flash-forward. We're at war, kicking human butt, all as planned, then you guys show up and turn the tables. Everyone like freaks— even our Commander who never freaks, freaks. But to me, what you guys are was so obvious.

"So I go back to my boss with my data, and now he's willing to really look at it, and he sees what I've been saying all along. So he takes me to his boss, who takes me to his, who takes me to his, yadda yadda yadda, next thing I know, the Commander's back on the vessel, and he summons me to an audience.

"And he frikkin' loves me! Swear ta God! I'm like the only one who knows what you guys are and how to defeat you, and he even wants to do me now—me, the dumb chick who couldn't make it as an observer spy is suddenly like his top advisor with her own department. And it's all thanks to you, sunshine," she said as she kissed his forehead.

"Then how about letting me go?" Julius replied.

"Oh you're so adorable, I could just eat you up.

"Anyway, the problem is that the lit on you guys is like all over the map. Some say garlic harms you, some say not. Crucifixes—some yes, some no.

Almost all of it says sunlight kills you in a jiff, only a couple of very old tomes and one or two recent novels say it's only the sun itself. So who can know f'sure, right? And on that note, ready?"

"Ready for what?"

"To find out which of your lore is true and which is bogus, silly. Haven't you been paying attention? Bad boy."

And with that, she placed three silver crucifixes upon his naked chest. They sizzled and burned into his flesh. The holograms showed his heart beating rapidly, his lungs swelling, the lobes of his brain quivering, and he cried out in pain.

"Cool," Mary said pleasantly. "Awesome start."

CHAPTER THIRTY-SIX

Africa awoke inside her casket feeling refreshed. Gone were the scars that the sun's rays had inflicted, and her heart was pumping strongly. She could sense that there was no sunlight outside the casket even though it was only late afternoon. She willed the lid open then slowly rose, now strong enough to easily break through the aliens' metallic net and cast it aside.

She saw that she was in the penthouse suite of the Omni Hotel that the humans had assigned as her and Prague's quarters. The windows were sealed—the entire hotel had been rendered sunlight-proof the day prior—but Africa could only focus on the empty spot where Prague's casket had once lay, and it made her cry.

"Did you sleep well?" asked a voice that only added insult to injury.

Africa turned quickly toward the sofa "What brings you hence, slayer?"

"We have matters to discuss," Laurel answered. In truth, the slayer would have far preferred to be by Denison's side right now, saying her last good-byes to her Guide, her mentor, her lifelong best friend, but Denison himself would have insisted that she fulfill her duty first. This was for him. "Do you know about Prague?"

"Yessss," Africa answered with a venomous hiss. "I know about Prague."

"And Julius?"

"What about Julius?!" Africa snapped, but she didn't need the slayer to answer—she could sense her leader's absence from the world. "He's dead," she said softly.

"Most likely," Laurel said, trying to keep her conflicted feelings concealed and remain professional. "He has been taken. If not dead yet, he will most likely be soon."

"You must be so pleased."

"Believe it or not, I am not."

"Liar."

"Be that as it may, we—you—have much work to do, Queen Africa."

"What did you call me?"

"With Prague no more and Julius taken, you are the eldest and the strongest, and hopefully the wisest. Either way, you are the new queen."

"Why are *you* telling me this? If not here to slay me, is it not the custom of the Guide to relay such information?"

"Denison has passed as well."

"Good."

"Excuse me?"

"Guides are just as bad as slayers. Worse. They're the ones who strategize our demise, who train you slayers to do their bidding while they sit on the sidelines like the cowards that they are. That's your precious Denison, a murderous coward."

Laurel wanted to slap the bitch, ram her wooden stake through the monster's ugly heart, but she knew that there was a far more important task at hand.

"I was under the impression that you were amongst those who like humans."

"Yesss, I am fond of humans. But I detest *your* kind of human."

"Well, as queen, you would have the authority to end our truce," Laurel said sadly, hoping that the new vampire leader would never choose such an option.

"Stop calling me that! Julius never referred to himself as 'king'."

"My apologies. What wish you to be called?"

"Nothing. I am Africa, nothing grander, nothing lesser. I cannot be the senior."

"Yet you are. And if you so decline, then who in your stead? Plato? Trung Nhi?"

"Plato is but a boy."

"A two-thousand-year old boy with much strength and little discipline. What if factions arise to support Plato and Trung Nhi each against the other, since neither has rightful claim? You know the lore that preceded Julius's reign—the tragic, bloody contest that brought Athena to rule. Is that what you long for?"

"You understand nothing, slayer. Despite my centuries, I have always been with Prague. From the moment I was made. When she became an elder, I was but her precious, pretty tagalong. I was the playful one, the silly little girl. I paid no mind to the ways of leadership. Only she did. She was the one ordained to succeed Julius, not I. I would not know how to perform such a burden if I desired it, which I do not."

"The role has fallen upon you by right, Africa, but also, from what I have studied, by qualification. So I ask once more, if not you, *who*? Good luck with your decision."

And with that the slayer walked out of the room, leaving the would-be-queen to fall back into her casket to ponder.

CHAPTER THIRTY-SEVEN

The hotel bar and the restaurant alongside it were packed to capacity as human and vampire alike celebrated their monumental victory of the night before. Civilian trainees served as bartenders, and every kind of music from Mozart to Kanye blasted through the loudspeakers so that all could experience the varied lifestyles of their new compatriots.

"To Prague and Julius!" Plato shouted as he raised his clamato juice to the air.

"To Prague and Julius!" responded the humans and vampires around him, even though most of the humans had no idea who Prague or Julius were.

"I love Vs!" shouted Johnny as he burst into the joint, fashionably late to the party. He took an open stool at the bar next to a knockout Marine Lieutenant, then turned to the bartender. "Beer please!"

"Juice and sodas only," said the civilian trainee. "The President's orders, we're all still on active alert. But I can mix 'em anyway you want."

"Cool. Mix me a gin and tonic," he told the boy then turned to the pretty Marine beside him. "How ya' doin'?"

"You're the pilot, aren't you?" she asked, Johnny's achievements preceding him. "Is it true that you saved one of them?"

"Yeah," he answered sadly. "But I really wanted to save *two* of them."

"Oh," responded the girl, slightly less impressed than before.

"But hey, I'll take credit for the one," he countered quickly then turned back to the bartender. "Whatever the lady wants! Put it on my tab!"

"They're free," smiled the Marine.

"In that case, make it a double."

"Oh you're terrible," she laughed.

Just outside the bar in the lobby proper were tables that hotel management had set up to create a faux outdoor experience. All but one of the tables remained vacant because most everyone wanted to be part of the celebration.

Harve sat outside the bar deep in thought but perked up when he saw Johnny enter. He had gone to question the pilot at his quarters over an hour earlier because that's where the log had said he would be, but there had been no answer when he banged loudly on the door. He had looked everywhere, asked everyone—but at a time of active alert, when all whereabouts were to be accounted for, his sole suspect had been nowhere to be found. Harve had a bad feeling that something nefarious was about to happen, and that had been the time during which Johnny had set it up.

He had spent all day combing the computer banks, forgoing sleep to find even one other suspect. He had questioned countless officers and enlisted men, anyone who seemed even remotely suspicious, but they all checked out. With Johnny it was just the opposite—the questions were mounting. Where had he been? What was he up to? And how had he dodged all those alien blasts? Yes, he had pulled off some super-fancy flying, all sorts of tricks, but could anyone be *that* good? Or was it truly that the bugs didn't want to lose their inside man? Not hard evidence, true, but it was the only answer that made sense. Besides, the newbie detective had no more leads to follow, not a single other suspect before him.

"Lieutenant!" he heard the Captain-with-the-scar bellow from across the way. "I've been looking for you."

Harve snapped to his feet and saluted. "Yes sir!"

"At ease, Lieutenant," said the Captain. "About this spy business, I need to take a look at your notes."

"But the President said I should report directly to him."

"And you shall continue to report directly to him," the Captain indignantly snapped. "But as head of base security, I need to know how your investigation is proceeding. You've never done this sort of thing before, and I have, many times. So hand 'em over."

"But –"

"That's an order, Lieutenant."

"Yes sir," Harve said, as he gave the superior officer his little notepad.

Harve watched with dread as the Captain-with-the-scar skimmed through his chicken-scrawled findings. It wasn't only the conflicting orders that concerned him, but also whether his notes would make sense to anyone else, if there was a proper way to run an investigation that he had never learned, if he was totally off base with Johnny, and he was embarrassed. It felt like high school again, his shabby homework being graded by an admonishing teacher while he stood by helplessly.

"You have no hard evidence here," criticized the Captain-with-the-scar. "This is nothing but raw speculation and theory. You do know that, don't you?"

"Yes sir," answered the humiliated Lieutenant.

"But the theory is solid, I'll grant you that," the Captain conceded as he kept reading. "Definitely holds water. Strong. Not bad, Lieutenant. Not bad at all. Now go get me some real evidence to back this up. No matter what it takes. Be a cop."

"Yes sir!" Harve shouted with an internal sigh of relief as the Captain moved off to the bar to join the party. Harve smiled, vindicated. If the security chief concurred that it was most likely Johnny, than Johnny it certainly was. He sat back down when he noticed that the dark vampire was now seated at one of the tables across the way.

Africa had just concluded her conversation with Laurel, and she had to admit that the slayer had made some strong points. Both Plato and Trung Nhi would make abysmal leaders, and the power struggle that would ensue would quite likely lead to a savage vampire civil war. She knew that Julius would command her to assume the coveted role as a moral imperative, and that Prague would say she deserves it.

She knew that her first decision, if she were to accept the post, would be whether to continue the truce with the humans. Julius would, she knew, while Prague most likely wouldn't. Which one would be right? She thought she could gain some insight on the matter by watching vampire and human in harmonious celebration, but her confusion only worsened as she watched them. How can the vampires rejoice when their leader had been taken, when her lover had died? How can the humans laugh and smile when so many of their kind had perished? With no insight to be found, she asked herself the most poignant question of all. How can she assume leadership when she simply didn't know what to do?

Her eyes met Harve's, and she sensed in the human an inner conflict not too dissimilar from her own—and it made her rescuer even more attractive to her than when she had first laid her eyes upon him.

"Thank you for saving my life," she said to him.

"Was just following orders, ma'am," Harve responded curtly yet honestly, feeling wholly uncomfortable around these disciples of evil.

"Then thank you for following your orders."

He smiled. That was a polite and clever response on her part. Despite his abhorrence for these creatures, they were his allies whether he liked it or not—the Commander in Chief had decreed it, so it would be rude to be rude. "I'm sorry about your friend," he offered.

"As am I," she replied. "Why are you not celebrating with the others?"

"Lots of good people died in this thing. I see nothing to celebrate."

She nodded her agreement—hadn't she just been thinking the very same thing herself? Maybe this one could provide her with the insight for which she searched. At the very least, she could rid him of the propaganda he had been hearing about her kind all his life.

"We're not evil, you know," she said as she got up and joined him at his table.

"I never said you were."

"You think it."

"Who says?"

"Vampire brain," she answered with a smile. "We know things."

"Well, you do kill us for food."

"You kill cows and chickens and pigs and fish," explained the vampire. "And you enslave them first. We let our food roam free, and we only hunt what we need."

"It's not the same thing," Harve chuckled at the ludicrous argument.

"It is exactly the same thing. Like you to your animals, we are simply higher than you on the food chain for our brains function at a higher level."

"Look, I know I'm not the brightest bulb on the planet, but we humans have our geniuses same as you."

"A vampire can hear a new language and be fluent within minutes. We can enter a factory in which we have never been and operate every piece of equipment flawlessly. And we can cause anyone to fall madly in love with us just by willing it."

This was going too far, thought the soldier. Yes, she was beautiful. Yes, her eyes were so alluring, so inviting. But he was far too strong to let Lucifer's minion entice him into the darkness. "I'm not falling in love with you," he said pointblank.

"I have not been trying to render you so. I wished only to make a point. Besides," she added with a coy, knowing smile, "you are a little."

This is crazy, thought the Kentucky boy. Even if she wasn't an agent of hell, it still could never work—she's black.

But those eyes . . .

*****

THE HEFTY NURSE PUSHED the cart of meds and food toward the quarantine area, and she was just a bit frightened. She had taken extra-special care to make certain that the yellow biohazard suit that she wore had not a single tear, and that every zipper and snap was securely fastened. She had no way of knowing that the air would be the least of her worries.

The last time she had entered the space, all the quarantined soldiers had been asleep. She had left them each a tray of food but none of the meds. Of course, the meds wouldn't cure the brave warriors of their mysterious virus, but hopefully they would help to ease their pain.

As she approached the door she could hear the banging and howling from within, and her heart went out to the poor souls. She unlocked the wooden door with her key and pushed her cart inside.

"Dinnertime! How are we all feeling today?"

Her mouth dropped open in terror as hordes of snarling zombies staggered toward her. Before she had the wherewithal to run, the two closest were upon her, knocking her down against the door, swinging it shut and automatically locked. A dozen more zombies dog-piled onto her plump body and gorged on all her juicy fat, leaving no openings for the other two hundred, zombie-Sanchez among them.

The sudden introduction of fresh meat without the opportunity to consume it made the two hundred go mad. They howled. They staggered hard into the glass walls once more in their pathetic mindless attempts to break free. The glass vibrated but held, but there was no telling for how long. A small crack emerged in the glass.

"Me want eat!" zombie-Sanchez would have cried if she had had words. "Pretty eat! Pretty pretty eat eat!"

CHAPTER THIRTY-EIGHT

"It's like totally amazing," Mary said to Julius as the alien soldier tried to force a scimitar through the vampire's belly. "I mean, the results we're getting have like no basis in science. I mean, of course they do—anything that is, is. Science is just what explains it all—but the science we've got has no explanation for *you*. So I may get to discover like a whole new field. I'm so glad you hit on me, sunshine.

"But we'll get to that when we get to it. For now I'm just supposed to stay focused on like *'what'* kills you not like *'why'* it kills you."

They had been at it for hours, Mary whipping through her long checklist of conflicting legends, lore and literature to find the truth behind them, each result matching some of her source material but only sunlight being consistent with all.

Silver bullets, no; silver crucifixes, no to cause death but yes to cause anguish and only upon direct contact; crucifixes in general, no; silver in general, no; fire, anguish only; garlic, no (in fact, he enjoyed eating it); twisting or cracking of bones, anguish, yes, loss of consciousness, sometimes, but healing occurred too quickly for it to be of any true value; chopping off his head, too early in the process to risk testing; wooden stakes, most likely—she had stabbed a few into his abdomen and his vital signs went crazy as he screamed in agony, the high probability therefore being that one through his heart would be fatal; the Sangue Debolezza virus (or vampire disease), so far untested, but spies on Earth were searching for a sample.

They had shot him in his arms and legs with fifteen different kinds of guns, and the bullets had merely made tiny dents in his skin—pulling out the compressed slugs being as simple as peeling off a scab. They had blasted him with their own time-space weapons—a one-inch void emerging in his belly then filling up just as quickly. (It was only as mist that the beams sailed straight through him, and they dared not let him turn to mist.) They had stabbed, poked and prodded him with twenty different kinds of swords, and the blades had merely snapped in two.

And through it all, she would not stop talking. She explained in great tedious detail the Dwellers' strategy of drawing the human forces to a single spot to defeat them en masse, why swarms were arranged in groups of seven and the awesome power of that fourth prime number, how their soldiers were conditioned to aim only at the human heart so that a miss could still render severe damage, and why the aliens were focusing their military attention exclusively on North America.

"It's like, everywhere else on Earth, everyone's freaking out. Riots, civil wars, human killing human. It's like the stress that we *might* attack is doing almost as much damage as attacking —we got it from an old *Twilight Zone* episode. By the time we start in Afro-Eurasia, humans will have done like half our work for us. Plus, by then, we'll have already annihilated the biggest and the baddest so the Afro-Eurasians will be all demoralized and everything, so totally easier to kill."

On she went. She explained how Peyton had turned out not to be the doofus they expected and the measures being taken to get rid of him, she complained about her underlings who resented her meteoric rise, she described with sordid specificity her carnal encounter with the nine-foot insect Commander, and she explained why the Dweller Vessel, with its wormhole technology, took so long to reach Earth.

"The larger the mass going through the wormhole, and the greater the temporal or spatial distance of the jump, the harder the jump is to accurately calculate. It's like, a pitcher on the mound can throw a hundred miles an hour with pinpoint accuracy. An outfielder at the wall can throw to the plate pretty hard too but not with the same degree or consistency of accuracy because we've increased the distance—although Barry Bonds got pretty close most of the time—actually, a ton of the time he nailed it—you just could never know f'sure in advance. But if we increase the distance *and* the mass, give Barry like an eighty-pound boulder to hold over his head and make him throw to the plate, who knows where the thing will land, right? This is a really bad analogy but you wouldn't understand the math.

"So sending individuals back and forth from tons of light-years away was easy as pie—we'd rarely be more than a bunch of kilometers off, if that—but something as humongous as our vessel? It's loony bird. So every three months we'd jump it a mere point-two-five light-years, which is the equivalent of traveling at lightspeed, which even Earth people know is impossible. Yet we were. But we weren't. But we were. But we weren't. You know what I mean, right?"

On and on she'd go, and Julius could only wonder which was the greater torture—the wooden stakes and silver crosses, or her incessant babbling.

And when all but one of the categories on her list was crossed off, she sat on the stool beside him, took his hand and smiled sweetly. "How we feeling, sunshine?"

"Couldn't be better," groaned the vampire. "How are you?"

"You're so hot," she giggled as she kissed him on the forehead. "So, listen. You're probably wondering why we haven't done any sun experiments yet."

"Never crossed my mind."

"'Kay, every time you say something adorable, I'm going to kiss you," she said as she kissed his forehead once more. "So, anyway, we're going to fiddle around with the intensities on the window filter to see how much sunlight you can actually handle—you know, find your breaking point and all that. But in case we go overboard—'cause, you know, stuff happens—I wanted to make sure we got everything else tested first. Makes sense, right? So, 'kay, g'luck."

She kissed him again, then coughed an order. The insect at the holographic keyboard tapped on some of the keys, and the room became a little brighter. Julius's body went rigid. Sweat flooded from his pores, and he panted heavily. The holograms of his heart and lungs swelled, the one of his brain pulsated rapidly.

"That's one notch up," said Mary. "Let's see what happens if we go two."

She coughed another order. The room went brighter still, and Julius screamed in mortal agony. The holograms of his heart and lungs swelled beyond the physically possible, the one of his brain contracted by a third, pockets of flame ignited on his chest, arms, legs and genitals, and he could barely gasp for air.

"Nice," smiled Mary. "One more up and you're dead f'sure, right? Two more, f'sure-f'sure. No way you could handle that, right? Wanna see?" She coughed a new order. The alien at the keyboard tapped on some keys, and the room dimmed back to its original level of brightness. Julius panted, his torture session ended, for now.

"I was just teasing, sunshine, I'm not going to kill you. Duh. I love you. You *made* me fall in love with you, remember? Besides, without you to study, I'd lose my whole department. No, I'm going to keep you around for a long, long time."

CHAPTER THIRTY-NINE

B OOM!

Without warning, the WTLV television station exploded into giant flames, the sickly black smoke made even more ominous against the backdrop of the early evening sun. Soldiers raced out of the Omni Hotel and onto the street to witness the devastation firsthand, and it was clear that there could be no survivors.

"Get hoses!" shouted the Captain-with-the-scar. "There's a firehouse three blocks east! Let's go! Move it!"

"What happened?" asked Harve as he sprinted onto the scene.

"The damn bugs took out HQ," the Captain explained. "Everyone who was inside is dead. The Canadian. The Majors. Colonel Williams. And the President!"

"Oh Jesus," gasped Frank. "Then who's in charge?"

"I am," answered the Captain with what Harve thought may have been a flicker of a smile. "Until we find someone who outranks me, I am."

The ground shook violently as a giant wormhole opened back down in Southpoint only blocks from where Peyton had left his troops, exactly as he had predicted. Alien swarms sprinted into strategic positions, opening fire on the move. Major Shaughnessy had no choice but to return fire, and the new battle had begun.

"Get me a walkie!" the Captain shouted. "Now!"

It was only a matter of moments until he was talking with Major

Shaughnessy but their conversation only served to exacerbate the chaos. The Major, his soldiers and his untrained trainees were heavily outnumbered and hunkered down in the midst of ambush, and he had no sense of a big picture or how to proceed. But when the Captain ordered him to fall back to base to regroup and strategize, the Major shouted back that the Captain had no authority to give a superior officer any orders at all. Add to that the roaring barrage of gunfire, the weak walkie-talkie connection, and the fact that the two men never liked each other in the first place, it seemed that the aliens' plan to render havoc was working to a tee.

"Every bleedin' order till now has been to hold position whether I *crackle crackle crackle!*" the Major's voice boomed over the walkie. "I can't bloody well reverse that on a *crackle crackle* junior officer! Now get me the *crackle crackle . . .*"

"Oh my God!" shouted Frank. "No one's in charge! We're all on our own!"

Frank may have been the first to verbalize his anxiety, but he certainly wasn't the last, and an even deeper panic swept through the human ranks.

"No one else is here, Major!" the Captain-with-the-scar shouted into the walkie. "Do you read me? Everyone is dead! You must fall back! If you won't take my order, take my suggestion. Please, fall back, sir!"

"Bollocks! *Crackle*! Where is the Colonel? Where's the bleedin' President?!"

"They're dead!" yelled the Captain. "Do you hear me?! Everyone is dead! The other majors are dead! The Colonel is dead! The President is dead!!!"

"The President's not dead," said Peyton as he jogged out of the hotel toward the Captain, buckling up the belt on his pants. "He was just taking a dump."

He grabbed the walkie from the Captain and roared into it. "This is President Willis. Hold position as before! Help is on the way!" He tossed the walkie back to the Captain then turned to one junior officer after another. "You, take fifty troops and double back around. You, get your squad in position on Salisbury Road. You . . ."

Despite the dire situation, waves of calm permeated among the troops for their leader had returned. Within seconds, soldiers were brandishing weapons and sprinting to battle.

Harve awaited his orders as he noticed Johnny approaching from the hotel. "Where have you been?" he asked suspiciously.

"In the bar with everyone else," the Californian answered innocently.

"Before that. I was looking for you all day. Came to your quarters around four, banged hard on the door, no one answered."

"I must've been in the shower."

"Was anyone with you?"

"No, but believe me, I tried."

"And you!" Peyton bellowed to Johnny. "Get your team in the air! Now!"

Harve had to think fast. Johnny was responsible for the explosion, of course he was. He had set it up while he was missing earlier that day— Harve had virtually predicted it, and the Captain had called the theory strong. There was still no hard evidence, but this was war, and to let this guy run amuck would only cost more lives. Getting him out of action and figuring out the rest later was the only safe course.

"I'm sorry, Mr. President, but he can't do that," Harve said, as he spun Johnny around and proceeded to handcuff him. "John Kester, you're under arrest. Mr. President, he's the one who blew up HQ. *He* is our alien spy."

"What?!" shouted Johnny.

"You son of a bitch!" Peyton shouted, then delivered a sharp right cross to the handcuffed pilot's jaw, sending him falling to the ground, unconscious.

CHAPTER FORTY

Scores of new casualties were raced into the lobby of the St. Vincent Medical Center—some from the battle that had just began anew, others who had had the misfortune of being in the vicinity of the exploding television station.

The cacophony of war boomed and echoed everywhere, making the quarantined zombies crazy with seduction. Over and over they bounced into the glass walls, causing one new crack after another, howling uncontrollably.

Lance, oblivious to the zombie threat, worked alone in the large, dingy, ninth-story records storage room putting the final touches on what would become the new command central. He had realized the prior morning, right after he had seen his first surveillance system sabotaged, that if a new HQ would be needed it would be needed fast—but he had never expected it to be this fast. His fear had been that the bugs would try to cut their electricity—he was still surprised that they had missed something so elementary—so he chose the hospital as the new locale because of its plethora of backup generators, the bleak, windowless storage facility being the only room not currently filled with wounded soldiers.

He supposed that it hadn't occurred to any of the doctors and nurses that old hard copies of medical records, X-rays and the like were redundant in this day and age of digitized data—and he certainly wasn't going to tell them because he needed the space. With official authorization from Colonel Williams, he recruited four civilian trainees to help him pilfer flat-screen

TVs from an abandoned Best Buy and hang them on the storage-room wall while he designed a whole new surveillance system from scratch. Then, to create the necessary space for the military brass, he ordered his recruits to help remove the many file cabinets and boxes, and dump them in the parking lot outside. Even if he was wrong, he thought, even if the X-rays and such had yet to be digitized and the sunlight destroyed them all, it was a small price to pay for the preservation of the species.

*****

DENISON LAY ON A gurney against the wall in the hospital lobby, the staff being far too busy caring for the wounded to properly tend to the deceased. Laurel stood by his side with her two hands clutched around his, unsuccessfully trying to hold back her tears as she delivered her lifelong companion's eulogy to no one at all.

"The Marines will give you your due, old friend," she said softly. "But you were so much more than they could ever have known—a loyal servant and brave warrior of the Society; a stalwart and fearless protector of a species unaware of your heroic deeds. And in the end, you led the monsters to battle, shook their hands in mutual victory, and they called you 'friend.' It is the stuff upon which legend is forged, and the Society will remember and honor you till the end of days."

With a sniffle, she removed her silver crucifix from her neck and placed it in his shirt pocket. She buttoned it closed, patted him on his chest, and wiped the tears from her eyes with the back of her wrist.

CRASH!

The glass walls of the quarantine area shattered, the curtains fell to the ground, and two hundred zombies staggered into the lobby toward the front door and the clamor of battle. Doctors, nurses and orderlies screamed in terror, which only served to draw the zombies' attention. The undead tore into them with rotted teeth and blackened fingernails, and it was only seconds until they seemed to be everywhere, unknowingly cutting off all means of human escape. On instinct, Laurel brandished the wooden stakes from her belt and assumed a fighting stance.

"Psssst!" she heard a voice. "Shhh, no!" whispered Lance who was crouched down only a few yards away behind a dolly stacked with metal file cabinets. He darted to the former First Lady, grabbed her by the arm and led her back to his hiding spot only to find zombies now blocking their way. Without hesitation, he spotted a small nook in the wall, pressed Laurel and himself against it, then put his index finger to his lips to encourage her silence.

The zombies killed, ate and devoured everything that made even the slightest noise as they made their way out of the hospital toward the seductively loud battlefield. The unconscious wounded went unnoticed, but the barely conscious who moaned in pain were devoured along with the screaming staff.

Lance and Laurel stood pressed against the nook in the wall, completely visible but utterly silent and motionless, barely even willing to breath, as three zombies brushed right past them, their cold, dead breathe filling the slayer's nostrils.

When the last of the zombies left the hospital, Lance took one of the wooden stakes from Laurel's hand and moved toward the nearest zombie victim.

"How did you know to do that?" Laurel asked.

"I'm a total geek," Lance said proudly as he plunged the stake through the zombie's skull. "I love zombies." Then he moved to the next victim to do the same.

"Zombies?" asked Laurel.

CHAPTER FORTY-ONE

"Zombies?" asked Peyton from his new director's seat in the new HQ, aka old records storage room. "Zombies?! Zombies?!!! Well, of course there are zombies! Why wouldn't there be zombies? But are they good zombies or bad zombies?"

"Um, neither, sir," Lance answered timidly. "They're just zombies. But you should probably tell the men to stop shooting and, uh, moving."

"And why would I do that?"

"Peyton, listen to the boy," pleaded Laurel. "What I am to vampires, he is to zombies."

"I just like the movies and TV shows," Lance confessed with a shrug.

"Well, we've got to do something," Peyton acknowledged.

*****

MAJOR SHAUGHNESSY WAS AGHAST when the President's new directive reached him. He had followed his Commander's initial order to a tee, leading his men forward into tactical positions along and inside the various buildings to hold the enemy in place, stalling the bugs until the V reinforcements could arrive, dusk being less than an hour away.

"Stand down, Major!" the President's voice had boomed through his earpiece.

"Again, sir?!" the Major had asked in bewilderment. "Please repeat!"

"Lower your weapons!" the President reiterated. "Wherever you are, stop moving and don't make a sound!"

"But sir —"

"Shhhh!"

Orders are orders, the Major told himself as he passed down the word. It made no sense to him until he saw what could only be described as a few hundred drunkards staggering to battle. The aliens shifted their focus and blasted into the drunkards' chests as they had been trained. Perfectly round one-inch voids ripped through the drunkards' hearts, but they just kept staggering forward, passing the silent humans, desperate to gorge on the source of the blasts. (Unlike the force of a bullet, the white beams that whizzed through them had no dynamic effect at all.)

How many mythical creatures do these humans have? the Alien Commander wondered. And how the hell did his researchers and spies miss them all?

Even at close range, the ferocious alien weapons proved inconsequential. The zombies converged upon the front line of the enemy soldiers three, four at a time, their rotted teeth tearing through the chitin scales of the aliens' heads, thoraxes and abdomens. But cannibalistic zombies thrive on human (not insect) flesh, so the moment a bug stopped blasting its weapon, stopped coughing out in pain and misery to lay silent on the ground, the zombies would lose interest and move onto the next closest soldier that was dumb enough to keep shooting.

The Alien Commander was confounded. The creatures were slow, weak, and he had them grossly outnumbered—but nothing seemed to stop them. He coughed out orders for the swarms to reposition themselves, to fire from different angles. He coughed an order to open communications with Mary, his resident expert on all things mythical, and quite a tasty tidbit to boot. But what he didn't do, the only thing he should have done, was to order his troops to cease-fire. And the zombies kept coming.

"Not too shabby," Peyton smiled as the stolen TV sets showed two hundred zombies devouring ten thousand aliens who simply didn't know how to kill them.

With everyone in the room gleefully consumed with the on-screen action, Rog wheeled himself inside to get his Captain's signature on a security authorization related to Johnny's arrest. The Private stopped cold when he saw the zombies on the screens, and he knew that he had screwed up big-time—but he was too embarrassed to say anything just yet. So he remained in his wheelchair in the back and watched the imminent victory like everyone else.

The Alien Commander was at a complete loss. He could clearly see that his quantum weapons were of no use, so he coughed out new orders for his troops to engage in hand-to-hand combat, but his soldiers still didn't know where to strike. They jabbed their rifle butts into the zombies' chests, backs, even legs, or they attempted to physically overpower the weak creatures, allowing the zombies close enough to bite or scratch them to death.

With the ruckus of blazing rifles gone, it was now merely the sounds of alien grunting that attracted the zombies' attention. Zombie-Sanchez found herself drawn to a particularly loud one and staggered toward him, but the bug rammed his weapon hard into her belly before she could get close. The zombie flew backward through the air to land on an alien flatbed, whereupon an electronic metallic net slithered toward her and wrapped itself around her legs. When she tried to stagger up to her feet, she tripped off the vehicle and fell back down to the concrete road.

She struggled to free herself, but the net merely wrapped itself tighter around her, as if of its own volition. She rolled on the ground as she fought it, inadvertently rolling under a parked Toyota Prius, and the net magnetically latched onto the hybrid's underbelly to hold her in place. She struggled more, causing the net to grow ever tighter, elevating her off the ground and pressing her against the car's bottom. Struggled still more, and the net wrapped itself across her face and mouth, and she began to chew on it. And there she would remain for some time, suspended in midair under a Japanese car, gnawing on metal, out of sight and forgotten.

"Bad eat," she would have said of the metal if she had had words. "Me want good eat. Good eat, me. No bad eat, me. Good eat, me."

Meanwhile, the onslaught continued. Mary had proven of little use to her Commander, claiming she believed the creatures were called "zombies" but that was all she knew because she had never studied them the way she had vampires. The Commander told her to appoint someone to learn about them fast and for her to get back to him. She was thrilled as the department she headed continued to expand.

Of course, it was only a matter of time till one of the alien soldiers happened to bash his rifle butt into a zombie's head to crack its skull and end it, and then barely any time at all for the rest of the bugs to follow suit. One by one, the stupid things went down, and it was clear to anyone watching that it wouldn't be long until all of the undead would be dead-dead, the forgotten zombie-Sanchez excluded.

"Dammit," Peyton muttered disappointedly from the windowless HQ. "If I only had a few thousand more of those things."

"Um, well, actually, sir," Rog stammered nervously. "You kinda do."

"I do?" Peyton asked.

CHAPTER FORTY-TWO

Patrick took his last bite of the last bit of the beef jerky that he and Rhiannon had shared. Their food was all gone now, and he was afraid. What good was being safe from the zombies if they were just going to starve to death anyway?

The phone rang, which both kids found quite strange. Patrick hoped it wasn't someone requesting police service because he clearly couldn't provide it, and he had long since given up expecting any help from the outside.

"Heartsoot Creek sheriff's office," he answered.

"Please hold for the President of the United States," came Rog's voice.

"Okay," Patrick said then turned to Rhiannon. "It's that jerk from before who wouldn't help us. Says I should hold for the President of the United States."

"Put it on speaker! On speaker!" Rhiannon said as she raced to the desk.

Patrick complied when a new voice began. "This is President Peyton Willis," said the General from the old hospital storage room, also on speakerphone.

"Bull!" shouted Rhiannon.

"Shhh!" Patrick whispered, recognizing the voice because he had done nothing but watch the news since they got trapped there. "It's him."

"Congratulations on your promotion, Mr. President," he said to the phone.

"Thank you, son. Now, to whom am I speaking?"

"Patrick Hutchins, sir. I'm twelve years old from Heartsoot Creek, Georgia."

"And Rhiannon Montadel of same. I'm the brains of the operation."

"Nice to meet you both. Now, I understand you kids are having a bit of trouble down there."

"Yes sir! The whole town's gone zombie!"

Lance did some quick Internet research and announced, "Heartsoot Creek, Georgia, population twenty-four thousand."

"Outstanding," Peyton replied then turned back to the phone. "So, kids, you think you can find your way to bring all your zombies down to me in Jacksonville?"

"Peyton!" gasped Laurel. "You can't put them in this! They're children!"

"American children," the great man answered. "With twenty-four thousand zombies at their disposal. So why risk the lives of our living when we can just as easily risk the lives of our dead?"

"We can do this, ma'am," Patrick insisted. "We *want* to do it, Mr. President."

"You bet we do!" Rhiannon piped in. "We'll win this war for ya!"

"I know you will, kids," Peyton said. "So let's figure out how."

*****

OUTSIDE THE SHERIFF'S BUILDING, thousands of zombies milled about, staggering this way and that, having no memory of how they ended up in this particular location but lacking the wherewithal to wonder about it.

A liquor bottle with a flaming rag in its top soared through the air to land on the hood of a Dodge pickup parked across the street. Bottle and truck exploded with a deafening boom as a second bottle blew up a 1967 Chevy Impala parked behind it. The zombies staggered away from the sheriff's building toward the explosions, several allowing themselves to be burned to a crisp in the process.

The kids stood on the roof about to light new bottles when Patrick stopped cold. "That's enough. We can get out now. Let's save the other bottles just in case."

"Good thinkin'," the little girl answered with a smile.

"Let's roll," the boy smiled back.

*****

THE SUN WAS SETTING in the West as Patrick and Rhiannon, freed from their imprisonment in the sheriff's office, sat upon their bicycles half a mile up the road from the zombie hordes that circled the burning cars. They had their backpacks on their backs, their rifles strapped to the side of their bikes, and two pistols each holstered to their sides.

"Ready?" Patrick asked.

"You betcha," Rhiannon responded.

"Hey stupid!!!!" Patrick shouted at the zombies as loud as he could.

With the explosion over, Patrick's voice was significantly louder than the sizzling of the fire so the zombies turned toward him.

"Bet you can't catch us, you freaks!" shouted Rhiannon.

"Dumb dead idiots!" yelled Patrick.

"Smelly rotting poop-heads!" yelled Rhiannon.

The zombies mindlessly, ominously staggered toward the children. The kids pushed down hard on their pedals and began to bike away.

"Slow down," said Rhiannon. "We don't want 'em to lose us."

And thus began their long, treacherous journey.

CHAPTER FORTY-THREE

The sun had set, its rays were gone, and the darkness of night prevailed. Africa walked onto the terrace of her penthouse suite wearing only the bathrobe that the luxury hotel provided its VIP patrons. She walked as close to the edge as she could, her midriff a mere inch from the handrail. She gazed out upon the dark splendor of the Jacksonville skyline, the lights of the abandoned city unlit, the town illuminated only by the flame of human guns and the white beams of alien rifles.

Like a whip, she thrust out her arms and her robe fell to the ground.

"Come to me, my children!" she shouted into the night.

Her naked body glistened in the moonlight, every curve and contour of her body perfectly proportioned, the visual definition of feminine beauty, strength and sexuality.

The black sky was suddenly rendered even blacker as scores of bats emerged from all corners of the world. They perched upon her outstretched arms, her head, her shoulders. They lay at her feet, hovered around her impeccable frame. Only once they were settled and all was still did she continue.

"Fill me with knowledge, my children, my teachers!" she cried out. "Fill me with the wisdom of leaders and secondaries past! Fill me with their souls and their hearts and their minds! Fill me with your love, my children, my teachers."

The bats frantically flapped their wings, brushing against her as they clicked and screeched. A wave of euphoria swept over the exquisite vampire as she felt the very essence of Prague, her cherished love and lover, miraculously come to life within her heart, her mind, her loins. She felt the great vampires of time immemorial enter her soul through her every orifice. She felt wiser, stronger, kinder and happier than she had ever felt before.

But she did not feel Julius.

It meant that he was still out there somewhere. If not, she would have felt him too. And if he had remained in the physical realm thus far, he would continue to remain, and he would soon escape his captors—she somehow knew this with certainty.

And that meant that she was only to be the *acting* queen, and only until the true king returned. It would be a temporary post, and that was a role that she was willing to fill.

The only question that remained was had she waited too long to assume her rightful position?

CHAPTER FORTY-FOUR

Where were the vampires? Harve wondered.

With the alien spy in custody, his detective duties fulfilled, and no pilot left to fly the humans' sole remaining helicopter, he had been sent back to join the ground forces to hold the bugs in place until dusk when V-Company could come out of hiding. His new squad of ten—which included his trusted sidekick Frank—were holed up in an apartment building, taunting the alien soldiers into engagement while doing everything they could to keep them at bay. They had arrived on the scene equipped with gas masks so the bugs' tear bombs proved inconsequential, and Harve had ordered two of his men to each of the five building entrances—front door, two side doors, back door and garage—so despite the enemy's vastly superior numbers, they were unable to break through the bottleneck that the doors provided. But their ammo was running low, and the human forces were all-in with no runners left to bring additional bullets. There seemed no end of alien soldiers emerging to supplant their fallen, and with the sun having set almost twenty minutes prior, Harve could only wonder—where the heck was V-Company?

He wasn't the only one wondering this, of course, but he was the only one who had increasingly growing feelings for one of them, and the only one struggling to keep these demonic passions from his mind.

But no one was more fraught with worry than Peyton. Laurel had briefed him on Africa's reluctance to assume command, the uncertainty of whether she'd continue the truce if she did, and the pending vampire clash if she didn't.

He was running out of options. He knew it was crazy to put too much stock on the Georgia zombies arriving in time, if at all. The best of his civilian trainees were still not close to combat-ready, and he felt like a heel for having already put a thousand of them in harm's way.

Then it happened!

A soaring gray mist blanketed the dark sky of night, and colonies of shrieking bats cast black specs upon the gray. Still a mile from the action, the vampires' mere appearance altered the course of the battle as the lion's share of alien soldiers moved away from the buildings and repositioned themselves along the roads in preparation of the flying onslaught, leaving behind only the bare minimum of swarms to keep the human soldiers out of it.

"They're here!" shouted the now-jubilant Corporal Frank Hatteras, echoing the gleeful cries of his comrades. "V-Company is here!"

Africa-as-mist soared miles above the others of her kind, unseen by the bugs, with only her new lieutenants Plato and Trung Nhi by her side. Her plan was for the vampires below to attack the first line of enemy soldiers only so as to keep their leaders in the rear calm, to keep the leaders from wheeling themselves back into their sunny meadow, and then to pounce upon them and suck them dead.

In the control room, Peyton and Laurel breathed a heavy sigh of relief.

"You did well," the President said to the former First Lady.

"We got lucky," replied the slayer.

But in the next few seconds, something began to feel off to the former General. The bugs had positioned themselves all along the streets, had dropped to their knees using one of their lower arms to balance themselves while they aimed their weapons upward, calmly awaiting the vampires to fly into range.

He had seen them adopt this stance before, but why now? After yesterday's devastating victory, the bugs should be running from the invincible Vs for dear life. So why weren't they?

"Something's wrong," he said with a dire tone. "Go tight on their weapon."

Lance did some fast tapping on his laptop as one of the screens zoomed in on an alien rifle. It looked different than it had the previous day, modified with some kind of long alloy tube welded to its barrel like a scope. But it wasn't a scope!

"GET THEM THE HELL OUT OF THERE!!!" Peyton screamed.

But it was too late. With the vampires in range, the bugs pressed the buttons to activate the modification. A low, bassy hum permeated throughout Southpoint. A soft yellow light shined out from the alloy tubing—simulated sunshine—and the front lines of the flying vampire mist instantly burned to a crisp!

"*Se recipite!*" Africa shouted down from miles above. "*Se recipite!!!!*"

She and her two lieutenants were high enough to reverse course and fly back to safety, but the formation of the mists below them was too tight for the Vs to get out quickly. They skidded to an aerial halt only to be bumped forward by their brethren behind them; they flew upward only to be blocked by those above, all while the bugs had a field day showering the vampires with deadly warm sunshine.

"We're doomed!" shouted Frank as panic spread among the humans.

But Harve remained focused, and saw an opportunity.

"Major Shaughnessy!" he shouted into his wrist-mike. "The bugs are so consumed with the Vs they left the back of our building unguarded. There's a five-story structure across the road. We can take the rooftop! The high ground!"

"Aye, soldier!" the Major shouted back. "Take it!"

"Everyone! On me! Now!" Harve shouted to his men.

His squad sprinted to him but before he could tell them his new plan, he noticed two new swarms approach the building that he had intended to capture.

"They heard us," he gasped in dismay. "They must have our frequency. They've been monitoring every transmission we've made!"

"Oh God," Frank wailed. "How much worse can this get?!"

"Actually, wait a sec. This could be a blessing in disguise," Harve responded, then began to write on a small piece of paper. "This could be *better* than taking that rooftop. We can make those bugs think whatever we want them to think, and then we do the opposite. Frank, you've got to get this note to the Major."

"How? The bugs own the street."

"It's dangerous, yeah. Crazy maybe. But what choice do we have? And after all our years serving together, there's one thing I know—if anyone can do this, it's you. The whole war may depend on it. You gotta do this for me, buddy."

Frank took a deep breath, touched by the plea of friendship. "All right, Harve. Whatever you need."

He snatched the note and tore out of the building at full speed. The bugs in front of the building were so startled by the recklessness that it took them a moment to brandish their weapons, by which time Harve and his men shot them dead.

With the bulk of the aliens focused on the vampires, Frank combined stealth and speed as he tried to make his way to the Major five blocks away. He hid, he sprinted, he ducked, he rolled, he zigged, he zagged. He burst unnoticed into a Macy's one block north from where he had left Harve, ran like Usain Bolt through the women's shoe section to exit the other side, when he found himself face-to-face with two alien soldiers!

"Holy smoke!" shouted Harve who had been watching it all with his squad.

For a brief second nothing happened for the two bugs were as stunned as Frank. The Corporal then tore off in the opposite direction. The aliens raised their rifles and fired.

And they missed.

Although only a few feet away, they missed!

It was a doggone miracle, thought Harve. Or was it? The aliens never miss, especially not at such close range. It took the Lieutenant but a moment to put two and two together, and a furious rage swept over him as it all started to make sense.

"You lying sack of dirt!!!!" he shouted as he burst out of the building and onto the street, blasting his M16 into the head and back of his former best friend.

Frank howled as he fell to the ground, the imperceptible seams of his human skin tearing open from the gunfire, the costume slipping off his insect frame like loose pants as he took his last breath of the natural Earth air.

But Harve never got to see any of it because the two bugs blasted voids into his chest, and he too was down.

FRANK

The real Frank Hatteras never knew his parents, or any living relative for that matter, and he had no friends. He had spent the bulk of his early years shuttled from one abusive foster parent to another, one cold orphanage to the next, lonely school after lonely school. At fourteen he began to experiment with drugs—by sixteen it was no longer an experiment. No one ever knew if the overdose from which he died was an addict's carelessness or a purposeful suicide but it didn't matter to the Vessel Dwellers. The boy was perfect.

He had grown up in "the system" so there was a giant paper trail to validate his human existence, and the fact that no one cared about him made it easy for someone to slip into his life and build it anew. So perfect was he that had he not died by overdose, the Dwellers would have killed him anyway just to make the switch.

The new Frank, the Dweller Frank, had designed his human skin and drafted his persona years earlier with the help of his younger brother and sister. He would be goofy-looking and dim so as not a threat to anyone, but not so ugly or stupid that he would ever stand out. He would be affable, pleasant, laugh at everyone's jokes, and tell a few bad ones of his own. He would be the type of man that everyone was happy to have around but never noticed when absent. He would be there but not there, liked but never missed.

He became fluent in English, Spanish, Russian and French (the latter of which he flaunted just before murdering Jean-François) to prepare himself for any appointment, but he was thrilled when he was assigned to the United States because that was where the most challenging parts of the extermination were to take place.

It had been easy to wormhole unnoticed into dead Frank's room that night so many years ago. Two vessel-mates removed the boy's corpse, and the new Frank went straight to work—that is, right after he took a few deep breaths to soak in the natural Earth air and chug down a glass of natural Earth water.

He packed up a few of the real Frank's belongings—including birth certificate and Social Security card—and placed them in the real Frank's backpack, then snuck out of the house while the real Frank's foster parents were asleep. Just another teen runaway. He walked to the local bus station and caught the first bus out. No one in Frank's hometown would miss him, and no one in the new town would know him.

He got a small apartment with the cash he had been given by his handler, spent the next two years in an array of odd jobs—paying his taxes to lay further track of a human past—and made new friends as he perfected the art of being "liked but not missed." He got a driver's license—the first government issued photo ID in the name of Frank Hatteras, making him the "real" Frank once and for all. In 2001, he enlisted in the Army as planned, and was shipped off to Iraq where he met Harve.

He could tell that there was something special about the soldier because of how the other members of the division responded to him. Even as a buck private, low-level officers and noncoms were struck by young Harve's strength and moral certitude, asking him advice on both military tactics and life. Frank knew this was someone to latch on to, and he set out to make himself the Kentuckian's best friend.

He could also tell that Harve would be easy to manipulate—not because he was dumb, but because he was smart. All Frank had to do was plant the seed of a good idea then back off and let Harve come up with it on his own.

Frank had been an instrumental part of the team that had laid the explosives that blew up the South Dakota Army Base, but to make his way off-site before the detonation, he needed Harve. He scoured the logs for an excuse until he saw that Johnny had never returned from leave, then brought the information of the AWOL to his Sergeant's attention by "thanking" him for letting it go and giving them an easy evening at home. As expected, the stalwart MP insisted they find the absent soldier the moment he learned about it, allowing Frank to bitch about the "hassle" for the rest of the night.

He had employed a similar tactic just the other day. Although it was Frank who had informed the Dwellers on which rooftops the human snipers would land, he knew he would have to find a safe way back to base because his usefulness to the cause was growing exponentially. He just couldn't be the one to suggest it.

"I don't get it, Sarge," he had said as he fired his M16, grazing the lower arm of his brethren, a minor wound by Dweller standards but enough to guarantee that no human would doubt him. "Why aren't they exploding the chopper? They're just leaving it right there in the open. It's like they're giving us a way out."

It was less than a minute before Harve came up with the plan that Frank had wanted all along. He then volunteered to be the Sanchez boy's decoy in order to get out of sight just long enough to let his Dweller comrades know that he was one of them. He instructed them to let the helicopter fly away safely, that he and the pilot (his ride) were not to be harmed, and that the others were expendable.

It had been nothing but a stroke of good fortune when his best friend was charged with the investigation of the alien spy. Frank had already laid the groundwork for Harve's ill feelings toward Johnny so it didn't require much to move the Lieutenant the rest of the way. "Maybe the bugs missed us on purpose 'cause they didn't want to kill their inside man." This, of course, was true, but it had nothing to do with Johnny.

The moment Harve took the bait, Frank did a fast about-face and leapt to the pilot's defense, countering Harve's suspicions as he prodded him along, insisting that Johnny must have killed some bug soldiers only so he could add, "I did, you did, the girl did." This was an outright lie for Frank would never kill any of his own kind, but it sounded good, and who had been watching?

And with Johnny's humanness soon to be uncovered, Frank had every intention of using the wrongful arrest as a personal validation since he had been the one to tout the pilot's innocence, during which he would plant the seeds of his next bogus suspect.

But how could he have anticipated that he'd be sprinting along some Florida road to deliver some stupid note to some stupid major, and that he would come face-to-face with his own brother and sister who had helped him design his human skin?

He knew his end was near the instant he saw them—either they would fire upon him to protect his true identity, or Harve would figure it out and kill him. And as he lay bleeding on the ground, preparing to become One-with-All-Matter, his final thought was of regret. He had come to like his Sarge over the years, and he was sad that the little human had to learn that he had been duped for his entire adult life.

CHAPTER FORTY-FIVE

Julius lay on the gurney scarred, burned, branded. He panted heavily, and his striking naked body was soaked in sweat. With dread, he awaited the next experiment to be performed, his next torture. It had been almost twenty minutes since the last one, and the bugs rarely gave him that much time between sessions.

Mary was in debate with one of the lab-coat-wearing aliens, one who had been a particular thorn in her side from the start. Julius had witnessed these smoker-cough arguments before but he was finally coming to understand them.

"*The sun-weapon is successful,*" coughed the subordinate. "*Supplemental experimentation on the vampire is wasteful of resources.*"

"*The retreat is inconclusive,*" Mary answered all business, all ditziness gone. "*They may acquire new skills, heightened immunities. Much to be learned remains.*"

"*I urge we wait for instruction from superior.*"

"*Your urge is ignored. I am chief. We experiment onward.*"

"If it makes any difference," Julius piped in weakly. "I'm okay with waiting for superior."

Mary and the others turned to him in shock.

"You understood us?" Mary asked as she moved toward the gurney. "You learned our language? So fast? OMG Sunshine! That's amazing!" She pulled up the stool and sat down next to him. "Say something in it. Pleeeese?"

Julius stared into her fake blue eyes with an icy-dark look of death in his own, and he coughed. *"I shall end you."*

"Well you don't quite have the larynx for it, but your grammar and vocab are like dead-on," Mary said with an impressed smile. "Say s'more. This is awesome."

"You will lose this war, Mary," he coughed softly, the pain of his torture having taken its toll. *"Because there is something about vampires of which you know not."*

To the aliens, this was nothing short of a miracle, another scientific enigma. But the more the vampire coughed, the weaker he became, the softer his voice grew, so the other aliens, not permitted to leave their posts, had to lean in to hear him.

"Something that has been kept from the lore and the legends," the vampire continued, his coughs now barely a whisper, the aliens leaning in ever further, the soldier by the window now blocking a small piece of the sun.

"From a time before history began, when man had yet to be born."

The soldier by the window leaned forward to such an extent that he blocked the sun completely, shielding Julius, which had been the vampire's plan all along. In a flash, Julius transformed to mist and flew through the leather straps that bound him, soaring straight at the alien by the keyboard. He knew he'd lack the strength to hold his mist for long but all he needed was enough to kill four bugs, three of whom had no military acumen, and he had the element of surprise on his side.

He held the bug in place with one arm while his sprouted fangs sucked her dead, using his free hand to type the command to engage the window filter at full strength, typing faster with one hand than the bug had with all four. The room went dark. The new nourishment gave the vampire a touch of added strength. The soldier by the window whipped his modified rifle off his shoulder and took aim, but Julius was already behind him, tearing into the bug, siphoning out the green pus of his life.

The other two bug scientists screamed a ghastly cry akin to the wretched sound of gagging and vomiting. Julius ripped his fangs into one, growing stronger with each suck, while holding the other in place by her scaly insect neck. After the first went down, he drank only enough to kill the second one because Mary was by the door, banging frantically on the keypad to unlock it, making her getaway.

The door clicked open for but a second before Julius slammed it shut. He towered over the terrified girl in his solid human form, staring down upon her with fury, his fangs dripping saliva and green blood as he savored his revenge.

"But I thought we were like bff's," she said innocently. "Seriously. I mean, like I love you. I said so a ton of times. I thought when we were done here we'd like go grab a smoothie or –"

"Will you please . . . just . . . STOP . . . TALKING!!!!" the vampire shouted then bit into her hard and fast, sucking out every last drop. She howled and struggled as she shed her human skin, then at last collapsed to the floor, emptied.

Julius panted, satiated, as he watched her lie motionless and still. Silent.

"Finally," he said to no one at all.

*****

"HMMMMM. MMMMMM. HMMMMM."

Julius sat naked on the floor in a lotus position as he uttered the soft, low vibration. His mind had entered a timeless state that could have lasted minutes or hours or days—he didn't know. But when it was done, his full strength had returned, and his scars and burn marks were gone—only the black imprints of the silver crucifixes remained, permanent reminders of the torture he had endured.

He got his clothes from the shelf on which the aliens had kept them neatly folded and got dressed. He transformed to mist and flew through the space under the doorway to find himself in some kind of corridor, consistent with his earlier assessment of an East Coast building. He flew through the space that separated the elevator doors, down the shaft, and into a lobby. The glass front door and windows showed the sun shining brightly, but it had no effect on him so he flew outside.

He came out of what appeared to be a ten-story brick building. A building within a ship was odd enough, but what he saw next he could not believe at all. He reverted to his corporeal form because it made no difference, and he just stood there gaping, taking in his surroundings in bewilderment.

He was standing in the heart of Manhattan, across from the Flatiron Building on the tri-corner of Broadway, Fifth and East Twenty-Second Streets. Aliens were everywhere, many wearing human skin only partly fastened, their human heads flapping on their backs like hoodies. Some looked fully human, some looked fully alien, but all acted like typical New Yorkers. They walked quickly with purpose, they drove cars and yellow cabs in bad traffic, they sold hot dogs, and they yelled at each other for no particular reason. It was NYC to a tee, a perfect replica, except that Julius could see the bridges from where he stood. On the other side of the Brooklyn Bridge lay Paris, across from the George Washington stood Tokyo. The ceiling was a hundred feet high, electronically painted as a perfect blue sky with a golden sun.

Julius was aghast.

Now what? he wondered.

CHAPTER FORTY-SIX

Johnny awoke from the anesthesia confused as to why he was in a hospital room, and why the door was open. They had put him under before regaining consciousness from Peyton's right cross so the brash Californian had assumed he'd be waking up in some cell. He was unaware of the surgery that had been performed on him, unaware that the aliens had rendered the vampires irrelevant, unaware of the existence of zombies, unaware that he had been the subject of a brief yet highly charged civil-rights debate, and unaware that he was going to be a very rich man.

His jaw was stiff and sore, which made sense to him, but what he couldn't understand was the excruciating pain that shot through his belly when he tried to sit up. He looked at it to find a large patch of gauze covering the center of his midriff. He peeled back the tape to see that he had been cut into, far and deep to the bone.

Of course, he thought. That's how they had proven that he wasn't an alien, why the door was open, and why he wasn't shackled. The bastards.

And that had been the precise topic of the debate.

White House counsel, JAG Corps attorneys and the Chief of Staff in D.C. had pleaded over the speakerphone for Peyton to rescind the order. Peyton had taken the call in the St. Vincent operating room while the military medical team stood perched over Johnny's anesthetized body, awaiting their Commander in Chief's final instructions. (All the civilian doctors and nurses had refused to participate.)

"Mr. President, we cannot do this," the Chief of Staff had pleaded. "It violates every civil-rights law on the books."

"If he's a bug, he has no civil rights," Peyton had insisted.

"That's not how it works, sir," a lawyer had countered. "Unless he's proven *not* human, legally speaking, it must be assumed he *is*. Innocent until proven guilty."

"Then tell me another way to figure this out," Peyton had shot back. "X-rays and MRIs don't tell us squat. If he's the spy, we've got to know. Yesterday."

"That's not the point, sir. Under the law –"

"I don't have time for the law!"

"Mr. President, if we cut into this boy and it turns out he's human, he is going to have a massive lawsuit against us."

It took Peyton but a moment to respond. "If we cut into this boy and it turns out he's human, pay him."

*****

JOHNNY COULD NOT HAVE been angrier as he braved the searing pain in his bandaged gut, moving through the hospital corridor toward his desertion.

It was the incident all over again, he told himself, and he had been so sure it would be different this time, so sure that he was somehow making amends for the terrible thing he had done, and that the military had turned a new leaf. He had drank the Kool-Aid and risked his life for them—had actually felt good about it—only to have them randomly cast him as their villain, again, and cut into him while he slept.

"Fool me twice, shame on me," as his grandmother used to say.

His plan was to steal a jeep, then find some remote spot where no bug or human could ever find him—no matter who won—and if he could convince some hot babe to tag along, all the better. But first he had something to get off his chest.

Harve lay wheezing on a gurney in the hospital lobby, his squad having raced him back north the moment he had been shot. (They informed the head of base security about Frank's true identity shortly thereafter.) The triage doctor diagnosed Harve with a collapsed lung and a ruptured pulmonary artery then tagged him black, the color for "deceased." Harve may have had a chance if they had had a full medical team available to operate for hours into the night like on TV, but hundreds of other soldiers would have died as a result. Harve was just another grunt, and the doctor's job was to save as many lives as possible. The fact that the Lieutenant had lasted this long was only a testament to his strength of will.

Johnny had heard that Harve had been wounded, and had every intention of laying into him. "What the hell did I ever do to you?" he planned to say. "What kind of bogus, cockamamie horse crap led you to the moronic conclusion that I was a bug? 'Cause you didn't like me? 'Cause I don't buy into your idiotic religion? That's a reason to lock someone up and cut them open? You stupid, bigoted, Christian freak!"

Of course, once he saw the extent of the injury, saw the soldier dying on the gurney, he knew he would say none of it. And before he could utter any word at all, their eyes met and a wave of shame swept over Harve's face.

"Johnny," he said weakly, barely audible. "I . . . I am so sorry."

Johnny could feel the depth of the sincerity, appreciated the shame, and he was touched. But it wasn't enough. "It's okay," he lied.

Harve flashed the tiniest of smiles, relieved for the absolution before meeting his Maker. "Go get your new orders, my brother."

"Thanks anyway, but I'm done with the military. I just came to say good-bye."

Harve sighed sadly. "Coward."

"Coward?!" Johnny said, barely able to contain his anger. "I'm a coward?"

"Army needs you. You run. Yes, coward."

"Let me tell you something about your precious army," Johnny said with venom, suddenly motivated to kill the dying soldier's faith in the institution he so admired. He grabbed a stool and sat, knowing full well that he wasn't allowed to repeat his story under penalty of life in prison—but who could Harve possibly tell?

"Back in Afghanistan, I was flying Apache Longbows—attack helicopters, best there are. We got orders to take out an al-Qaeda training camp in Pashtar. Blew 'em to bits. Only someone goofed because it wasn't an al-Qaeda camp—it was just some impoverished village of widows and children. But someone had to take the fall.

"I spent the next six months rotting in some cell waiting for my court-martial. But the army didn't want a court-martial—it didn't want any record of the incident at all—God forbid it went public and someone forced actions to stop such things from ever happening again. So instead they made me an offer. I could insist on a trial that was already rigged for me to lose and spend twenty years in Leavenworth. Or, I could sign a confession stating that I had gone rogue, and that no faulty orders had been given. I'd get a mild reprimand, bumped down to private, and oh yeah—spend the rest of my life in the service so they could keep an eye on me just in case.

"It was a delicate détente we had. I didn't want to go to prison, and they didn't want the story out. So they let me do whatever I wanted, and it really sucked.

"Oh, and one more little kicker. The Chairman of the Joint Chiefs of Staff at the time was Four-Star General Peyton Horace Willis.

"And today he gave the order to cut me open because someone didn't like me.

"So, 'coward'? Yeah, maybe you're right. Maybe I should have just gone to prison and forced the story public in the first place. But the real coward, as I see it, is the United States Army, and I will not serve these bullies one day longer."

"This bigger than you," Harve wheezed. "Bigger than army. This . . . about . . . mankind extinct."

"Well, maybe mankind deserves to go extinct. Ever consider that? We're paranoid, petty, judgmental, greedy, and just plain mean to each other."

"No. We love . . . and help . . . and pray."

Johnny found it interesting that at no point did Harve defend the military, but only clung to a resolute faith in the fundamental goodness of man. It was inspiring. Or stupid.

"You're a good man, Harve. A terrible detective and a religious nut, but a good man." Then he stood up and snapped a salute. "But I'm out."

*****

NONE OF THE PARKED cars or jeeps on the abandoned night streets had keys in the ignition, and the searing pain in Johnny's gut was making it too hard for him to keep searching. He stared at the helicopter, *his* helicopter, as he debated the morality of stealing the Army's *only* helicopter.

"What the hell," he finally said. "No one else can fly it anyway."

He crawled inside, fired up the engine, then flew off into the night as far from the battle as he could, saying good-bye to mankind, going AWOL for the last time.

At least, that was his intention.

CHAPTER FORTY-SEVEN

Julius strolled along the Times Square of the alien vessel with the confident air of a distinguished gentleman in jeans and a jean jacket. Given the many aliens in human skin, no one gave him a second thought. He had no trouble understanding the snippets of conversations all around him, knew he could communicate if need be, but he also knew that it was risky for he had yet to perfect the phlegmy, wet sounds of the alien tongue—didn't quite have the larynx for it, according to Mary.

He wasn't exactly sure for what he searched. A way out? A way to defeat the bugs? Both? Or was it merely an intellectual's curiosity about the enigma that was the alien vessel?

He looked through the glass window of a storefront that had all the appearance of a garment-industry sweatshop. Hard-working aliens "sewed" flawless human-skin costumes then put them on racks that were wheeled to the back.

The next storefront had more of an upscale feel to it, the neon sign above showing alien symbols that loosely translated to "Rosetta Stone Language School." Rows upon rows of bugs in headphones sat at small cubicles, staring at images on small screens as they repeated the sentences that only they heard.

"The mother bakes a pie for her children," said one.

"*Le garcon mange un pomme de terre,*" said another.

"他们去公园," said a third.

A well-kept man in his sixties came out of the building, and smiled at Julius. The "man" wore an expensive three-piece suit and a top hat, and coughed a friendly phlegmy greeting. *"Good day, fine Dweller. Do you study here as I do?"*

Julius knew that any coughed reply could give him away, but it would be too suspicious to say nothing at all.

"Ah ah ah," he cautioned in his redneck drawl, commensurate with his jeans and jean jacket. "English only, pardner. That's the rules they done gave me."

The "man" smiled and tipped his hat. "Quite right, dear sir," he answered with an upper-class British accent. "The Queen's only indeed. Dreadful sorry."

"Don't sweat it, buddy. Ya take care now."

And then he moved on.

The next storefront into which he peered showed the aliens' new sun-gun attachments being mass-produced on a giant assembly line at a staggering speed. Only because of his vampire eyes was he able to ascertain what in fact was being manufactured—to a human, it would have been merely a blur.

The machines spit the finished weapons into large crates on conveyor belts that carried them out the back of the shop. Julius's curiosity was piqued. He made sure that no one was paying attention to him—and as he was in a replica of New York City, there was not much risk of that. He transformed to mist, flew under the shop's doorway, then hid between two of the crates on the belt and went for a ride.

The alley behind the shop seemed to be one giant conveyor belt stretching for miles. Julius could see that the belt was heading toward an opening at the base of the World Trade Center (which in this world had never been destroyed), the higher portion of the North Tower protruding up, through and beyond the fake sky ceiling.

The tower interior was more akin to Grand Central Station, albeit for elevators. The conveyor belt on which Julius rode attached itself to a mini-belt inside one of the elevators, click-clack-click-clack, then left him and the crates—along with several racks of human skins—to go for a vertical ride.

The elevator shot up fast and smooth. The panel beside the door showed that he was thirty levels from the top with seventy levels beneath, each level signified by a number and the Earth cities it represented—"Los Angeles-Tangiers-Jerusalem," "Moscow-Montreal-Shanghai," "New Orleans-Santiago-Macau," and the like. He could not make out the words for the level to which he was being sent.

The doors opened, and Julius was aghast once more. It was another "elevator central station" but infinitely larger. Unlike the prior station, it made no attempt to mask the fact that it was part of a massive space vessel. The floor, girders and ten-foot ceiling were of a faded gray metal, and there was neither a wall nor end in sight. Miles of conveyor belts interconnected and merged like a giant highway system, whizzing their cargo in every possible direction toward their elevator destination.

The elevators themselves abounded in predetermined spots like gates in an airport, their alloy casing shooting up through the ceilings and down through the floors at vertical and diagonal angles of all stripes. Alien signage marked the general location to which each section of elevators traveled, such as "rural," "island," or "wasteland." The section from which Julius had come was labeled "metropolis."

Tens of thousands of aliens flooded through the port, entering or exiting one elevator to transfer to another (since there seemed to be no actual exit), walking or riding motorized carts to their respective sections, or waiting patiently in queues at their gates. Julius could only wonder if this was the central hub of the vessel or if there were dozens more like it. There was no way to know for certain.

The crates between which he hid finally arrived at their predetermined section, labeled "military." After just a few quick conveyor belt transfers, click-clack-click-clack, he and his crates were carried to the back of a giant freight elevator, roughly the size of an Olympic swimming pool. One by one, new crates of sun-guns from God-knows-where were automatically loaded into the space. Only once filled to capacity did the doors close, and the elevator begin its downward plunge.

Julius's gut leapt to his throat as he felt the intense speed—more like a vertical Japanese bullet train or a Six Flags ride than any elevator he had ever experienced on Earth. He could see from the panel that the beastly machine would descend over one thousand levels without a stop before it could open its doors one level at a time.

At long last, the beast slowed down and opened its doors on level ninety-nine (from the bottom.) A new conveyor belt attached to the one inside, the front eight crates were automatically carried out, and Julius perched up to get a better look.

Hundreds of thousands of alien soldiers were in the midst of military drills. He could not see what lay beyond some of the grassy hills, and he wondered if their numbers were even greater than that. The blue sky and yellow sun were once again but painted ceilings, and an officer's booming voice coughed orders over a crackling loudspeaker.

It was the other side of the wormhole that he had seen on Earth, the grassy meadow from which the aliens had come and gone. Or so he thought.

The elevator made further drops on levels sixty-four, forty-five, twenty-five and six, before it unloaded the last of its cargo on level four—and each level was identical. Julius rode the conveyor belt out of the elevator along with his crates, then dropped down to the grass to watch the soldiers, hovering as mist unnoticed.

Assuming that the parts of the meadow that he couldn't see were just like the part that he could, and assuming that the hundred levels at which the elevator hadn't stopped were identical to those at which it had, Julius calculated over three billion combat-ready soldiers; and that didn't account for the possibility that there could be other sections of the vessel just like this one, nor the possibility that there could be millions of other soldiers scattered elsewhere throughout the ship.

The truth that Peyton had chosen to ignore days ago was indisputable. There were just too many alien soldiers for the beings of the Earth to ever defeat!

But the vampire couldn't readily accept this fact either—no one wants to accept the death of all they've ever known and loved, the end of their world. Perhaps the assumptions that he had made were wrong, he told himself. *They had to be!*

As crackly orders continued to boom over the loudspeaker, Julius-as-mist slithered through the blades of grass, hoping to discover that the as-of-yet unobserved parts of level four were barracks or hospitals or storage facilities—anything but soldiers! It could alter his calculations considerably.

"*Officer Cough-Cough, to the Bridge,*" coughed the loudspeaker. "*Officer Cough-Cough, report to the Bridge.*"

One of the senior drill instructors quickly ordered the swarms under his command to report to another instructor, then jogged toward one of the elevators.

Bridge? Julius wondered. That could be interesting.

CHAPTER FORTY-EIGHT

"If I stuck around they'd just pin something else on me," Johnny muttered his rationalization as he flew the stolen Bell 407 northward. "I could kill every damn bug single-handedly and they'd probably try to bust me for murder."

He wasn't sure where he was going—he hadn't thought it out that far— he only knew that there was no army left to look for him, and his new concern had to be surviving an alien victory. They can't kill *every* human, he thought. There'll have to be a few stragglers they miss, surviving in the middle of nowhere, living off the land and staying out of the bugs' way. He saw no reason he couldn't be one of them.

Then he happened to glance down below.

"What the hell?" he said to no one.

*****

"C'MON, STUPID ZOMBIES," SAID a bored Patrick as he led twenty-four thousand zombies down the country highway on a girl's bike. "Gotta keep up, stupid zombies."

"Blah blah blah stupid zombies," said an even more bored Rhiannon.

They weren't afraid. The zombies were a safe distance behind and too slow to catch them as long as they kept moving. But they were so tired.

"This way," Patrick said as they peddled up the ramp to the I-95.

They were close to the mouth of the interstate when the zombies behind began their ascent so turning back was no longer an option. And that was when they saw roughly forty thousand new zombies in front of them, staggering right at them!

"Holy poop!" Rhiannon shouted. "Where the heck did they come from?!"

*****

THE YUPPIE MAN AND woman in the BMW convertible who had promised to bring help to zombie-Joey and his parents in the totaled Silverado on the lonely country road back in Chapter Fifteen had tried their best to keep their word.

Their first mistake was continuing on their original course east instead of turning back toward Heartsoot Creek, which was just a few minutes to the west. It was during that time that the man lost consciousness as the zombie virus (which he had received when zombie-Joey bit him) began to gestate. The woman assumed it was an aspect of the "weird" feeling of which he had complained, blasted her alternative-rock mix and kept her eyes on the road.

It wasn't necessarily her fault that she drove over a broken beer bottle and got a flat tire. There was still no cell-phone reception to call Triple-A so she attempted to awaken the man, but he was out cold—it was her first sign that the "weird" feeling may have been more severe than either had given credit.

She had never changed a tire before so she had to figure it out from scratch. It took her more than two hours to complete the task by which point the dozing man's metamorphosis had begun to take form. The grease-stained woman jumped into the car and floored it. In not too long, she saw a rundown motel on the outskirts of Happenstance, Georgia, population forty thousand, and that was when the man's dead eyes popped open, and he jammed his rotted teeth into her arm. She let go of the wheel to fight him off, but he kept chewing. The BMW, being an automobile of fine alignment, continued on course until it plowed into one of the motel rooms.

The innkeeper, his wife and teenage son ran out of the office to help.

JEFF ABUGOV

The wife and son sped to the unconscious woman while the innkeeper tended to the man. He unbuckled the seatbelt whereupon the zombie tore into his flesh. The son sprinted across to help his Dad, yanked the zombie over the convertible door and onto the ground, and the zombie began to gorge upon him. The wife bolted into the office, then back out blasting her rifle into the air, but it only lured the zombie toward her. She shot into him at point-blank range as he approached her, and then he ate her.

It wasn't until nightfall that the woman, the innkeeper, his wife and son had completed their gestation, then joined the zombie-man who had been staggering aimlessly by himself all afternoon. The five zombies staggered aimlessly together for hours more, then somehow found their way into town. You can figure out the rest.

*****

PATRICK AND RHIANNON SAW no way out. The forty thousand Happenstance zombies were in front of them, the twenty-four thousand Heartsoot Creek zombies were staggering up behind, and they were too high up the ramp to jump off safely. It wasn't death that they were afraid of but injury, for certainly the zombies would follow them down to the road below and devour them.

"I don't wanna become one of 'em," Rhiannon wept. "Kill me."

"I can't kill you," the terrified boy answered.

"Then you want me to kill you?"

Patrick looked around to realize the girl was right. Better to be dead than one of them. "Okay," he said. "We'll each kill ourselves. Together. On three. Ready?"

Rhiannon nodded then tearfully pressed her pistol against her head. "You're a good egg, Patrick."

"You too, Rhiannon," he sniffled as he did the same. "One," he said.

"Two," she said.

They cocked their triggers.

Wait!" he shouted when he heard the strange noise.

They both turned toward it, and they couldn't believe what they saw. It

246

was a helicopter! Flying low and fast along the I-95, just a bit above ground level, barreling through the Happenstance zombies like a steak knife through Velveeta. Scores of undead were bulldozed over the freeway girders to the road below, and even more were crushed to oblivion as the chopper made its way to the side of the ramp where it hovered just a few feet from the kids, and the man inside yelled, "Get in!"

The children looked at each other and nodded, jumped off their bikes and leapt toward the machine. Patrick made it easily through the open space behind the pilot, but Rhiannon was only able to latch onto the skid. She clung for dear life as her body swung desperately in midair, the zombies on the ground below salivating as they awaited her fall, the zombies on the ramp staggering toward her only to tumble off the interstate because they were too dim to know to jump.

"Help!" she cried.

The pilot jammed the cyclic between his knees and reached out toward her. He screamed in anguish as one of the nineteen stitches on his belly ripped open but it didn't stop him from grabbing the little girl by the wrist and yanking her inside.

The great bird floated up and away from the whining zombies with ease, at which point Johnny looked over his shoulder to address the children.

"Didn't your mother ever tell you not to take rides from strangers?"

CHAPTER FORTY-NINE

Harve had only enough consciousness to feel his life slipping away. He hung on as best he could, fighting with all his will to keep death at bay, although he didn't know why. Habit, maybe.

He felt the ceiling and walls around him start to move. No, he realized—he was the one who was moving. They were taking him somewhere? Where? Why? But he didn't have the strength to ask out loud.

He found himself in a very large space with many empty unmade beds. It was the quarantine area where the zombie soldiers had gestated but he couldn't have known that. He felt the gurney stop moving, and then he saw the dark vampire slide a stool by his side to sit down.

"There has been too much death," she began. "Too much sorrow, too much loss. You saved my life, and I can give yours back to you. Do you understand?"

He tried to answer but he was too weak.

"Shhh," she said as she gently took his hand. "I have but one question, my darling, and you need not speak your answer. Merely blink once if it be yes, twice if it be no. Do you want to die?"

Harve closed his eyes and opened them while Africa awaited the second blink, but none came, only a single tear that rolled down the dying man's cheek. This was God's final test, Harve knew, the devil's last seduction. Life everlasting in exchange for evil servitude.

Africa was saddened but not surprised. Hadn't Prague given her the same choice so long ago as she herself had lay dying in a gutter, a once proud Carthaginian noble raped and beaten by the Roman invaders? And hadn't she too chosen death over becoming what she had believed to be a pagan demon? But Prague hadn't accepted her answer, and Africa had been grateful ever since. So too will the human.

She sprouted her sharp fangs, then bit hard into his neck. He had no strength left to fight her as she sucked out all but a single ounce of his life. She then bit into her own wrist, gasping in pain as she sliced open her veins. With her red blood dripping from her arm, she placed her open wound a hair's breadth from his mouth.

"Yet still, I leave the choice with you," she told him.

It was life, Harve knew, somehow he just knew. His very survival lay in her blood. Immortality less than an inch away, all he had to do was pucker up and take it. No! he shouted in his mind. It's a test! No!

But his will to survive was too strong. As his brain continued to shout its protests, he could not stop himself from pursing his lips to taste of her sweet nectar. Those first few drops alone gave him the strength to tilt up his head to drink of her further, deeper, which in turn gave him the strength to lift his arms, grab hold of hers, and helplessly, uncontrollably suckle her very essence into his own.

Africa writhed in ecstasy as their souls intertwined. The Kentucky Christian devoured her, growing stronger with each swallow, while the lady vampire panted and cried out in orgasmic delight. The holes in his chest closed, his lung filled with air, his artery healed, and a vitality he had never experienced before coursed through his veins, making his desire to consume the woman all the more insatiable.

And she was more than happy to be consumed.

CHAPTER FIFTY

Zombie-Sanchez was sad. She had yet to stop her instinctive gnawing on the electronic metallic net that bound her under the Prius, and she could hear the sounds of war—her precious "booms"—moving away. She didn't know it was because the tide of war had turned, that the aliens had been advancing all night and that the humans were fleeing in retreat—she no longer knew what aliens or humans were. All she knew was that the lovely noise was growing fainter with each passing moment. So when the last vehicle in the far rear of the great alien battalion drove past her and away, all the poor zombie could do was howl in wretched sorrow.

Peyton had run out of options. His command staff had been whittled down to his young Lieutenant aide, the Captain-with-the-scar who sat in place of the late Colonel, the handicapped Private, Laurel and Lance—the latter two having no military background—and the vampire Plato who seemed to be there only to watch.

He had put much of his hope on Jean-François's promise of using the bugs' own weapon against them, but the Frenchman had been found dead, and the weapon gone. His trained soldiers now numbered less than a thousand, and he had ordered them to fall back—although fall back to where he didn't know. If this had been a normal war, he would have surrendered in order to spare his soldiers' lives, but how do you surrender to an enemy whose singular goal was to watch you die?

He had done everything he could, he knew, had strategically outthought his enemy time and again. If this had been a chess game, he'd have taken significantly more of their pieces than they had of his, but he was down to the king and a few pawns while they just kept replenishing their board. How could anyone defeat that?

"Ding-dong! Zombie delivery!" a merry voice crackled over the loudspeaker.

Lance quickly altered the angle on one of the monitors to show Johnny's low-flying chopper leading sixty-five thousand zombies like the Pied Piper.

"Good morning, Mr. President!" the kids shouted in unison.

"Sorry we took so long," Johnny added. "But you'll get your next order free."

And with that, he soared the bird skyward and beyond, letting the roar of battle lure the sixty-five thousand the rest of the way, the children's package delivered.

"Yes!" Peyton shouted as he waved his fist in triumph.

The Alien Commander's bug mouth gaped open, and he coughed an involuntary gasp that could best be translated as, *"Oh crap."*

Then a bug at the front of the alien lines took a shot at the chopper. Johnny darted right at the last second but not quickly enough. The white beam blasted a hole through the tail rotor, sending bird, pilot and children spiraling out of control.

*****

NOT TOO LONG BEFORE Julius had sucked the life out of her, Mary had begun her initial research into the zombie phenomena. She had carefully dissected the zombie corpse that had been brought to her from their first onslaught, but there is no difference between the brain of a dead zombie and that of a dead human. A chemical analysis of zombie fluids showed blood, urine and saliva to be a highly toxic mix of human and Dweller, slowly infectious to humans while instantly poisonous, instantly deadly to Dwellers. This, of course, was interesting to her as a scientist, but did nothing to help her uncover a method to destroy the creatures outright.

She had assigned her new subordinates the task of skimming through the lore and bringing her a summary, but their quick reports also uncovered nothing of use. The zombie literature was even more conflicting than that of the vampires. There was the *Plan 9 from Outer Space* variety in which slow-moving zombies were resurrected human corpses; there was the *28 Days Later* type in which super-fast-moving zombies had contracted an accidental virus; even *The Walking Dead* seemed at times inconsistent between its own graphic novel and TV show.

In the end, all she could suggest was that if bashing zombies in the head kills them, then shooting them in the head would, reasonably speaking, do the same.

And she was kind of wrong.

*****

THE SWARMS OPENED FIRE, blasting the zombie hordes right through their blank eyes with impeccable precision, yet barely one out of a hundred fell, the rest continuing their relentless stagger forward. How could the bugs have known (even though Rhiannon did) that most of the zombie brain was already dead, and only one tiny part of one tiny lobe was all that kept these undead alive? There was a decent chance that a single shard from a shotgun's spray would pierce the miniscule target, and a blunt object bashed through their soft skull would shatter the whole brain at once, but a perfectly clean shot of white nothingness through the eyes had no effect at all. Only the bugs' misses had a chance of hitting the target, and the bugs rarely missed. Say, one out of a hundred times.

But the Alien Commander would not be dissuaded. If hand-to-hand it must be, then hand-to-hand it would be. He had beaten these creatures before, and he would do so again. Even at a ten-to-one loss rate, he had more than enough soldiers to complete the task. And so he coughed the order for his troops to charge!

Meanwhile, the 407 was still spiraling out of control. Patrick and Rhiannon bounced from one wall to the other, from ceiling to floor, as wooden crates of weapons and explosives (which had never been removed) bashed against the walls and splintered open. Johnny, securely belted in the only seat, struggled with the controls, dumping power and pushing over the cyclic as the helicopter spun straight toward the brick wall of a fifteen-story condo unit.

At the last moment, he managed to pull up just enough to get the front of the bird above the top edge of the roof, the forward thrust lurching it over the rest of the way, the skids ramming hard into the brick wall and collapsing under the fuselage. The metal bottom scraped fiery sparks against the roof's edge as the 407 climbed a few yards above the gravel floor, then crashed back down on its side. The blades screamed as they bent and crumpled while the machine slid sideways across the building where it would inevitably fall over the other side to plummet back to the ground fifteen stories below.

"Jump!" Johnny yelled. "Get out! Now!"

The kids didn't need to be told for their imminent doom was clear. Rhiannon, closest to the door, leapt out fast, landing in a perfect drop-and-roll (which she had learned from television), then sat on the ground panting, watching, and wondering why the other two hadn't jumped as well.

"I'm stuck!" Patrick shouted, his legs pinned against the wall by one of the wooden crates. "Help me!"

Johnny hurriedly unlatched his seat belt and climbed back to the boy. He tossed out the debris that blocked him like yesterday's garbage—loose weapons, binoculars, walkies. He groaned from the searing pain in his abdomen as he shoved the crate away from the boy. Patrick stood up fast but immediately fell back down.

"My leg!" he cried. "I think it's broken! I can't move!"

With the bird only feet, seconds, away from careening over the edge, Johnny lifted the boy into his arms—barking obscenities as two more of his stitches ripped apart—then leapt out the open door to safety just as the helicopter slid off the building, exploding into a giant ball of flame on the ground below.

The three lay on the roof, panting. Johnny clutched his belly as he watched the smoke rise from the crash. "I bet they're going to make me pay for that," he said.

*****

IT WAS ALMOST AS if the explosion was the cue for battle because that was the precise moment in which the charging aliens came face-to-face with the zombie hordes. The battle was brutally ugly as the swarms bashed their rifle butts through the zombies' soft skulls, while the brain-dead undead sunk their rotted teeth and gray fingernails into the bugs' crusty scales. The chaos was more akin to a battle of ancient times, one in which Marc Antony or Achilles may have fought, certainly not one in which a race that has mastered quantum mechanics would be involved.

Under the Toyota, zombie-Sanchez continued to instinctively gnaw on the electronic net that bound her. She didn't know why she did so, didn't know that the constant scraping against the metal had made her decayed teeth razor sharp, and she lacked the brain capacity to wonder about either. Nonetheless, her scalpel-like molar at last punctured a small crack in the metal. Purple steam—the net's energy source—sprayed out like air from a balloon. The net deflated to a flat, thin material that tore apart against the zombie's weight, and she fell to the ground.

She crawled out from under the car and rose to her feet. She was almost a mile behind the alien rear, which was another mile from the vicious battle, but she could hear the grunts and groans and yells and screams of the dying warriors. She would have smiled if the part of her brain that controlled such things were alive, but instead, the contented zombie merely staggered forward to war.

"Pretty noise," she'd have said if she had words. "Pretty pretty noise noise."

Peyton and his motley staff watched the battle on the monitors, and the Commander in Chief was pleased. According to Lance—who seemed to know *everything* about these creatures—zombies had no secret vulnerability the way vampires did. The only way to end them was an assault to the head, but the bugs already knew that, and they were still losing. Unlike the Alien Commander's initial estimation, the loss rate was more like twenty-to-one, and the zombies had outnumbered the bugs by a factor of more than six from the start. The fact that no new replacement bugs had yet to arrive was odd, and Peyton could only assume that the Alien Commander was pondering a full retreat as he had against the vampires.

"Mr. President?" Lance began. "What're we going to do about all the zombies after the bugs are gone?"

"One enemy at a time, son," Peyton answered. "One enemy at a time."

But the thought grated on him. What good was saving the world from aliens only to have the planet overrun by zombies?

"How'd they get rid of them in that Brad Pitt movie?" he asked.

"They gave all the people in the world a lethal injection."

"Well, that doesn't seem smart," answered the President.

On the ground, the Alien Commander watched the carnage through his scope. The heavy loss rate his side was suffering didn't concern him for he knew that he had billions of brave replacements itching to jump into the fray. But where were they? His standing orders had been for the replacements to wormhole to battle with no delay at all, so where the *cough* were they?!!!

He ordered his Sub-Commander to look into it, only to have the subordinate inform him that the vessel had shut down all communications.

And for the first time, the Alien Commander began to worry.

CHAPTER FIFTY-ONE

Africa and Harve held hands like schoolkids as they walked up the stairwell. They had been watching the battle through the hospital lobby window, but with the sun soon to rise they knew that that would not be an option much longer.

Although the windowless old storage room would be a safe place to spend the day, Harve had serious misgivings about popping in on the Commander in Chief without having been summoned. Africa, embracing her new role as mentor, was delighted to point out that Harve was no longer a mere lieutenant in the United States Army but the mate of the acting vampire queen.

The soldier took it in with a nod, but he was still having trouble adjusting to his new identity—although he appeared more handsome than he ever had in his life. "Okay, but I'll tell you right now. I'm not going to kill people."

"You have killed many people in your time," she casually responded.

"Enemies," he countered emphatically. "*Bad* people."

"Then bad people it shall be. We shall voyage to the Middle East in which there are villains aplenty on whom you may feast."

"That's a thought," he considered, then he opened the HQ door for his lady. They walked inside and quietly took their seats next to Plato in the back.

"What about that zombie TV show?" Peyton was asking Lance. He knew full well that the billions of aliens hovering above remained a grave threat, but with his eyes glued to monitors showing zombies killing bugs at an alarming pace, he was determined to find a solution for the next challenge he would possibly have to face.

"TV show, sir?" Lance asked. "You mean *The Walking Dead*?"

"Yeah. How'd they get rid of *their* zombies?"

"They didn't," Lance answered. "It's a TV series. Zombies every week."

"Oh yeah. That makes sense."

*****

THE ALIEN COMMANDER FOUGHT back the fear that grew inside him like a parasitic cancer. He had wormholed one of his officers back to the vessel to uncover the root of the communications problem, but the soldier never returned, the communication issue was never fixed, and the Commander's anxiety mounted. But his unacceptable rising fright only served to heighten his insatiable desire to win, which in turn ignited his colossal brain. All his years of training suddenly kicked in like an explosion, all those years of baffling his drug-induced amnesiac self with confounding impossible challenges of his own design—and then he saw it! In one mad bolt of inspiration, he knew exactly how to destroy the zombies en masse, and the now pesky humans would be sure to follow. It was perfect, and he knew it.

With intense focus, he watched the zombies push his troops back toward him. They were getting too close for comfort, and he deemed it prudent to pull the command vehicle back to the safety of the vessel meadow before initiating his plan. He tapped a series of symbols on his keypad to divert the power source from the vessel's main brain, and plugged directly into the central core of the quantum generators. But before he could tap the next sequence of commands, a burning pain shot through the human flesh that surrounded his thorax. The two thousand pound behemoth gagged, wretched and dropped dead to the ground, crushing almost all of his high command, pinning in place the sole surviving Sub-Commander.

For the alien brass had been so transfixed on the zombie hordes that lay ahead that it never occurred to them that a single zombie could be behind, staggering up onto their vehicle unheard over their Commander's coughing shouts.

Zombie-Sanchez lay upon the nine-foot monstrosity, joyously feasting upon his flesh. She had no comprehension of the vast contribution to the war effort that she had just made by killing the enemy Commander—she didn't even know what war was anymore. All she knew was that he was delicious, juicy and fresh, his flabby human meat made even more delectable by the tart green blood that flowed within.

"Yum," she would have said if she had had words. "Yum, yummer, yummest."

In the control room, cheers abounded.

On the rooftop, Johnny and the kids watched through their binoculars.

"Well, look at that," Johnny said with a smile. "Y'know, I almost dated her. First day we met, she vowed that she'd kill that guy some day. So let that be a lesson to you kids. No matter what life may throw at you, never give up on your dreams."

Then the President's voice squeaked out from the walkie-talkie on the ground. "How about that other zombie movie? How'd they get rid of their zombies?"

"Which movie, sir?" Lance asked.

"You know. The one with the guy from the Facebook movie, and the other guy from the *Cheers* reruns."

"Um . . . *Zombieland*?"

"Yeah."

"Didn't see it."

"Oh," the President answered.

On the ground, zombie-Sanchez continued to gorge on the Commander's fine flab and sinew. The Sub-Commander finally managed to wriggle out from under his superior's hulking corpse and then whipped his rifle off his back to ram its butt into the head of the unsuspecting Sanchez when he noticed twenty zombies headed straight at him. So he jumped off the flatbed and ran.

The twenty zombies, far more attracted to the scent of the Commander's fleshy flesh than that of the scaly bug, climbed onto the flatbed and converged upon the Commander's corpse, wholly unaware that they were stepping on, lying on, rolling on the activated keypad strapped to his lower forearm, banging on the alien symbols as they jockeyed for a better feeding position.

The ground shook more ferociously than ever before. A giant wormhole opened—twice the size of any the aliens had thus far unleashed. Hazy moments of Earth's past randomly flickered in and out of the void as the zombies continued to stomp on the keys. Lincoln is shot; man discovers fire; Mardi Gras; the first Ice Age; Elvis in concert; pioneers travel west in covered wagons; the first two amoeba join together; the final episode of *Friends*; an early creature crawls out of the sea; a picnic in a park; and on and on. But it didn't take long until the zombie's relentless thumping cracked the light alloy casing and ruptured the sophisticated technology, and the wormhole stuck on a time long forgotten in which tens of frenzied Deinonychus were embroiled in deadly battle with two crazed Tyrannosaurus rexes. The dinosaurs stopped dead in their tracks to look into our present-day, and they were utterly confounded by what they saw. Even the highly intelligent Deinonychus could not make heads or tails of it.

The Alien Sub-Commander had been trained to assume command, but he had never been trained for conditions such as these. His army was in shambles, and the undead were converging all around. Their only hope was to outrun the zombies, but their only escape was into the wormhole behind them, into a world and toward strange beasts he knew nothing about—but the zombies were too close to give that consideration its due.

"*Retreat!*" he coughed as loudly as he could, then led his few hundred remaining soldiers to charge into prehistory.

The dinosaurs didn't know what was happening. Rex and Tyrene roared. The Deinonychus shrieked. The Sub-Commander panicked and coughed out an order!

"*Fire!*" he shouted, and his soldiers did as instructed.

The roars, the shrieks, and the deafening explosions of the alien rifles caused Dinah to stir awake just in time to see the Sub-Commander blast a hole through Tyrene's head exactly where Claw had been clutching her, killing them both with one shot. Dinah shrieked in horror. Rex roared in fury. The great Tyrannosaurus bolted at the aliens, as did Dinah, as did the thirty-seven remaining Deinonychus.

But despite the aliens' impeccable accuracy, the Deinonychus' movements were too jagged for them to get a clean shot. The Deinonychus pounced upon one bug after another, their dagger claws and razor teeth slashing through the bugs' thoraxes, heads and abdomens. All the insects could do was keep running and try to fire on the move.

Rex's giant body absorbed the alien blasts like annoying mosquito bites. The gaping holes popping open along his massive frame missed his vital organs because the bugs didn't know where to aim, and it only made the giant beast all the more enraged. The bugs had seen that a shot to the head could take down the T. rex, but he was so fast that he would be upon them before they could fire, trampling them with his massive weight, biting off their heads and spitting them out. The few soldiers able to hold still long enough to take proper aim were pounced upon by the ferocious Deinonychus who slashed, clawed, and bit them to death, while those who ran back in full retreat found themselves face-to-face with the encroaching zombies who had been lured into the past by their precious booms.

Even the little ones pitched in. Donald leapt upon the back of an alien soldier, but the bug easily grabbed hold of the hatchling before he could do any real harm, threw him to the ground and took aim. Donald landed hard on the trigger-button of a dead alien's rifle, which then blasted a perfect void into his bug assailant's chest. The highly intelligent Deinonychus smiled as he assessed what had happened in an instant, then purposely hopped up and down on the button, joyfully blasting bug after bug to death —and the fact that he had no concept of technology or sophisticated weaponry took none of the fun out of it. It wasn't too long before Daffy and Dizzy followed their big brother's lead, jumping up and down on alien weapons of their own finding, blasting the mysterious, deadly beams to their hearts' content.

The Alien Sub-Commander was on the run, having long since given up on the futility of shooting. He found a nice little hiding place behind a tree so he could focus on the keypad strapped to his lower arm in order to wormhole his brethren to safety. He banged frantically on the symbols to bypass his vessel's main brain and plug directly into the quantum generators when two things happened: (1) Dinah leapt at him from the right and sunk her razor-sharp teeth into his lower abdomen, and (2) Rex charged him from the left, engulfing the entire bug head in his mouth.

Both Dinah and Rex recognized the Sub-Commander as the killer of their mate, and they each yearned for vengeance. A vicious tug-of-war ensued—Rex yanking from the top, Dinah's teeth dug into the bottom. Dinah soared through the air as Rex thrashed his mighty head but she would not let go. Only when the bug's thorax ripped in two did the contest end, green pus and organs spilling everywhere.

All the while, the other enraged Deinonychus sprung from one alien to the next, slashing and severing bug after bug till not a bug remained.

With all the aliens dead, the dinosaurs turned their wrath on the zombies—we're all aliens to them—and they charged forward into the twenty-first century. The zombies' rotted teeth and fingernails could not penetrate the dinosaurs' thick hides, and it took the Deinonychus all of a minute to determine how to best kill them—far quicker than it took the aliens because the dinos had no concept of external weapons. With great speed and agility, they slashed at the fragile zombie skulls, stabbing, biting, clawing. Rex alone was worth twenty of them as he trampled, chewed, and crushed the creatures into nonexistence. The zombies' only advantage was their numbers—there were just so many, and they never tired.

That advantage was not lost on the Commander in Chief. For although the mood back at HQ was positive, Peyton had seen what sixty-four thousand zombies had done to an impeccably trained alien army, and he didn't like the odds.

"There are still too many zombies! We need more dinosaurs!" he shouted, then added, "did I just say that?"

Johnny and the kids heard Peyton through the walkie-talkie. Patrick, who had been thinking the very same thing, elbowed Johnny to get his attention then pointed off in the distance. Johnny looked through his binoculars and immediately saw what the kid was getting at, and he smiled.

"Nice," he told the boy, then reached for the walkie and cockily spoke into it. "We got this one, Mr. President."

He stood up, grunting from the searing pain in his belly, then picked up one of the RPGs that lay on the ground—part of the debris he had tossed from the helicopter when he had saved the boy. He focused the scope on the clearing in the prehistoric woods where hundreds of Triceratops, Stegosaurus, Brontosaurus and other dinosaur breeds grazed peacefully, aware of some kind of commotion but considering it the sole business of the nasty carnivores. Johnny took aim and fired a grenade over the far side of the expanse.

BOOM! The herbivores spooked! They bolted away from the explosion in a mad stampede as Johnny fired another rocket behind them.

"Zombies for dinner!" he shouted with a smile, then fired yet another to keep them moving. "Get 'em while they're hot!" he screamed as he fired again to keep them on course. "Don't be the last of your friends to kill one! Eeeehaaaa!!!!"

The docile herbivores weren't specifically looking to kill anyone as they stampeded into our world. They had nothing against zombies—they were just so crazed and so enormous that they couldn't help but trample the creatures en masse.

Herds of Stegosaurus swung their tails wildly as they charged, impaling zombie after zombie upon their spikes.

Droves of hulking Triceratops, blocked by dormant alien tanks, dug their armored heads under the rims of the vehicles, flipping them up to the sky and back down to the ground, squashing scores of zombie skulls in the process.

Mobs of giant Brontosaurus stomped through the city, their towering necks plowing across electric cables, yanking the wooden beams out of the concrete road. The live wires floated to the ground to electrocute the thousands of zombies they touched, the bolts of electricity extinguishing the last of their tiny brains, zombie-Sanchez among them.

"Aww," Johnny said sadly. "Now she'll never go out with me."

The violence and mayhem continued on and on, and it would through the rest of the day and into the early evening. Herbivores and carnivores alike. Slash, stab, bite. Impale, squash, electrocute. Even little Donald, Daffy and Dizzy took down zombie-Jeb, zombie-Marcus, zombie-Joey and the plethora of zombie children. It was a zombie bloodbath. Carnage, carnage, carnage.

Back at HQ, the mood was joyous and even relaxed, as all but Peyton sensed the end of the war a mere matter of time—with ten billion bugs or more up in the sky, he knew that this war was far from over—but for the others, their relaxed, victorious thoughts turned to other matters.

"So if you're queen," Harve asked his new lover. "Does that make me king?"

"Only to me, my treasure," Africa answered with a loving smile. "Only to me."

"'Kay," he said, as he took it in. "And am I going to have to talk like that, say stuff like 'my darling' and 'my treasure'?"

"No, my flower, you may speak in whatever manner you feel comfortable."

"'Kay. But, you know, another thing. 'My flower' is kinda gay. Can we just stick to 'darling' and 'treasure'?"

"Harve?" Johnny asked, hearing his old captor over the walkie. "Is that you? Shouldn't you be dead by now?"

"Well, more like undead."

"You? A vampire? *You*, you religious freak? How the hell did that happen?"

"Well, she was hot and she liked me," the Lieutenant answered, calling back to a more innocent time between them. "What was I going to do, *not* be a vampire?"

"The circle is now complete."

"So what are you doing here anyway? I thought you gave up on humanity."

"I tried, man," Johnny answered with sincerity. "Swear to God, I tried my ass off to give up on humanity. Maybe there's just something in us that makes us care, even when we don't want to care. Something in us all that just needs life to go on."

"Tell me about it," replied the Baptist vampire.

"All right, people! Enough!" Peyton shouted at last. "Let's not go licking our strawberries just yet! There's still a few billion bugs flying over our heads, and we need a goddamn plan for when they come back! Because they will!"

Then a crackly voice came over the loudspeaker. "Oh, I wouldn't worry about them anymore, General."

One of the monitors suddenly flickered to snow, and a new image flickered back in its stead. Julius sat on the plush captain's chair on the bridge of the alien vessel, looking out at sun and stars through a wall-sized filtered window, surrounded by a dozen alien corpses lying dead on the ground. The vessel's alarm system blared a deafening "whoop whoop whoop" while bug soldiers tried to break through the gray alloy bridge door from the other side.

"Julius!" shouted a gleeful Africa as she jumped up from her seat.

"You're alive!" shouted a thrilled Laurel.

"Welcome back, son," said the President. "I'm glad you're all right."

"More than all right, General," said the vampire. "You see, it occurred to me that it's not only vampires. Too much sun isn't good for anyone."

"What are you talking about?" Africa exclaimed, already ahead of him.

"Oh no! Sir!" shouted Lance. "In all the commotion, I stopped checking. The bug vessel left our orbit some time ago, and it's on a direct course toward the sun!"

He quickly punched keys on his laptop, and then a wide shot of the alien vessel careening toward the sun popped onto one of the screens.

"Julius! What are you doing?!" demanded Laurel.

"What I always do," the vampire answered as his skin began to sizzle. "What must be done."

"But you'll die!" Africa shouted as her eyes welled up. Harve moved beside her and wrapped his arm around her for comfort.

"Yes, Africa, I will die, so that you all may live."

"But we need you here, Julius. *I* need you here."

"You got this, my Queen," he told her.

"I don't."

"You have a generous spirit and an untapped wisdom, Africa. Say it for me, my Queen. You got this."

"Julius . . ."

"Deny not your dying leader's last request."

"You can do it," Harve whispered softly, lovingly in her ear. "I'll make sure of it. I got your back, my treasure."

She gazed into her Lieutenant's eyes, sniffled once, then turned back to Julius. "I got this," the new Queen softly conceded.

"My liege," Julius answered as he bowed his head and tipped an imaginary cap in royal deference, then turned back to Peyton. "It was an honor to serve under you, my General."

"Um, you too," the President replied sadly, at a loss for words. "Take care."

"Julius, you don't have to do this!" Laurel insisted. "There's got to be another way."

"But alas there is not. Fare-thee-well, slayer. Fare-thee-well, y'all."

Then his skin began to bubble from within, and he groaned in anguish. Patches of fire erupted from his pours. His face melted to a creamy goo that dripped off his vampire skeleton. His wretched screams of agony were soon joined by billions of aliens who screamed and cried and melted and burned as well, and the monitor flickered back to snow; and the screen of the vessel exterior showed the craft growing ever smaller as it streaked into the sun, becoming a tiny spec, and then nothing at all.

Africa buried her head in her lover's chest and cried, and he held her tight.

Laurel bravely held back her tears as she blew a loving kiss to the monitor. "Be at peace, my monster."

CHAPTER FIFTY-TWO

The sun was setting in the West for it had taken the whole day for the dinosaurs to crush, slice and decapitate first their alien foes, then the zombies. With the last of the undead lying vanquished on the ground, the exhausted, panting animals found themselves standing still amidst a sea of strange-looking corpses, surrounded by towering constructions they could not comprehend, utterly confused by the very world in which they stood, unsure how they even came to be here at all.

Dinah and Rex locked eyes with grave hesitation. They began their day as enemies in a war of their own, only to find themselves the most unlikely of allies in a land that made no sense to either.

What's next? their eyes asked of each other.

Dinah waited for the hulking T. rex to gesture an answer, one way or the other. He was by far the stronger—and the dumber—so it was his move.

The colossal beast pondered for only a moment before he shook his massive frame like a wet dog, as if shaking off the bizarre events of the day. It had begun with the loss of his son, then the loss of his mate, and that was enough loss for one day. He was tired. If the pesky Deinonychus were as weary as he, good. They would all live to fight another day, but only in a world he could understand.

He turned and slowly trudged back through the wormhole. Dinah sighed, relieved—she felt no more urge for continued war than he. She followed him home, as the other Deinonychus followed her, and as the herbivores followed them.

The Deinonychus hatchlings brought up the rear, skipping and prancing and shrieking their personal battle highlights in boastfulness. They were not tuckered out like the grownups, but invigorated by the whole adventure, thrilled that they had been allowed to participate as if adults themselves. Nor had the modern world felt particularly strange to them—they were so young their own world was still full of mystery. And as one final "screw you," little Donald jumped onto the severed thorax of the Alien Sub-Commander, but he lost his balance on the slippery scales and fell hard onto the bug's lower forearm, and onto the keypad that was attached.

The ground shook violently, and the wormhole closed, and then vanished.

There was a moment of stunned silence in the streets, in the buildings, on the rooftops, and inside HQ. Is that it? Did we really win? And the silence was finally broken when Peyton breathed a smiling sigh of relief. "It's over."

"Praise Jesus!" shouted the vampire Harve.

Cheers, applause, handshakes and high fives abounded; a single tear rolled down the creviced cheek of the Captain-with-the-scar; and Harve and Africa kissed.

"We must find you a proper vampire name," she said to her new love.

"What's wrong with 'Harve'?"

"It lacks majesty," she answered with a smile. "Vampires draw names from great lands to which they feel connected, or transformative figures who inspired them. Plato titled himself after the great philosopher, Julius after the mighty Caesar."

"Okay, I get that," Harve answered as he considered. "Then I'll be . . . Reagan."

"We'll work on it," she smiled, then kissed him passionately once more.

On the battlefield, the surviving soldiers emerged from the buildings in which they had remained silent and motionless for so long, and they too cheered, laughed, shouted, and they threw their helmets in the air.

On the rooftop, Patrick and Rhiannon exchanged a high five, then offered their hands out to Johnny to do the same. "You did well, kids," he said as he slapped their palms in celebration. "Amazingly brave. I'm proud of you. Everyone is."

"So are you going to adopt us now?" asked a gleefully optimistic Rhiannon. "And take care of us and send us to good schools and love us forever?"

"Come on, guys," Johnny replied. "Wasn't what we just went through horrifying enough?"

But back at HQ, Petyon knew that there was still much work to be done. "I want a plan on how to dispose of the enemy bodies," Peyton ordered the Captain-with-the-scar. "Make sure to keep a few for science— those guys cream over this stuff. And keep Lance involved. He knows zombies like nobody's business. As for the rest," he added as he leaned into the microphone, "nice work, everyone. I thank you. Mankind thanks you. Vampirekind thanks you. Open the bars and serve the booze!"

The sounds of cheering soldiers on the ground grew even louder. Peyton's aide, the young Lieutenant, quietly approached his President to fulfill one of the earliest orders that he had been given.

"Your, uh, medicine, sir," he said as he handed Peyton the small silver flask.

Peyton smiled as he took it from the boy and unscrewed the cap. He raised it to the room in toast, moved it to his lips, then paused. "After I win reelection," he said as he screwed the top back on and placed it in his jacket pocket.

And on the far side of the room, Africa approached the slayer that she had always despised. "No matter what transpires forward, Laurel," she began as the two other vampires lingered by her side, "I wish only to say to you, thank you."

"On the contrary, Africa. It has been a privilege to watch your ascent. You will make a fine queen for your kind."

"I shall endeavor to prove you right. Yet if it should come to pass that we must face each other in battle –"

"Let us hope that it does not."

"Yes. Let us hope, my friend."

Laurel smiled, honored, so proud of all that she had been able to accomplish.

And that was when her eyes met with Peyton's. The President clasped his hands to his heart, extended them out to her in a gesture of love and friendship, and mouthed, "Thank you."

She mimicked the gesture back to him, paying no heed to Plato who was now standing behind her, salivating as he stared upon her luscious slayer neck.

"No, Mr. President," Laurel mouthed back. "Thank *you*."

In a flash, Plato sprouted his fangs and lurched towards Laurel's throat. But just as quickly, she thrust her left arm backward and up into the small vampire's chest, stabbing him in the heart with the wooden stake that she had been quietly holding in her hand all along. Plato dropped dead to the ground.

"Truce over," said the slayer.

The Queen leaned toward her new protégé and whispered, "We'd better go."

And with that, Harve and Africa transformed to mist and flew out of the HQ, out of the hospital, and into the night.

EPILOGUE

It was very late that same night when Rog wheeled himself into the office. There was still much work to be done, bodies to be burned, bodies to be donated, bodies to be buried, and medals to be allotted. It would require an endless sea of paperwork for the Captain-with-the-scar and hence an endless sea for Rog himself—and the formerly homeless man couldn't wait to get started.

He was surprised to see that the light in his Captain's office was on, and even more surprised to hear a soft sobbing coming from behind the Captain's partially open door. Rog's heart went out to the man to whom he owed so much so he quietly wheeled himself to the edge of the door to see what was what.

The Captain-with-the-scar was standing alone in the center of the room. His human skin was peeled back as he tapped repeatedly on the keypad strapped to his lower forearm but to no avail—the quantum generators that powered it were gone forever. He cried softly over the billions of his kind who had needlessly perished, and for his friends and family that he had held so dear.

Rog wheeled himself out of the office and then back to his quarters.

He never said a word.

Indie books and authors rely on support from their readers. If you enjoyed this book, please take a moment to leave a review. Thank you!

ACKNOWLEDGMENTS

There are so many people who so generously gave their time to help me with this book that I don't quite know where to start. They were all invaluable. I suppose, since my made-up science is such a big part of the story, I will start there.

But first, I must point out that at any point in the process, if accuracy or fact conflicted with a compelling narrative, I always chose the narrative. In other words, despite my heartfelt gratitude to my many expert consultants in so many varied fields, I didn't always listen to them. So if you're their buddy or coworker and catch a mistake they should have caught, don't give 'em a hard time. It was probably me.

It was my goal for my made-up science to be scientifically correct wherever it could be, and to *sound* correct wherever it couldn't, which was most of the time. It was a bit intimidating to ask respected experts in their field, "Hey, I conjured this up out of whole cloth. Can you make sure I'm using the right words?" But the two Davids, as I call them, did so much more than that.

David Saltzberg, UCLA professor of physics, and David Jefferson, spacecraft navigation engineer, Jet Propulsions Laboratory (JPL), not only gave their time and expertise, but their warmth and humor. Working separately because they don't know each other, they corrected me when I was factually wrong (I had forgotten about relativity at one point, oops), and they pushed me to go even further with the science fantasy whenever applicable. This book is better because of them both.

Regarding the military aspects of the story, my goal was to be one hundred percent accurate as to tactics, behavior and jargon—you know, other than the fact that my soldiers were fighting aliens, avoiding zombies, and allied with vampires. In this category, I lucked out too. Retired Army Major Leonard Gomberg and former Army Sergeant and Police Detective Julia Torres (the latter of whom also taught me how to properly swear in Spanish), approached the book from entirely different perspectives but each to the same positive end. Also working separately, addressing their comments was at times as easy as swapping one word for another; others, it seemed the whole story was about to collapse. But they never shied away from the long tactical discussions that followed, digging in till we came up with something militarily credible while remaining dramatically compelling. I thank them both.

Writing a screenplay in which a helicopter is about to crash into a brick wall or is ducking alien beams of white nothingness would require little more than the words I just used in this sentence, the rest being up to stunt coordinators and special effects teams. But a novel requires every detail spelled out and hence, an actual knowledge of the machine. I began this effort with no such knowledge, and have ended it with plenty. But pilot Laurie Pitman did far more than teach me words like "cyclic," "collective" and "skids." She targeted some of the stunts I had in my first draft as utterly impossible, commended other stunts that were improbable but cool, and even threw in a few tricks of her own. She also explained how helicopter pilots don't care for the word "chopper;" a word that had been all over the early drafts. I deleted the offensive term from Johnny's mouth and thoughts, but sometimes it just felt like what certain characters would say. Sorry Laurie. And thank you, Laurie.

I want to thank Dave Engdahl for teaching me about the city of Jacksonville, and Audrey Samz for her knowledge of Key West, neither of which I've been to but both of which seem beautiful. (The original plan was to have the main war in Miami but that didn't make tactical sense from a military perspective.)

I want to thank my copy editor Amanda Pisani for her scrutiny, her tireless devotion, and her willingness to fight me on most everything; Patrick Gomez for the Latin; Keith Nolan for teaching me how to type with an Irish accent; and Josie Abugov for typing the one Chinese sentence into a Word Doc. (It means "they go to the park.")

But my greatest thanks must go to the friends and family who read my pages along the way—some Part by Part, some chapter by chapter—sometimes even versions of the same chapter over and over as I neurotically asked them to weigh in on changes that I had made. Their encouragement kept me going, and their brutal honesty kept me honest. Only because they would sometimes say the pages were confusing, or stupid, or dull, hurting my feelings terribly, was I able to believe them when they said they loved it, giving me the inner security to move on. Without being able to quantify their invaluable help, I list them alphabetically. Thank you to Adam Abugov, Aria McKenna, Don Foster, Sandra Bettencourt and Will Kleist.

Lastly, I want to thank you, dear readers, for getting this far. I take that to mean that you enjoyed this tale, and I hope you will like my next one even more.

ABOUT THE AUTHOR

Jeff Abugov graduated from Concordia University Film School in Montreal where his two student films won national awards at the Canadian Student Film Festival. He began his professional career writing freelance for the NBC hit *Cheers* for which he eventually became a staff writer and then story editor. He served as executive story editor on *The Golden Girls*, then went on to write and produce such hit shows as *Roseanne* and *Two and a Half Men*. He served as executive producer of *Roc* and *Grace Under Fire*, and most recently of the animated series *Fugget About It*. He also wrote and directed the feature film *The Mating Habits of the Earthbound Human*, starring David Hyde Pierce and Carmen Electra. He has received a Golden Globe Award, a Peabody Award, and three People's Choice Awards, as well as being nominated for a Humanitas Prize, a Canadian Screen Award, and a second Golden Globe.

After having achieved success writing and producing within the Hollywood system, doing as he's told and playing nice, Jeff has at long last decided to let his imagination run rampant and do it his own way . . . and he's having a blast!

He hopes you're having as much fun reading his stories as he's been having writing them.

ALSO BY JEFF ABUGOV

"The Autobiography of @" (a short story)

JOIN JEFF ABUGOV ON THE INTERNET

Website: www.jeffabugov.com

Facebook: www.facebook.com/jeffabugov

Twitter: @jeffabugov

You can sign up for Jeff's newsletter or email him at:
www.jeffabugov.com/contact

Made in the USA
San Bernardino, CA
13 December 2015